# I WANTED YOU TO KNOW

LAURA PEARSON

Hope you enjoy it.

Laura x

## ABOUT THE AUTHOR

**Laura Pearson** has an MA in Creative Writing from the University of Chichester. She spent a decade living in London and working as a copywriter and editor for QVC, Expedia, Net a Porter, EE, and The Ministry of Justice. Now, she lives in Leicestershire, where she writes novels, blogs about her experience of breast cancer (www.breastcancerandbaby.com), runs The Motherload Book Club, and tries to work out how to raise her two children.

* * *

www.laurapearsonauthor.com

facebook.com/LauraPAuthor

twitter.com/laurapauthor

instagram.com/LauraPAuthor

ALSO BY LAURA PEARSON

Missing Pieces

Nobody's Wife

PRAISE FOR *I WANTED YOU TO KNOW*

'This book will tear you apart, but leave you forever changed for the better.' — NJ Crosskey, author of *Poster Boy*

'One of my books of the year.' — Louise Beech, author of *The Lion Tamer Who Lost* and *Call Me Star Girl*

'A beautiful novel that will leave you wanting to live your best life.' — Lauren North, author of *The Perfect Betrayal*

'Another courageous and powerful novel from Laura Pearson. Her best yet.' — Fiona Mitchell, author of *The Swap*

'Laura's special power is to pack love, warmth, and wisdom into the darkest places. The result is beautiful.' — Francesca Jakobi, author of *Bitter*

'It broke my heart, brought tears to my eyes and got me thinking — about cherishing those we love and never taking life for granted.' — Joanne Burn, author of *Petals and Stones*

PRAISE FOR *MISSING PIECES*

'A convincing, patient portrait of loss — beautifully written.' — Fiona Mitchell, author of *The Maid's Room*

'I've not stopped thinking about *Missing Pieces*...it's such a good book. Heartbreaking and hopeful.' – Amanda Berriman, author of *Home*

'Elegant, honest, and breathtakingly beautiful...an impressive and raw portrayal of how one tragedy affects an entire family.' — Christina McDonald, author of *The Night Olivia Fell*

'A gripping, devastating, heart-stealing read.' — Tamsin Grey, author of *She's Not There*

'Fabulous.' — Jane Shemilt, author of *Daughter*

'A stunning story of loss and survival. Beautifully written, heartbreaking and hopeful.' — Francesca Jakobi, author of *Bitter*

PRAISE FOR *NOBODY'S WIFE*

'It's astonishingly good. Breathtaking assured writing and a deftly told story about sisters and love with characters I can't stop thinking about. Utterly sublime.' — Clare Empson, author of *Him*

'I felt every moment of this book. It was beautifully written, acutely observed, and utterly addictive...this is just stunning. I devoured it in twenty-four hours, and highly recommend.' — Louise Beech, author of *The Lion Tamer Who Lost*

'A beautifully crafted and deeply honest story of marriage and love.' — Lauren North, author of *The Perfect Betrayal*

'A heart-breaker of a tale that will stay with you long after reading it.' — Cass Hunter, author of *The After Wife*

'A heartbreaking page-turner of a read — deftly exploring the complexities of family relationships and the dark nature of obsession.' — Isabel Ashdown, author of *Little Sister*

# A LETTER FROM LAURA PEARSON

Dear Reader,

When I was thirty-five, and five months pregnant with my second child, I was diagnosed with breast cancer. No one expects to have to face cancer at that age; no one expects their body to turn on them just when they are busy creating new life. I waited, with my heart in my mouth, to be told I was going to have to terminate. Instead, I was told I could be operated on during my pregnancy and start chemotherapy after the birth.

The first question I asked after diagnosis was whether I'd be able to breastfeed my daughter. I didn't ask whether I was going to die. Perhaps I wasn't ready to, but I always put it down to the fact that when you're carrying a child, your instinct is to put that child first. I felt like I had to bring her into the world safely, no matter what. And with the help of the incredible NHS, I did.

When my daughter was seven days old and miles away from home in a special care unit after an incredibly shaky start, I had the first of six rounds of chemo. I'd held her perhaps twice at that point. She hadn't been home. I wasn't able to be any sort of a mother. I followed all the instructions I was given. *Lie still while we surgically insert this port for administering the chemo drugs. Take this medication. Call us if your symptoms are worrying you.* And in the back of my mind, I wondered whether I would survive it. Whether I would get to be her mother at all.

My son was two and a half. We were still counting my daughter's age in days. If I died, neither of them would remember me. It seems so impossible, that, when you've been a mother for more than two years and all those hundreds of days have been spent taking care of your child. When you have fed him from your body and sung him to sleep. When you have held him so often you can feel the warmth and weight of his body even when he isn't there. But I knew that he would forget me, if I died, and she would never know me. And I wondered what I could leave them, what they would need if they didn't have a mother.

When my treatment was over, I set myself the challenge of writing a 50,000-word first draft of a novel in the month of November. It wasn't easy. My daughter was home by then and both my children needed me. I was tired from the chemo and I had a small operation during that month and another big one ahead of me. But I'm stubborn, and I don't always take the easy road, and this was one of those times. Day after day, I added 2,000 words to my document. This book that I was calling *I Wanted You To Know*. It was written in letters. It was about my fears, and it poured out of me, and every day I felt a little lighter for getting it out of my head and onto the page.

Of that initial draft, not much remains. The title, the characters of Jess, Jake, Gemma, and Edie. The disease that Jess and I share. I've rewritten it a couple of times. It was elusive; it was hard. But in the early months of 2019, I rewrote it from scratch and something clicked. It poured out again, and this time it was right.

One of the best things about writing novels is how they can surprise you. I planned this novel out chapter by chapter, and though I didn't deviate from that plan, it became something I hadn't expected it to. I thought it was a love story, and it is, in part. But I didn't know that it would be a love letter to friendship, to women, to life. That it would be a celebration as well as a tale of loss. That it would champion the wisdom of ordinary women; their compassion, their incredible strength in the face of tragedy.

The book you hold in your hands is the story of Jess and the people who matter to her. It's about fear and virtue and bravery and love. I hope it strikes a chord with you. I hope it makes you want to reach out to those you love, and pull them a little closer. Thank you for reading.

Laura

# I Wanted You to Know

LAURA PEARSON

First published in Great Britain in 2019 by Agora Books

Agora Books is a division of Peters Fraser + Dunlop Ltd

55 New Oxford Street, London WC1A 1BS



Printed and bound in Great Britain by Clays Ltd, Elcograf S.p.A.

*This book is for my children, Joseph and Elodie.*
*I once wrote you a letter like the ones in this novel,*
*and I hope you never have cause to read it.*

*It's also for the women who are named on the following page.*
*I am truly grateful for the times we've shared, the ways we've*
*laughed and informed and lifted one another. I never wanted*
*to have cancer buddies, but I'm glad you're mine.*

*Adriana Ford*
*Amy Buller*
*Bethan Butcher*
*Beth Hooper*
*Carie Stainsby*
*Cynthia Murphy*
*Donna Drew*
*Emily Devane*
*Jackie Buxton*
*Marianne Doherty*
*Michelle Downe*
*Rachel Kitching*
*Robin Schacht*
*Sheena Ellis*

## CHAPTER ONE

Jess understood all the words in the sentence, but she couldn't make them hang together properly. She looked at the doctor, sitting opposite her with his hands neatly folded in his lap.

'Can you say it again?' she asked.

'I'm sorry, Jessica. We've found evidence of breast cancer.'

Jess looked down at her feet, where Edie's car seat was resting. Edie was stirring, and Jess took hold of the handle and rocked her a little, and Edie closed her eyes and went back to sleep. She was holding the edge of her knitted blanket in her tiny fist. Jess had been a mum for a handful of weeks. She was still learning, still felt untethered and lost. She'd gone to the doctor, initially, because she'd felt a lump when she was feeding Edie. She'd gone to the hospital clinic, ready to be told it was a blocked duct. To be told it was nothing and sent on her way, another overcautious new mother.

'Jessica, I know this is a shock. Do you have any questions for me?'

Jess tried to focus on his face. He was in his forties, she

thought, with small round glasses and a receding hairline. She wanted to ask him whether he had a wife, whether he had children. Whether he understood this new feeling she was grappling with – that her life was no longer her own. That she owed this tiny new person everything. She couldn't have cancer. How could she? She was a mum. She was a new mum. And she was twenty-one years old.

'Are you sure?' she asked.

The doctor's face changed a little at that. He smiled a sad smile and she saw that he was probably very kind, that he was sorry for her.

'I can show you the scan, if you like? The lump you felt, in your right breast, it's definitely a malignant tumour. It's roughly 30 millimetres in diameter. We hope you'll make a full recovery. But look, I don't want to bombard you with information right now. Do you have anyone with you?'

Jess looked down at her sleeping baby and back up at the doctor. 'Only my daughter,' she said, her voice catching as if on a hook. Something about looking at Edie made it all harder, made it worse.

'Asha, here,' the doctor gestured at the nurse who was hovering a little way behind his chair, 'is going to be your breast care nurse, and she can take you into a room now for you to process this news and ask any questions you might have. Okay?'

Jess nodded. And then she was being ushered out, into the corridor, where she'd waited ten minutes before, making faces at Edie, back when she hadn't had cancer. Or hadn't known, at least, that she had cancer. Asha put a hand on Jess's arm, the arm that wasn't carrying the car seat. It stilled her.

'Let's go in here,' Asha said.

She pushed open the door to a small room with a sofa and an armchair. There were framed prints on the wall, cushions, a coffee table with a box of tissues on it. This was the room where they brought you after the bad news. This was where you began to come to terms with it. Cancer. Jess's grandfather had died from lung cancer when she was fifteen. Her mum's dad. And she'd had a friend at school once whose sister had died from cancer, but she didn't know what kind.

Asha put a pile of leaflets and little booklets on the table between them. 'Some reading for you,' she said. 'Listen, I know this is a shock. I see women receiving this news all the time, but you're one of the youngest I've ever known. And your baby, still so tiny…'

Asha broke off and Jess realised she was trying to hold back tears. This stranger, this nurse who dealt with cancer every day of her life. 'I'm sorry,' she said, her voice a little stronger.

Jess realised that she hadn't cried, that she wasn't crying. And just as she thought it, Edie woke with a howl and Jess unstrapped her and lifted her, held her to her chest and stroked her wispy hair. She lifted her top and pulled down her nursing bra and began to feed her daughter. And then it struck her.

'Will I be able to keep feeding her?' she asked.

Asha shook her head. 'I can't say for sure. It depends what the treatment is. But if you have chemotherapy, I imagine you'll have to stop. Don't think about that now, though.'

Jess wanted to ask her what she should think about. Her head was a mess, her thoughts jumping from one thing to another. Cancer. The question she really wanted to ask was whether or not she was going to die. Whether this tiny baby, who needed her for every little thing, would have to learn to live without her. But she didn't know what words to use, and she was frightened of the answer.

'I can't tell my mum,' Jess said.

'Why not?'

'I just can't. I'm an only child, and my dad's not really been in my life. It's just the two of us. Well, the three of us, now. She won't be able to deal with it.'

Asha pressed her lips together and tilted her head to one side. 'Try not to worry about other people. For now, just think about dealing with this news yourself. It's a big blow, Jessica. It's okay to be upset, or angry. It's okay to fall apart.'

But it wasn't, Jess thought. It wasn't okay to fall apart when you had a baby.

'Is the baby's father...?' Asha didn't finish the sentence, though Jess gave her plenty of time to.

'He's not around,' she said, when Asha's discomfort became too much. 'He's not in our lives and he never will be.'

'Okay,' Asha said. 'So what does your support network look like?'

Jess thought about that. She lived with her mother in a small town in Cheshire, had always lived with her mother, apart from the couple of years she'd spent away at university, and, even then, she'd always come home at holidays and for the odd weekend. Her mother was her support network, wasn't she? But could one person be an entire network? There was Gemma, too. They'd been best friends for years, since the early days of secondary school, and they'd known one another for years before that. Gemma was caught up in most of Jess's memories of being a teenager, and she'd been great throughout the pregnancy and since Edie had been born. She told Asha, about her mother and her best friend. And it didn't seem like a lot, suddenly. She felt as though she should have more people to offer up.

'There's my dad,' she said, eventually. 'I didn't grow up with him, but he lives nearby, and I see him now and again.'

Asha smiled. 'Okay,' she said. 'Well, I think we've told you everything you need to know for today. There'll be more tests, I'm afraid, but we can get in touch about those. I'd advise you to go home and break the news to those people you've just told me about. You're going to need their help and support more than ever, now. How are you getting home?'

'I'm driving,' Jess said. She'd borrowed her mum's car for the appointment. She'd said she needed a few bits and pieces in town. It had felt easier, at the time, than explaining.

'And are you sure you're okay, going home on your own?'

Jess looked down at Edie, who'd finished feeding and was lying in her arms, her face all contentment. She wanted to say that she wasn't on her own. That she was with Edie. But she just nodded and thanked Asha as she strapped Edie back into her car seat. When she got outside and the cool winter air hit her face, Jess stood still and inhaled it for a moment. And then just as she was about to struggle to the car park with Edie's car seat in the crook of her elbow, she heard her name and turned, and Asha was behind her.

'You forgot these,' she said, brandishing the pile of leaflets. 'And I've written down my number. You can call me if you think of any questions or want to talk to someone.'

'Thank you,' Jess said, putting the car seat down and stuffing the paper into the changing bag.

It seemed, for a minute, as if Asha was going to say something else, but then she just rested a hand briefly on Jess's arm again, before dashing back inside.

It wasn't until she was in the car, Edie secured and her own seatbelt on, that she cried. Cancer. There was something about that word. It reeked of death. And it was for old people, people who'd lived. Not women who were just starting out. Not new mums. Jess cried hard for twenty minutes, until her eyes were sore from it and she felt empty. In the back of the car, Edie slept on, oblivious. And then, feeling that it was out of her system, Jess turned the engine on and drove, slowly, back home. When she got there, she sat in the driveway for a while, feeling like she lacked the energy to move. It was peaceful, with Edie sleeping. The jolt of removing the car seat from the car might wake her. Why not sit for a while?

Cancer. Breast cancer. Jess reached down and touched the place where she'd found the lump. It was close in to the nipple, hard to the touch. She wondered why she'd never noticed it before, or whether it had only recently become pronounced enough to be felt. She'd always had fairly small breasts, and then in pregnancy they'd become much larger, and now that she was feeding, they were sore and variable, rock hard when Edie was due a feed and then soft as soon as she was finished. She'd been so sure that this lump was a part of that, of those changes. She'd been so sure.

Jess knew that her mum was out, that she was at work. She worked in a call centre answering the phone for hundreds of small companies and passing on messages. Jess didn't always know what shifts she was doing, but she knew she was at work that afternoon. She'd gone on the bus because Jess was using the car. So when Edie opened her eyes and Jess carried her inside the house, she knew it was empty. And part of her was glad, because she wasn't ready, yet, to share this news with anyone else. But part of her was sad and felt horribly alone. For the first time in weeks, she thought about calling Jake. And then she gathered herself. She put Edie in her bouncy chair, carried it into the bathroom and had a shower, avoiding the lump when she covered her body with shower gel. She washed her hair. When she stepped out, dripping wet, and reached for a towel, a few drops of water fell on to Edie's head, and she did a funny little wriggle. Jess laughed.

It was so hard, being a new mum, and yet every day — every hour, almost — Edie did something to make her laugh, and Jess remembered to be grateful for her. Remembered that she'd made the right decision, when those two lines had turned blue. She might be missing out on her final year of university, but she was doing something else. Something better. Or she had been. Now, she wasn't sure what she was doing. Or how long she had left to do anything.

'I want to promise you things,' Jess said. 'I thought I could promise to always be here with you, but now I don't know.' She knew that tears were coming again. 'Edie, you're my love. My big love. And I'll do anything I can to make sure I'm here to look after you. But if I can't do that, I'll make everything right for you for when I'm gone. I'll make sure you're always looked after by people who love you.'

She would wait for her mum to come home, she decided. And then she'd sit her down and tell her. And her mum would know what to do. That was how it worked, with mums. Jess wondered, for a moment, whether Edie would feel that way about her, when she was an adult. Whether she would believe that Jess had the answer to everything. And then the thought struck her, hard, that she might not be around to see Edie as a grown-up, and she sank on to her bed, a towel around her body and her hair still dripping. Edie in that chair, playing with her fingers. And the cancer inside her, growing.

# CHAPTER TWO

*Dear Edie,*

*I wanted you to know how I met your dad. I'd just started university in Manchester, and I got a job at the supermarket near my halls, operating the checkout for a few shifts a week. On my first day, the manager gave me a tour and we ran into your dad. He was stacking shelves. Soup, I think.*

*'Jessica, this is Jake. He's been with us a couple of months now.'*

*I smiled, and your dad put his hand out to shake mine.*

*'Hi, Jessica,' he said, and that was it.*

*His hand was warm and slightly dry, I could feel the skin was a little rough in places. There was something about the sound of my name in his mouth that made it seem new. And then the manager moved on to cleaning products, and I followed him. I tried really hard not to look back over my shoulder, but I did, and your dad had gone back to what he was doing. I wondered whether meeting me had had any impact whatsoever on his day.*

*Every time I went in for a shift, I thought about him, about whether he'd be there. But it was a pretty big place and he always seemed to be stacking shelves or marking down reduced items or shifting things around, while I was on the tills. More than once, I caught a glimpse of him just as I was leaving. And I felt irrationally cross that I hadn't seen him earlier, though god knows I wouldn't have said anything to him if I had.*

*I told my friend Gemma about him, in a letter. We'd written notes to each other throughout school, and I wanted to carry that on. Gemma thought I was mad and always replied by text. Anyway, I told her I couldn't stop thinking about him and that I'd barely met him, and he'd said about two words to me and I'd said nothing in reply. Gemma was bolder than me, more worldly, somehow, even though we'd both lived in the same little town our whole lives until I'd gone away to university. She asked me what he looked like. It was hard to describe him. He wasn't especially tall, he wasn't fat or thin. I couldn't remember the colour of his eyes. And his hair was brown, that most nondescript of colours.*

*The following weekend, I arrived at work and he was standing outside, leaning against the side of the building, smoking a cigarette. I felt my face start to flush, and I turned my head to the side, hoping he wouldn't see.*

*'Jessica,' he said. 'Jess?'*

*It was a miracle to me that he'd half remembered my name, even though his had been going through my mind for weeks, crowding out my reading and my half-finished essay. I turned back to him, willing my skin to return to its usual colour. I said he could call me Jess. He repeated it, and again, it sounded like an entirely different name to the one I'd carried around with me for eighteen years.*

*'Have a nice day, Jess.'*

*Edie, when you meet someone you really like and every minute is spent wanting them to notice you, a few words mean everything. My craving was sated. But as soon as he was gone, it returned. I was desperate to know when I'd get to talk to him again, whether I would have to wait another six weeks. I went inside, hung my coat up on the usual peg, and started my shift. But the dissatisfaction lingered.*

*It was winter, but not the good part when Christmas is coming, and everyone is feeling festive and throwing parties and eating too much. It was January, the bleakest month, when no one has any money and spring seems a long way away. I only lived a ten-minute walk from the supermarket, but I remember that my toes would feel frozen solid by the time I got back to my little room. I used to walk home as fast as I could, my hands rammed deep in my pockets, my hood up against the wind.*

*One day, I was nearly there when I heard a car pull to a stop at the side of me. I turned to look, and it was him. He was driving a red Volkswagen, and, when he wound down the window, I heard a blast of something loud from his stereo. He said my name, asked if I wanted a lift.*

*I thought about getting into that car beside him, about how our bodies would be closer than they'd ever been before, and how I would get to learn what music he was listening to and whether he was neat or untidy and how well he drove. I was still young enough that having your own car seemed very adult to me. I was living on very little money and owning something that big seemed so far away, almost exotic. I thanked him and said that it was okay, that I was nearly home.*

*I don't know why I said it. I had been wanting something like this to happen for weeks, and now it had, and I'd pushed it away. It was something I did, something I've always done. But I'm trying to do it less as I come to understand that opportunities don't always continue to present themselves. All my life, I've tried to train myself to reach out and grab the things I want with both hands. He shrugged and wound his window back up, and then he was gone, and it took a moment for me to realise that I should start walking again.*

*When I talked to Gemma, she always asked me how it was going with Jake, and I told her the tiny scraps of progress I had made. We had exchanged a few words outside the building one morning. He had offered me a lift home. She sighed loudly when I told her I'd said no. She told me I was useless, that we needed to do something about this. That she would visit, and we'd have a party.*

*At home, Gemma lived on the other side of town from me, in a small, squat house with her parents and her older brother, Dan. Gemma's parties were popular, because her parents didn't seem to mind going out and leaving the house in the hands of a group of drunk teenagers, and the neighbours rarely complained. And Dan was either busy or he just joined in. It was the rougher end of town, and arguments and parties were more frequent. People were used to noise. They didn't complain, because next week it might be them, and they didn't want the complaint to bounce back.*

*I thought about what kind of party she might arrange here, with only my small room in halls to host it. I wanted to say no, but she never responded well to that. When she arrived, a couple of weeks later, she looked around as if she thought the room might open up a little on closer inspection, then said that drinks in the pub would have to do. When I left her to go and do my shift, she told me to mention the drinks to Jake 'and some of the others'. I wondered what she thought it was like, whether she imagined there were crowds of us working there, making plans to socialise in the evenings. When I said I couldn't do it, she rolled her eyes and said I should leave it to her. And I believed that she would think of something. She was the kind of girl who made things happen.*

*She turned up later that day, and it was quiet, so we chatted for a while at my till. And when Jake walked past, I cleared my throat to alert her to the fact that this was him, the person we'd spent all this time talking about. But I needn't have done, because they made eye contact and they both smiled.*

*'Gemma Kershaw?' he asked, his head tilted slightly to one side.*

*'Jake Burton!'*

*He came closer and it looked like they might hug, but then they didn't, and it was a little awkward.*

*'Jess,' Gemma said, turning to me. 'You remember Jake, right? From school?'*

*From school? My head was spinning. This wasn't right. I was the one who knew Jake, who was supposed to be introducing him to my friend. We were thirty miles from where Gemma and I went to school. How could Jake have gone there too?*

*'I'd completely forgotten that this was where you moved,' Gemma was saying. 'You remember Jess, don't you?'*

*At last, Jake and I made eye contact. 'I didn't remember,' he said, and then he dropped his eyes to the floor, as if he'd said something he was ashamed of. 'But we know each other now, a bit.'*

*'Well listen, we're going out for drinks tonight. Will you come? Bring some friends, if you want to.'*

*'Cool. I'll give you my number.'*

*He pulled a tatty piece of paper from his pocket and I handed him a pen, and when he took it from me, his fingers brushed mine and I felt a shiver and wondered whether he felt something too. He passed the piece of paper to Gemma and disappeared. As he was walking away, Gemma and I widened our eyes at each other, and when he'd gone, we both collapsed into laughter.*

*'I can't believe you've come away to uni and you've got a crush on someone we went to school with for years!'*

*I was trying to remember whether he had seemed familiar to me, now that I knew. Gemma's brother seemed to have played football with pretty much everyone, so Gemma knew a lot more people than I did.*

*'So, what? His family moved here?' I was still trying to puzzle it all out.*

*'Yes, after his GCSEs, I think. His dad got a new job or something.' She paused, then went on. 'You know, I kissed him once, at a party.'*

*I didn't say anything, but I was devastated. I'd felt almost like I'd discovered him, like he'd always been standing by the tins of soup in that supermarket, had never been a little boy, or a young teenager kissing girls at parties. There was so much I wanted to know and couldn't find the words to ask. Like whether he was a good kisser or why I'd never heard about him before.*

*Edie, I'm sure there are things that are uncomfortable for you, here. Imagining your dad kissing Gemma, for a start. Thinking about us as young and vulnerable and romantic. Try to bear it, and keep reading. It's important.*

*When I'd finished my shift, I hurried back to my room to get ready. Gemma was in the kitchen I shared with seven other girls, drinking tea with a couple of them. She'd invited them along. I felt sick with nerves. It was entirely possible that Jake and I wouldn't speak that night, or that he wouldn't even come, and yet I somehow knew that it wouldn't go like that. I'd already decided what to wear, chosen my favourite pair of jeans and a black top that Gemma always said looked good on me. It had thin straps and it was silky, and another boy at another party had told me I looked sexy in it, and so it made me feel sexy. It made me feel like someone else.*

*I got dressed too early, brushed my long, dark hair until it shone. I put on some makeup, and took it off again, thinking it was too much, and started again, more careful and sparing the second time. All the time, Gemma and I talked and laughed, and she showed me the text messages she and Jake had sent each other that day. He was coming. He was bringing a friend. Gemma said she hoped the friend was hot.*

*She'd arranged to meet him at eight. At seven-thirty, I wrapped a chunky scarf around my neck and put my coat and boots on. And then I walked to the pub with my arm linked through Gemma's, feeling like I was heading towards a new beginning. Or do I only remember it that way now, knowing what I do? I suppose it doesn't matter much.*

*Gemma was wearing a red dress that showed off her hips and her boobs, both of which were large, but not too large. She had bright red lipstick on, and there was a smudge of it on her teeth, and I didn't tell her, and I wasn't sure why. She looked so glamorous, and I kept thinking about what she'd said, about kissing Jake once at a party, and I couldn't bear to imagine that it might happen again. Not that she was interested in him. She had a boyfriend that winter, called Mark, who was at college studying engineering. He smoked a lot of weed and took her to bars in the next town, and they were having sex. She talked a lot about the sex they were having – how much, and how long, and how big.*

*I'd never had sex. I'd had the opportunity a couple of times, but it had never felt right, somehow. I was scared of it, to be honest. It seemed like a line that you couldn't cross back from. Which it is, of course. I was stuck, in a way. Desperate to be more adult but terrified, too. I wasn't ready for a proper job or responsibilities. And I lumped sex in with all of that, as another thing that grown-ups did. Something I would do eventually.*

*Gemma and I had had a couple of drinks while we were getting ready. I loved the warm feeling that alcohol gave me. Just halfway through my first bottle of beer, I'd begun to relax, felt my confidence growing. Gemma had pulled a bottle of vodka from her bag and held it up to me, her eyebrows raised, but I'd shaken my head. A few times when we were at school, I'd misjudged it, and gone from being cute and bubbly to being blotchy and drunk before we'd even arrived at the party or pub. I wanted to pace myself, that night.*

*When we got to the pub, Gemma looked around for Jake, but I knew he wasn't there. I could sense it. And I sensed it when he walked in, too. The hairs on my arms went up. I wonder whether you'll laugh at this; whether you'll think I'm making it up. I promise I'm not. We didn't talk for ages. Gemma talked to him, and flirted with his friend, and I just stood there, feeling stupid. Jake and I exchanged quiet smiles. And then a couple of hours into the evening,*

*I went outside for a breather, the alcohol masking the cold. Even so, after a minute or so, I wished I'd brought a coat. I leaned against the outside wall of the pub, feeling tears prick at my eyes. I'd really hoped that something might happen. Gemma had got me all excited, and I'd been stupid, and started to believe.*

*I blinked away the tears, counted to ten. Told myself I would go back inside and keep pretending that everything was fine. But I only took a couple of steps, because then the door opened, and Jake came out. I hoped he would come over and hoped he wouldn't. For a second, I thought I might be sick, and then I was fine again.*

*'Jess,' he said, his voice steady, his eyes fixed on mine.*

*He was walking towards me and he didn't stop when I expected him to, didn't stop until he was inches from my body. I wondered whether he'd had too much to drink, whether he could hide it in his voice but wasn't quite so in control when it came to his movements. I said hi, my voice a croak.*

*For a moment, we just looked at each other, and I thought that he was going to kiss me. I readied myself, licked my lips, and then he didn't kiss me, and I felt stupid and disappointed and cold, suddenly. I shivered. He asked me who I was, and when I said I didn't know what he meant, he leaned closer still and said he didn't know anything about me. I was flustered. I started to tell him about my course, about my room in halls.*

*And then he did kiss me, and I wasn't ready for it, and although I'd thought about it for a long time and it felt wonderful, I couldn't stop thinking about him kissing Gemma like this, in some other garden at some other party. He put his arms around me, wrapped his coat around the two of us.*

*Although I felt so sure about him, that kiss somehow didn't feel like it was the start of something, like it would lead to all this, to you. Perhaps because I didn't dare to believe. It was just a kiss, a drunken kiss, I kept telling myself. It wasn't a relationship, wasn't a date. This is what we did, all of us, to pass the time. We got drunk and we kissed, because there was nothing else to do. And we were teenagers, with hormones running wild. It was just a kiss.*

*I wanted you to know how I met your dad. We met at a supermarket, and then at a pub.*

*With love,*

*Mum*

# CHAPTER THREE

The following day, Jess was in the living room with Edie when she heard her mum's key in the lock. They were lying on their backs on the brightly coloured playmat Gemma had bought when Edie was born. Jess was holding things out to her daughter, seeing if she would take them. Edie was waving her hands around. Jess braced herself. She heard her mum come inside, heard her unzip her coat. Any minute now, she'd enter the room.

'I'm back,' Caroline said. 'How are you two?'

Jess sat up and picked up Edie. She needed to have Edie close, she felt. Edie was her protection, somehow.

'I need to talk to you about something. Shall I make us a cup of tea?'

They went through to the kitchen and Jess's mum, Caroline, kept asking questions.

'Is it Edie? Is there something wrong?'

That gave Jess pause. At least it isn't Edie, she thought. At least it wasn't her baby. But for her mum, it was *her* baby. Hadn't her mum always said, when she was three and fourteen and twenty, that Jess would always be her baby? That's just how it was, once you had children.

Jess flicked the kettle on and grabbed mugs from the cupboard with one hand, holding Edie in place with the other. She was getting better at this, but her mum held out her arms regardless, and Jess put Edie in them.

'Edie's fine. Just give me a minute.'

When the tea was made and Jess had taken a packet of biscuits from the cupboard and she and her mum were sitting down, there was really nothing more she could do to put it off.

'I went to the hospital yesterday,' she said.

'I thought you were going shopping,' her mum interrupted.

'I know. I didn't want to tell you, in case it was nothing. But it isn't. So now I have to.'

Caroline's hands flew to her mouth, and Jess felt for a moment as though she wasn't in the room, but somewhere slightly above it, watching it, and she thought about how her mum was reacting the way you see people reacting to bad news in films or on TV. And she wondered how this could be her life, their lives, and how it could be that the news she had to impart was going to take a hammer to this cosy, domestic scene, and tear things apart.

'I've got breast cancer,' Jess said. The words were a jumble, and she hoped her mum would have heard her correctly, hoped she wouldn't have to say them again.

'Breast cancer?' her mum repeated, and Jess nodded. 'But you're twenty-one!'

Jess closed her eyes for a second. She wanted to say that it wasn't helpful to remind her of her age, that it wasn't helpful to disbelieve the news she'd just imparted. But she didn't have the energy. Her mum had always been a bit like this. When she had told her mum that she was pregnant, that she was dropping out of university to have the baby, she'd been a bit like this. And then, the news had been about a new life, and not about an illness. Nothing like this.

'Jessica, is this really happening?'

Jess nodded, and when her mum stood up, she thought she was going to give her a hug, but she was trying to pass Edie back to her. Jess took her. She was half-asleep, groggy, and she objected to the discomfort of being passed from person to person with a little whimper. Jess looked down at her daughter and promised her, silently, that she would never behave this way. That if she was lucky enough to survive into Edie's adulthood, and Edie came to her with something like this, she would be calm and supportive, full of love.

'How much do you know? What's the treatment plan?' Caroline asked.

She'd sat back down, now that she didn't have Edie to hold, and she looked like she had hundreds of questions like this, ready to fire. She was crying, too. And Jess realised that she hadn't cried all that much. But she thought she might, soon.

'I don't know anything, Mum. It was a shock.'

'But didn't you ask?'

'No, I didn't ask. I was on my own, with Edie, and it was a horrible shock. I couldn't take it in. Even now I don't know what the right questions are.'

There was a long beat of silence, and Jess could feel her mother's disapproval. She wanted to ask her mum to hold her in her arms. To tell her it would be okay. To tell her she would help her through it. But Caroline was up on her feet again, pacing the room.

'I had an aunt with breast cancer, do you remember? Penny. She used to live up near the school. We took a casserole round once, when she'd been in hospital.'

Jess didn't remember, but she thought there was little point in saying that. When her mum was fixed on something like this, she often didn't need input.

'She died,' Caroline said, softly.

And suddenly, Jess couldn't take it. She needed to be out of the house, away from the walls, which she could feel pushing in on her. She needed to breathe some fresh air and be alone.

'I'm going to take Edie for a walk,' she said.

If her mum heard the shake in her voice, she didn't mention it.

'Do you want me to come with you?' she asked.

Jess shook her head. 'I'm okay,' she said.

It took a while to get the two of them ready. Jess put her coat and scarf on, and she put Edie in a snowsuit. She'd never worn it before and it was too big, her limbs not quite reaching the suit's arm and leg holes. Jess lay her daughter flat in her pram, tucked a blanket around her. She bent to give Edie a kiss, and a tear fell from her face and landed on her daughter's, and she knew she had to get out quickly, because it was starting. She didn't want to examine her reluctance to let her mother see her crumble.

Jess opened the door, and she heard her mum calling something to her, but she pushed the pram out and closed the door behind her without looking back. The tears were coming fast, now, and she hurried to the end of the road, only slowing her pace when she knew she'd gone too far to be followed. A memory came to her, of being six or seven, curling up with her mum on the sofa to watch a quiz show they both liked. Her mum would call out the answers and Jess never knew any of them, but she liked the presenter, who always wore sparkly dresses and had the most beautiful curly hair Jess had ever seen. There was a catchphrase from the show, something about making it count, and Jess would sometimes shout it down the stairs when she was supposed to be asleep, and her mum would come upstairs to tell her to get back to bed, but she would be laughing, and they would always have an extra cuddle.

Edie was asleep. The gentle movement of the pram had soothed her. She was a good baby, Jess thought, although she had nothing to compare her to. She was happy, easy to love. Jess had thought about not having her. She'd been twenty, two years into a degree, and unexpectedly pregnant. She'd thought about making the whole situation go away. She knew others who'd done that, knew that it was an option. She didn't think it was wrong. But somehow, she'd known that she didn't want to do that. It hadn't been what she'd planned, but it had been what was happening, and she'd decided to just go with it.

Jess looked up. She'd barely noticed where she was going, stopping now and then to cross roads carefully, turning this way or that without much thought. She was near her old primary school. One of the windows was covered in red and green hand prints. In a few years, Edie would be in one of those classrooms, learning her letters and numbers. Jess looked down at her, her peaceful sleeping face all that was visible, and tried to imagine her at four years old. Jess had a hazy memory of her first day at school. Her mum had always said that she couldn't possibly, but she did. She remembered standing in the playground and her socks slipping down her legs, having to bend to pull them up. What would Edie look like, in a grey skirt and knee-length socks? And would Jess be there to see it?

Jess's mind kept flitting back to Jake. In the early days of her pregnancy, she'd dared to imagine the two of them doing this together, but it hadn't worked out like that. She remembered coming home that weekend, telling her mum, the way her mum had said they would look after the baby between them and who needed men, anyway? Sometimes, Jess scanned

Edie's face for signs of Jake. They were there, in her dark eyes and the shape of her chin, and Jess marvelled, again and again, at the fact that they had made a human, unwittingly, in those long days and nights they'd spent in bed together. That Edie was part her and part him, that she was theirs.

She'd left after a huge row with Jake about their future. Neither of them had had this in their plan, but while she'd quickly adapted to the idea of it, he'd refused to. Unable, possibly. Definitely unwilling. And she'd been so furious — all her fear of losing him turned to rage — that she'd said things that couldn't be unsaid and cut off all contact. And now he was travelling around the country, trying to get a music career off the ground, trying to make a mark. How could she interrupt that, with news like this? I have cancer. She couldn't. She wouldn't. And yet.

Edie snuffled and woke, just as they were walking past the park, its equipment dripping with the rain that had fallen overnight. Jess had never pushed Edie on a swing, never held her hand as she went down a slide. When did all that start, she wondered? When they could sit up, when they could crawl, or walk? She asked her mum, sometimes, about things like that, and Caroline would wave her hand and say she couldn't possibly remember. She would ask the Health Visitor, she thought, next time she got Edie weighed. She would ask how long she had to wait before she could push her daughter on a swing.

Jess turned for home when Edie began to cry. She was hungry, and Jess didn't want to sit and feed her on a wet bench. As Edie's cries grew in force and volume, Jess pushed the pram a little faster. They went past the church, past the Chinese takeaway and the Tesco Express. They were five minutes from home, and Edie was wailing now, and it was only then that Jess noticed her own tears had stopped. She put a hand to her face, wondered if it was red and puffy. As soon as they made it through the front door into the warmth of the house, Jess began pulling off their outer layers, knowing that Edie would be calm as soon as she put her to her breast. But before she could do it, Caroline swooped out into the hallway, reaching for Edie.

'There there, my darling. What is it, hey?' Caroline held Edie close and Edie turned her head, butting her forehead against Caroline's chest.

'Give her to me, Mum. She's hungry.'

Caroline handed Edie over, her face a little hurt. 'I wish you'd let me feed her sometimes. It would give you a break.'

'How can I let you feed her when she's breastfed?' Jess's voice was sharper than she'd intended.

Caroline held up both of her hands and backed into the kitchen, and Jess heard the sound of the kettle beginning to boil. She clamped Edie to her breast and went through to the lounge, sinking into the armchair. She was shattered. She'd fed Edie three times in the night, and between feeds she'd lain awake, wondering what all of this meant, what she should do.

When Caroline came into the lounge with a mug in each hand, Jess smiled at her.

'Sorry,' she said. 'She'd got herself all worked up and it got to me.'

'Love, are we going to pretend that none of this is happening?'

'None of what?' Jess asked, trying to keep her voice level.

'The cancer!'

'I'm not pretending anything. I still have to look after my baby, don't I?'

Caroline shook her head, as if this wasn't quite true.

'I'm thinking about getting in touch with Jake,' Jess said.

And then she wasn't sure whether she'd said it to antagonise her mother, or because it was true.

Caroline sighed. 'Why on earth would you do that? He obviously knows you've had her by now, and he hasn't been in touch, has he? I can't see him rushing to your rescue.'

Jess said nothing. There was so much her mum didn't know. Couldn't know. The way Jake had looked at her when they woke up together in the mornings, the way he reached out to touch her face or took a strand of her hair between two fingers, as if he was checking that she was real. The way he'd made her laugh, telling her stories about his childhood. The way they'd laughed together, eyes full of tears. The way he'd seemed to get beneath all the layers and really understood her, even when she was trying to hide from him.

The day Edie had been born, Jess had been desperate to call him, to show him, but she was exhausted from the labour and she'd fallen asleep, her mum sitting in the corner of the room with Edie in her arms, and when she'd woken up it hadn't seemed like such a good idea after all.

'I think I'm going to go up and have a lie down with her,' Jess said. 'I didn't get much sleep and she'll go off after this feed.'

'Okay,' Caroline said.

She sounded almost put out and Jess had to stop herself from asking what the problem was. She knew that the lack of sleep made her snappy, and she tried hard to keep it in check. Upstairs, she pulled back her bedcovers and got in with Edie, who'd finished feeding and was half asleep. Jess watched her, the way her face twitched and changed every few seconds, until she fell asleep herself.

She woke to a harsh ringing sound and realised it was her phone. She managed to answer it before it disturbed Edie.

'Hello?' It was almost a whisper.

'It's me,' Gemma said. 'Can I come over later?'

Jess had missed Gemma every day when she was away at university. And when she'd come back, without a degree and pregnant, they'd fallen back into their old ways. Spending weekends and many evenings together. Just without all the alcohol, at least for Jess. Gemma had simply shrugged when Jess had told her she was pregnant, and Jess had loved her for that. She often felt that without Gemma she would go mad.

'Yes, come,' she said. 'Straight after work?'

'I'll bring a pizza.'

Jess hung up and looked at her watch. It was almost lunchtime. Her mind whirred through a few things. Her mum, and whether she might be going out to work in a bit. And then it settled on Jake again, and Jess was surprised, and she checked whether she still had his number in her phone. Knowing all the while that she did.

# CHAPTER FOUR

*Dear Edie,*

*I wanted you to know about the first proper argument I had with your dad. It's important that you see things from both sides. I sometimes make our love story sound like a fairy tale, and it was, sometimes. But it wasn't always. It was six months or so after that first kiss, and we'd been pretty much inseparable. We timed our breaks at work and stood outside, whatever the weather, just kissing. Occasionally, the manager would stick his head out of the door to tut at us. There was nothing he could do, but he obviously thought it was important to show his contempt for the situation.*

*We bickered occasionally but only about silly things. What to see at the cinema or whose turn it was to buy the drinks. We didn't have much money, either of us. He was working at the supermarket full time, but it didn't pay much. I thought it was just a stopgap sort of a job. He made me think it was. He talked a lot about his big plans, to play in a band and to travel the world. We didn't talk about what would happen when I'd finished university. It was summer and we were in love and life was good.*

*Your dad played guitar. He often picked it up when we were at the house he lived in with his parents, holed up in his room. He sang me songs by bands like The Cure and INXS. I thought he was good. He had a soft voice but there was something underneath it, something raw and rough, and you could just make it out when he sang. It was different to other voices I'd heard. I thought he would make it. I asked him whether he'd ever tried writing his own songs and he shrugged me off. He just talked big about making an album, getting a drummer and a bassist to work with and hiring a recording studio.*

*One afternoon, when I'd finished lectures for the day and your dad was at work, I was wandering around town. I'd been thinking that I wanted to get him something, but I only had a few pounds and I couldn't think how to make it stretch to buy anything worthwhile. I was walking past the library when I saw a notice in the window. A local band was looking for a lead guitarist and singer. They listed bands they wanted to sound like, bands I'd listened to in your dad's bedroom, names I'd seen on posters on his wall. It was perfect. It wasn't a present, as such, but I genuinely believed it might be the start of his future, and I was so proud that I'd seen it. I pulled a notebook and pen out of my bag and wrote down all the details. I looked at my watch. There were another two hours to go before the end of your dad's shift. I didn't go home. I just killed time, going in and out of shops, impatient to break the news.*

*When there was only half an hour to go, I walked to the supermarket. It was a warm day, no breeze, and my hair felt heavy on the back of my neck when I got there. I lifted it up with both hands and then let it drop. There was a wall around the car park, and I sat on it. I pulled a book from my bag. I think it was Dickens. I had a seminar about it the following day and I had two hundred pages left to read. I was finding it hard going. I stopped at the end of every couple of pages and looked at my watch. I wanted to tell him about the band, but I wanted to see him, too. I wanted to feel his arms around me, the way he laced his fingers together at the small of my back.*

*And then finally, he stepped outside, his eyes adjusting to the bright sun. I jumped up and waved, and he smiled lazily, and it was enough to tell me he was glad to see me. When he reached me, I let it all out in one breath. I was dancing around, moving my face ever closer to his, waiting for his kiss.*

*'Give me a minute!' he said, and there was a sharpness in his voice that I hadn't heard before, and I stopped moving but stayed close to him.*

*He said sorry straight away, but repeated that he needed a minute, that he'd just got out of work. I said that I was just excited for him and I heard the whine in my own voice. I felt young then, and stupid. Was I supposed to ignore it or make a big fuss and storm away? I could feel tears starting to build and I didn't do anything to try to stop them. I looked up at him, to make sure he saw that he'd done this. He met my eyes for a second. Said he was sorry, that I shouldn't cry.*

*He folded me in his arms, and I resisted for a few seconds before letting my body do what it wanted to do. Then he pulled a packet of cigarettes from his bag, lit one and offered the packet to me. I shook my head. I'd started smoking, a little, just with him. It was something we did together. It felt like it was just our thing. It's stupid, I know. He pleaded with me to say something. But I didn't know what to say.*

*I said that I thought I should go home. He threw his cigarette end on the floor and ground it out with the heel of his black boot. And the smell of it was stronger, suddenly, and I was too hot, and I just wanted to be anywhere else.*

*He didn't argue. I wondered for a moment whether he'd shrug and let me walk away, but he ushered me towards his car, like always. I loved watching him drive. I loved the way the muscles in his arm moved when he changed gear, the way he checked his mirrors before pulling away or changing lane. Often, we'd put the radio on and sing along, but not that day. We didn't speak, and when he pulled up outside my halls, I reached down to release the seat belt, and he touched my hand.*

*'I'm sorry,' he said.*

*I said I knew. I did know. I believed him. When I walked into the shared kitchen, my friend Keisha was standing at the kitchen sink, filling the kettle, and she turned and asked what was wrong. I loved that she knew instantly, but I didn't want to talk about it, so I said it was nothing and went to my room to do some more reading. I lay on my bed for a couple of hours, trying to concentrate on the text in front of me, trying not to brood.*

*I was young, and I loved him, so the next night, I went to meet him from work again and we pretended nothing had happened. When he kissed me, it didn't quite feel like normal. He was being careful with me, I realised. And that was enough to make me forgive him. He took me back to his house and made me a cup of tea. When we'd been in his room for a while, he picked up his guitar. I asked whether he'd called about the band. I'd left the piece of paper with the details on the passenger seat of his car the day before.*

*He strummed a bit, then stopped and looked at me. Said no. When I asked why not, he said it wasn't his thing. I was speechless. It was exactly his thing. The right kind of music, the right role in the band. What was the problem? Unless he didn't really want the things he said he wanted, after all. Unless he was scared of not being good enough. Unless he was planning to stay at the supermarket forever, pretending he planned to do something with his life but never actually doing it.*

*I didn't say all of those things. I just said I thought he was scared. I watched his face fill with anger, but he kept it all inside, letting the words wash over him. He asked me to leave it, said he thought I should go.*

*The previous day, I'd been the one to put a stop to our time together. I'd been in control. That day, it was him asking me to leave. I felt my face redden, and I wanted to take the words back. Would have done, if I could. I cared more, at that moment, about being in that room with him than I cared about challenging him. I tried to say that it didn't matter, that I was sorry, but something had closed in him and he wasn't listening.*

*He always drove me home, but that day, he didn't offer, didn't stand to come with me or to see me out. I closed his bedroom door quietly, ran down the stairs and slipped out. And all the way home, I cried noisily, not caring what I looked like or who might see me.*

*We were having sex by then. I know, I know. You don't want to know the details, so I won't give them. But it's important that you understand why I was so upset. We were having sex, and I had thought he was the one for me, and that day I was scared that I'd got it wrong, that I'd lost my virginity to someone who didn't really care about me at all. So I cried, and I half walked and half ran home, where I shut myself up in my room and cried some more.*

*That night I called my mum and I told her I thought it was over with Jake, and that my heart was broken, and she listened. She said that first love isn't always the right love and told me a story I'd never heard before about a man she knew before she met my dad. And then she made a sort of snort and said that it hadn't been right with my dad either, obviously. It was strange to hear her talking about that, just as it must be strange for you to be reading about my teenage years. But it just made me more sure that it was all over. Perhaps I'd meet the man I should be with next. Second time lucky.*

*Jake didn't call the next day. I went to uni and walked home and caught up on some of the reading I'd been getting behind on since spending all my spare time with him. By the time he did call, the day after, I'd almost stopped believing that he would. But just hearing his voice, my heart leapt to my throat and I could barely speak. I had to think about breathing. That's one of the things love does to you. You have to remember that you need to breathe. He said he was sorry, and that he loved me, and asked if we could forget about it.*

*I wasn't sure, and I told him that. Pushed into a corner, he explained. He was scared to go after what he wanted. He was scared that he wanted a career in music too much, and he would never have one, and so sometimes he felt like it was easier to not even try.*

*He talked me round. I think I knew that he would, that I'd let him. I already loved him, you see. He'd already won me. When I told Mum that we were still together, she sounded concerned but said that I should do whatever made me happy, and that she'd always be there if anything went wrong. I knew from that that she thought I was doing the wrong thing. But it was my life, and I had to make the decisions, even if they weren't the right ones.*

*Things went back to how they had been before, very quickly, and we just didn't talk about it. And when anything like that came up again, I just didn't bother suggesting it. I let him get on with things. Which meant that his life changed very little over the next year. He stayed at the supermarket when I felt that he could and should have been doing something bigger and better. He stayed and I didn't push him to go.*

*I wanted you to know about our first argument. It was painful and it was over quickly. It wasn't the end of the world. It wasn't the end of us.*

*With love,*

*Mum*

# CHAPTER FIVE

The doorbell rang just after six. Jess was upstairs giving Edie a bath, just like she always was at that time. She'd learned the hard way that routine was crucial, and now the hour between six and seven was all about bath and cuddles and stories. A minute later, Gemma pushed through the door. She bent over the bath and gave Edie an enormous smile, plunging her hands into the tepid bathwater and tickling Edie's tummy. Jess loved that Gemma greeted Edie first. She also loved that Gemma then got on the floor and gave Jess a hug.

'Can you grab that towel?' Jess asked, nodding in the direction of the radiator.

She lifted Edie and laid her on the warm towel that Gemma had spread out on the floor. Wrapped her up. And then she picked up the bundle and carried Edie through to her bedroom, where there were nappies and new vests and sleepsuits. Gemma threw herself on Jess's bed and her hair fanned out around her.

'I'm knackered.'

Jess almost said that Gemma didn't know what tiredness was, that she had thought she knew, before having Edie, but now she waded through a different level of tiredness every day. But she stopped herself. It wasn't fair, and she knew her friend didn't mean anything by it.

'Work?'

Gemma worked in the nicest bar in town, which wasn't saying much.

'Yes, we had this big office party in, and they were such dickheads. Every single one of them wanted a different cocktail every time and they were hammered by three and pretending not to be because they were going back to work. And I'm pretty sure two of them were either doing drugs or having sex in the toilets.'

Jess laughed. 'How do you know?'

'They were just so shifty. Kept sneaking off together. I reckon she was his boss, too.'

'Scandal.' Jess enjoyed Gemma's stories. She knew half of them were made up, that it was something Gemma did to get through the long shifts, and she didn't care. Her world felt so small and she enjoyed having it widened in this way.

Jess manoeuvred Edie's little limbs into her clothes and then propped herself up with a couple of pillows and began to feed her daughter.

Gemma rolled over on to her stomach. 'I've been promoted to assistant manager, because Carly's going on maternity leave, which means more money for basically the same job.'

'That's great!' Jess hoped her words didn't sound hollow. She was trying really hard to mean them. It was just so incredibly difficult, sometimes, to see people her age getting on with their lives, while she was stuck in a sort of limbo. At home with a baby. Degree unfinished. She'd thought she would do that final year later, and then decide on a career. But now, her whole future was an unknown, and she couldn't think about it for too long without wanting to cry.

A little later, when Jess's mum had gone out to her book club, Gemma and Jess sat downstairs in the living room, eating pizza. Edie was in her Moses basket at the side of Jess's armchair. Her eyelids kept flickering and every so often, she would jolt a little, but she was fast asleep.

'Are you okay?' Gemma asked. 'You seem really sad.'

Jess smiled a little. She hadn't told her friend she had cancer. Hadn't told anyone, other than her mum. And it might just have been the perfect time. Edie was asleep, her mum was out, Gemma was ready and willing to listen. But somehow, Jess just couldn't find the words. And so she told Gemma the other thing that was on her mind, instead.

'I've been thinking about Jake,' she said.

Gemma raised her eyebrows, silently inviting Jess to go on.

'I thought he was so great, when we were together, and maybe Edie deserves more than just me…'

'She doesn't only have you,' Gemma interrupted. 'She has your mum. She has me. You're not on your own with this, you know.'

'I know,' Jess said. 'I didn't mean it that way. I know she's not short of love. But she is short of a father. And I grew up without one, pretty much, so I know how that feels. To always be waiting for him to make an appearance or get things together and decide he wants his child. It's not the nicest way to spend a childhood.'

'I didn't know you felt like that. You never said.'

Jess brushed away tears. 'I suppose I didn't ever want to seem like I was saying Mum wasn't enough. She did so much for me, tried so hard. But I want more for Edie. I want her to have two parents.'

Or one, Jess thought. At least one.

'So, what?' Gemma asked. 'You're going to get in touch with him? I thought things were pretty final when you came back here.'

Jess reached for the final slice of pizza, just as Edie started to grizzle. A wave of exhaustion came over Jess. It was relentless, this job she was doing. Edie fed, and then slept, and then fed again. It was boring, and so tiring. And yet it was essential. Without her, Edie couldn't survive. Most people had someone to share it all with, of course. The baby's father couldn't breastfeed, but he could listen while you told him you thought you were going mad. He could hold the baby while you cried. And if you had cancer, and you died, he could take over.

Jess put the half-eaten piece of pizza back on the plate. She picked Edie up and held her in the air so their noses were touching. 'Hungry again so soon, little girl?' She wearily unclipped her nursing bra and put Edie to her breast. And all the time, she was thinking about how to answer Gemma's question. Was she going to get in touch with Jake? Were things too final to be revisited?

'He said some things that I can't forget, I suppose. He was more interested in this chance he got with the band than with me and Edie.'

'You have to remember that she wasn't Edie then,' Gemma said, frowning.

'What do you mean?'

'Well, now she's this little person and she's a huge part of your life, but then she was sort of an unknown. Especially for him. You were growing her in your body, but to him she was just this abstract concept. I just think he might be different, if you let him back into your life. That he might be everything you want him to be.'

Jess thought about that, not speaking. Gemma had a point, but she couldn't let go of the hurt she felt at being left to do this alone. Every time she pictured Jake's face, she was furious. And yet, she did think about him a lot. There was unfinished business there, even if it was just an argument they needed to have.

'I'm going to get in touch with him,' she said. It felt good for the decision to have been made. 'And then we'll see.'

Jess's mum arrived home just as Gemma was leaving, and when Jess had closed the door with her mum on the inside and her friend on the outside, she felt suddenly tired. How had it come to this? She felt like the life she was supposed to have was walking away without her.

'Where's Edie?' Caroline asked.

'She's in her Moses basket, in the lounge. She's fast off. I think I'm going to take her upstairs and go to bed.'

'Will you have a cup of tea with me first?'

Jess wanted to say no. Her eyes were sore, and she probably had less than two hours before Edie would wake again, demanding a feed. But something in her mum's eyes made her nod her head. Was she lonely? Jess wondered. Had she been lonely those two years when Jess was away at university, only coming home in the holidays and for the odd weekend? Her mum had always been so self-sufficient, so strong, that Jess had never really considered it.

Caroline boiled the kettle and Jess got the mugs down from the cupboard. Caroline pulled two teabags from the box and Jess went to the fridge for the milk. How many times had they performed this little ritual, over the years? There was something comforting about it, but something a little sad, too. How many years would they go on like this, the two of them? And in time, would Edie find her role in this performance? Would it always be the three of them, with only one another to love?

'Is there something you wanted to talk to me about?' Jess asked.

'I just wanted to apologise. I don't think I've handled all this cancer stuff very well. It was so unexpected, and so awful, and I don't know where to begin with it.'

'It's okay.'

Jess was sitting on the sofa, now, in the living room, and her mum was in the armchair, and she wished they were closer. Wished they were the sort of mother and daughter who might sit together, side by side, one running a hand through the other's hair.

'Did you tell Gemma?' Caroline asked.

'No. I don't know how.'

Jess took a sip of her drink and didn't look up. She couldn't meet her mum's eyes. She was on the verge of tears, and she knew it wouldn't take much to start her off. And if she started, she had no idea how or when she would stop. She felt like she'd regressed, somehow, to childhood. Here in her mother's house. She willed her voice to stay steady as she changed the subject.

'I should tell Dad,' Jess said.

There was a slow silence and when Jess looked up, her mum's expression was one of hurt.

'He deserves to know...'

'I never said he didn't,' Caroline snapped.

It had always been like this. Jess had no memory of her parents ever being together, so it had always been her and her mum, at home, and her dad on the periphery of things, barely peering in. He'd been disinterested her whole life, only ever involved when she asked him to be, absent from so many birthday parties and Christmases and parents' evenings. Jess felt let down, but she could never quite bring herself to cut ties with him. And so, he was another person to tell. Another person to manage, to tick off her list.

'I can't imagine he'll care much,' Jess said.

As soon as she'd said it, she wished she could take it back. It was a stupid thing to say. He wasn't a monster. He was just careless. Selfish. She was his daughter and she was twenty-one, a new mum, and she had cancer. He couldn't not care. So she was surprised when her mum didn't challenge what she'd said.

'You know Tony.' Caroline's voice was bitter.

When she was a child, Jess had longed for a dad who lived at home and went out to work and played with her at week-ends. All of her friends had one, and it seemed so unfair that she didn't. Hers sometimes came to pick her up and take her out for the day, but he never seemed to get it quite right: taking her to the cinema on bright, sunny days when she would have preferred to run around at the park; splashing out on a day at a theme park when she was too young to really enjoy many of the rides. And then there were the cancella-tions, the let-downs. Often, she'd be standing at the door with her bag packed when she'd hear the phone ring, and her heart would drop like a stone. She would hear her mother's tight, fast responses and know that he wasn't coming. It wasn't as if he'd moved on, had another family. He'd always lived alone. Jess hadn't been replaced; she'd been forgotten. She wasn't sure which was worse.

'Did you ever love him?' Jess asked.

It felt like something she must have asked before, but she couldn't remember it, if she had.

'I'm not sure I'd call it love,' Caroline said.

Jess wished that, just for once, her mother would let go of her bitterness and tell her what had really happened. She never wanted Edie to feel this way, no matter what happened with Jake. But Caroline had never had a good word to say about Jess's father, which didn't make sense. Something must have brought them together, after all. They must have at least liked each other, once.

'Tell me,' Jess said, hoping her mother would recognise the need in her without her having to spell it out.

Caroline looked at Jess, her eyes searching. They'd both finished their mugs of tea. Edie was still, her chest rising and falling like clockwork. And suddenly, Jess wished she hadn't asked. Was it too late, now, to say she'd changed her mind? To pick up Edie's basket and take her upstairs and never know the full story? Because what if it was terrible? But no, she was overreacting. Her mum had allowed her dad to be in her life for all these years, so it can't have been all that bad, whatever happened between them.

'I met him at university, you know that,' Caroline began.

Jess nodded. Half of her wanted her mother to go on, and half of her didn't.

'He was clear from the start that he didn't want to be in a relationship, didn't want to get married or have children. He just knew that. But I was naïve, and I thought he'd change his mind when he got a bit older or fell in love. And we went on like that, in an on-and-off sort of way, for about four years. I kept thinking it would change, even though he kept telling me it wouldn't. And then I found out I was having you, and I told him, and he said he was sorry, but it wasn't what he wanted, that he'd always been clear about that.'

Jess felt like they were talking about someone else, someone distant, someone from a book or a film. Not her mother. Not her.

'Did he want you to have an abortion?' Jess asked.

'Yes, he thought that was the best solution. And I thought about it. Even booked myself in.'

Jess had never heard this. She tried not to flinch, but it was tough to hear, that you might never have existed at all.

'I couldn't go through with it. Didn't want to. He respected my decision, said he'd do what was right, financially speaking. Even then, I thought he'd change his mind when you were born. When you were real. Babies are real to their mothers from the time they find out they're pregnant, aren't they? But I don't think it's like that for the dad. I don't think it sinks in until the baby arrives.'

Caroline looked up and Jess tried to show that she was open to hearing this, but she mustn't have communicated it well.

'Oh love, I'm sorry. This must be hard. I just... you seemed like you wanted to know.'

'I do, it's okay.'

'Well, there's not much more to tell. You were born and I let him know and he came to see you three days later. Three days! You were his flesh and blood and he didn't race round to see you the minute he heard you'd arrived. I never understood that. I'd fallen for you instantly, I was totally gone, and by the time he turned up I was just sad for him, to be honest. That he was never going to know the love we had already. That he was too selfish to let it in.'

Jess thought about the similarities and the differences between her mum's story and her own. What must her mum have thought when she turned up at home, two years into university and pregnant? No father to be seen. It was history repeating itself, wasn't it?

'I want to get in touch with Jake,' Jess said. 'But I worry that it will be just like that. Just like Dad.'

Caroline wasn't expecting this sudden turn in the conversation, Jess saw, but she adjusted well.

'Is it because of the cancer, love? Are you thinking that she needs him around, in case...'

Caroline trailed off, not able to bring herself to speak the end of that sentence, even though they both knew what it was. Those unspoken words hung in the air, between them, making it harder for them to see one another clearly.

'It's partly that,' Jess said. 'Yes, that's definitely what's made me think about it all again. But it's just about him being her dad, too, and her deserving to know him.'

'Well, just think about it for a while. Don't rush into anything. In my opinion, having a father who isn't really interested can be worse than having none at all.'

Jess wanted to challenge her on that, to ask her how she would know. For her own part, Caroline had had loving, caring parents who were both present throughout her childhood. What did she know about how it felt to have a father like hers, or like Edie's? Her mother wasn't the one who had spent hours waiting by the window for a car that often didn't pull up. But she pressed her lips together and said nothing. It was getting late, and Edie would be up again soon. It was time for bed.

# CHAPTER SIX

*Dear Edie,*

*I wanted you to know what it's like to be without a dad. I grew up with half a father, at best. It wasn't that he was half a man. He wasn't broken or bereft or anything like that, to the best of my knowledge, at least. I wouldn't necessarily know. He just didn't want to be a father, so he barely was one. It might have been easier if he'd refused to have any involvement at all. That's why I go back and forth on the idea of bringing your dad into your life. But I can't just assume they're the same person. I want to believe that your dad is a stronger man than mine ever was. And I do believe it, almost all of the time.*

*In my early years, it was just me and Mum and that was fine. It was all I knew. I loved her ferociously, because she was all I had. There were friends and grandparents and all those people coming in and out, bringing presents and taking me to the park and playing games. But they were just background noise, as far as I was concerned. It was me and her. She was the one who put me to bed and was there if I woke up in the night and was scared. She was the one who cooked my food and held me all night when I was ill and took me everywhere she went. And I loved her for it.*

*I must have been about seven or eight when I started to notice that other families were not like ours. It was around the time that I was going round to friends' houses for tea, or to play, or even to sleep over, sometimes, and I saw that there was usually a dad around, and more often than not, a brother or sister. I asked her about it, one day. Why it was just us. And she must have known I would ask one day, but she wasn't ready for it. She said that my dad wasn't really able to be a dad to me, and I thought she meant he was physically unable. I thought he was ill.*

*That night, I crept downstairs and overheard her on the phone to him. Heard her say that I'd been asking, and did he want to come? I was hopping about with anticipation for the next few days, wondering what he might be like. Because I couldn't shake this idea that he was ill, I wondered whether he might be in a wheelchair or have a missing limb or something. But he was always so handsome, in my imaginings. Tall, with thick, dark hair. Like the dads I'd seen in films.*

*And then, the next Saturday, there was a knock on the door in the middle of the afternoon, and when I opened it up, there he was. It was the first time I'd met him, that I remembered. I'd expected to feel like I knew him, for him to seem familiar, to seem like he was mine, but he didn't. He was just an ordinary man, like all the other dads I'd seen. Nothing like the dads from films. He shuffled his feet and said hello, stuck out his hand for me to shake, and it felt cold and somehow a bit clammy at the same time, and I was disappointed. I'd built him up so much, and he was just a man.*

*He came inside and my parents shared a pot of tea and I tried to imagine them kissing or being a couple, like my friends' mums and dads, and I couldn't. They were polite with each other, both refusing the last biscuit on the plate until I shrugged and took it. I drank my glass of squash too quickly, and then I needed to go to the toilet, and I was afraid of missing something.*

*After that day, I saw him sometimes. Not regularly. Not every weekend or every other Thursday. He'd phone, sometimes, and Mum would say he was going to take me out somewhere, or he'd invited me for lunch, and I didn't once think about saying I didn't want to go. I think I was hoping that one day, he'd have turned into a dad. That he'd know how to talk to me and what might make me laugh and he'd understand the complexities of my friendships the way Mum did, but it never happened. He wasn't good at remembering what I did and didn't like to eat, or what my favourite colours were. When he bought me things, they were often wrong. And he was hard to talk to, too, because he didn't know how to be around children. He often tried to tell me about his work as an engineer, and I wanted to scream that I didn't understand.*

*I want so much better than this for you, Edie. I don't want your father to be a stranger or someone who's around but doesn't really understand you. I want you to love one another, to be a little team. I want that whether I'm around or not. But we are no longer together, your dad and I, and it's hard to be the one to make the first move.*

*I wanted you to know what it's like to be without a dad, but I don't want you to live it, like I did. I'm going to find him for you, Edie. I'm going to tell him. Not when you're seven or eight, but now. Because you deserve to know for sure. You deserve the best of everything.*

*With love,*

*Mum*

# CHAPTER SEVEN

Jess woke up the following morning feeling confident in her decision to get in touch with Jake. If he'd been on social media, she might have eased herself in by liking a few of his posts, but he'd always insisted all of it was a waste of time. She picked up her phone and went to their WhatsApp conversation, scrolled up and down. They'd talked every day, sending each other photos and jokes and telling one another the little stories that made up their days. And then nothing, since about a year ago. Jess typed the word 'hello', then deleted it. It was so easy to carry on a conversation, once it was flowing – she'd messaged him literally hundreds of times with almost every thought that had gone through her mind. But it was hard to start something up again after such a long break. Hard to know how to get the tone right.

Jess strapped Edie into her bouncy chair and carried her into the bathroom, where she took off her pyjamas and started the shower running. She handed Edie a rubber duck, which she immediately began to chew. She stepped into the shower, giving Edie a little wave through the door when her face began to crumple. While she shampooed her hair, Jess thought about Jake, about the time she'd gone round to tell him she was pregnant.

She'd shown him the pregnancy test and he'd taken it from her hands and said 'fuck'. And Jess had thought that surely no happy baby story starts with that word. She'd told him that she hadn't decided anything yet, that she didn't know whether she was going to keep it. It wasn't true. She knew she was having the baby. But she had wanted to see how he would react. And he had nodded and said that they should probably look into all the options. She had known, right then, that his heart wasn't in it, and that hers would break. She had known that she would be going it alone, and it was scary, and unspeakably sad.

They'd limped on, barely talking about the pregnancy, barely touching. And then a couple of weeks later he'd got that chance, to go on tour with his band, and that had sealed it. Looking back, it was shockingly final, the way it had happened. Jess stepped out of the shower and wrapped a towel around her body. And then, before she could change her mind, she tapped out a message on her phone, glanced back over it and took a deep breath. And then she pressed send.

**Hi Jake, sorry to get in touch out of nowhere after so long. There are a couple of things I want to talk to you about, if that's okay. Let me know. I hope the tour is going well.**

That last bit, about the tour, was a message, although she'd tried to make it seem casual. She wanted him to know that she wasn't angry about the decision he'd made. Not now. In other circumstances, she could imagine having been excited for him, having flung her arms around him when he shared the news.

It would have meant them being apart for a while, of course, but it was his dream, and that was worth some sacrifice. It was the fact that she was pregnant that had made it the worst possible news at the worst possible time. All of this was clear now, all these months down the line, whereas at the time it had been a mess of pain and panic. Jess leaned over Edie's bouncy chair and stroked her daughter's cheek. Wondered what Jake would make of this beautiful person they'd created. Whether he'd be able to forgive her for keeping Edie from him.

'Are you nearly ready, love?' Her mum's voice came up the stairs and into Jess's bedroom.

She tried to push all thoughts of Jake to the back of her mind and replace them with the steel required for a hospital appointment. Her mum had insisted on driving her there, and Jess knew she would try to insist on coming in with her, and she was half resolved to let her, because she still wasn't sure what questions she should be asking. Her mum would take a notebook, she knew, and write down what the doctors said. And while Jess would find it embarrassing and a bit silly, she'd be glad of that retained information later, when she'd forgotten it all.

They were quiet on the drive, Caroline driving, Jess in the passenger seat and Edie in her car seat in the back. After a couple of minutes, Jess reached forward and turned the stereo on, and a song from *Les Miserables* burst out. She caught her mum's eye for a moment, and they both laughed as she turned the volume down a little. The last time they'd been in this car together, they'd both sung along to 'On My Own' at the tops of their voices. And they hadn't known that Jess had cancer.

Most of the women in the waiting room were at least her mother's age, Jess noticed. In fact, the woman at the desk looked at Caroline, assuming she was the one with the appointment. And when Jess stepped forward and said that it was her who was here to see the breast surgeon, the receptionist looked at her, and then down at the car seat at her feet and flashed her a sorry smile. They took a seat and her mum fixed her eyes on the TV in the corner, which was showing a home renovation programme, but Jess kept looking around at the other women who were waiting. One looked about forty, and there was a man sitting next to her, and they were holding hands, both looking straight ahead. The man had tears rolling down his face and was doing nothing to hide or stop them. Another woman looked much older, maybe mid-seventies, and she was sitting next to a similarly aged woman (perhaps a friend or sister) and they were chatting non-stop, as if they were young and carefree. Did all of these women have cancer? How did they bear it? And then Jess's name was called, and she stood and lifted Edie's car seat.

'I can wait with her, if you want…' her mum said.

Jess smiled. 'It's okay, you can come in.'

As they followed a nurse down the corridor and into a small, clinical room, Jess felt her mother's hand at the small of her back, gently guiding her.

The same doctor who had diagnosed her walked into the room, clearing his throat. And he was followed by Asha, Jess's assigned breast care nurse.

'Jess,' the doctor said, 'it's good to see you again. And this is…?'

'I'm her mum,' Caroline said, and Jess detected a slight shake to her voice.

Jess thought that perhaps the reality of the situation was only now becoming real for her mum. For Jess, there had been time for it to settle, and become a part of her.

'I'd like to discuss your treatment plan with you today. At least, the parts we know about. We've discussed your case in our department meeting and we think the best way forward is to book you in for surgery first. Then we'll test the tumour and determine whether you need to have chemotherapy and radiotherapy based on what we find. Does that sound okay to you?'

Jess looked across at her mum, who had pulled her notebook and a biro out of her handbag, and written 'surgery, then chemo and radio' with a question mark beside the words chemo and radio. She almost laughed, at the absurdity of it all. But then she turned to the doctor, saw that he was looking at her with a serious expression, waiting for her answer.

'Look, I don't know anything. Whatever you say is the best thing, that's what we'll do.'

The doctor nodded and turned to Asha, who was holding another bundle of leaflets. Jess remembered that she had Asha's phone number scribbled on a piece of paper that was probably at the bottom of the changing bag.

'Asha has some information for you to read through, regarding the type of surgery. We're recommending a mastectomy rather than a lumpectomy, and there are various options for reconstruction, which she can talk you through if you'd like.'

It wasn't quite a question, but his voice lifted at the end of the sentence and Jess felt obliged to speak.

'Okay.'

'Would you be happy with a surgery date of 15th February?' he asked.

Caroline spoke up. 'That's in a couple of weeks.'

'Yes. We like to move fast. Tumours can grow at a surprising rate. Once we know what we're dealing with, we like to get on top of it as fast as we can.'

Jess didn't say anything, but she nodded. Two weeks. The day after Valentine's Day. She would go into hospital and they would put her under and remove one of her breasts. She was struck, again, by how unbelievable all of this was. Cancer had always been a word that meant nothing to her. That she read in books, or heard in conversations or on the TV, that she thought was synonymous with being old and with dying. She wouldn't have guessed, could never have guessed, that it would become a part of her life like this, so soon.

She didn't really hear anything after that, but she saw that her mother was scribbling things down, and she was grateful. In her head, over and over, words were repeating. Tell Gemma. Tell Jake. Look after Edie. She closed her eyes for a few seconds, and then she heard her name.

'Jess, are you okay?'

The doctor was standing up, ready to act if she needed him to.

'I'm tired,' Jess heard herself saying. 'I'm just so tired.'

'It's the shock,' Caroline said. 'She'll be all right. I'll take her home.'

The doctor nodded and gave Jess a smile that was more than half sadness, and Jess stood. When she reached down to pick up Edie's car seat, she thought that perhaps she didn't have the strength to lift it.

'I'll take that,' Caroline said.

And Jess bit down on her bottom lip to stop herself from crying. That recognition, from her mother, that ability to see just what she needed. It was everything.

In the car on the way home, Jess checked her messages. There was one from Jake. She held her breath as she opened it, glad that the car was quiet, her mum concentrating on the road, or at least pretending to.

**Hey Jess, of course we can talk. You know that. I'm in Ipswich. We're playing at a bar in town tonight and then**

**heading somewhere else tomorrow. I've forgotten where. It's nothing like I thought. Call me.**

Jess read it three times. 'You know that'. How did she know? Was she supposed to assume, because he'd been so wonderful when they were together, that he was open to hearing from her for the rest of their lives? She didn't know the rules, and she felt adrift, somehow. Each time she read the short message, she stumbled over the words 'It's nothing like I thought'. Did he mean that it was better, or worse? She found herself hoping that it wasn't working out, that he was on the verge of walking out, going home, but then she felt bad about that. This was his dream, after all.

But what about her dreams? She hadn't planned on being a mum at twenty-one, and she hadn't planned on having cancer. And though she'd never quite known what she wanted to do with her life, surely it wasn't fair that it had come to this?

'What do you fancy for lunch?' Caroline's voice broke into Jess's thoughts.

Jess wanted to scream. She didn't care about lunch. How could she bring herself to care about lunch, when there were these life and death issues going on?

'Just a sandwich or something,' she said, instead.

Her mum took her hand off the gearstick for a brief moment and placed it on Jess's. And the warmth of it was comforting, but then it was gone, and they were pulling on to the drive beside their house, and Jess took a few deep breaths and turned away from her mum's worried expression.

# CHAPTER EIGHT

Jess had been avoiding Gemma since her last hospital appointment, but she knew the time had come to tell her what was going on. She'd called her best friend, knowing she wasn't working until that evening, and asked her to come over. And now, Jess was sitting on her bed with an empty suitcase beside her, waiting for the doorbell to ring.

When it did, Jess ran downstairs to get it.

'Come in,' she said, almost pulling Gemma inside. 'Come up to my room.'

'What's going on?' Gemma asked. They were her first words and she was already halfway up the stairs.

Jess wished she could say that it was nothing, or that she had a secret she didn't want her mum to overhear. She thought of the times they'd raced up these stairs to her bedroom together. Aged eight, with Barbie dolls in their hands and entire worlds caught in their imaginations. Aged thirteen, with cups of tea, serious and moody, feeling like the advent of their periods and not being the youngest at secondary school meant they were all grown up. Aged seventeen, with bottles of coke spiked with vodka sneaked from Gemma's parents' booze cabinet. So many times, Jess had hurried her friend up to her room to tell her something, but it had never once felt like this.

When they were inside her room, Jess closed the door. Edie was on the playmat on the floor, where Jess had left her. She was squirming a little, waving her legs around.

'I have to tell you something, and it's really awful, and I don't think I can look at you while I say it.'

'What's the suitcase for?' Gemma asked. 'Are you leaving?'

Jess let a little laugh escape. Imagine if that was all it was. That she was running away, starting again. That those options were still open to her.

'I've got cancer,' Jess said. And she realised that she'd only said it once before, to her mum, and she was probably going to have to say it a lot more in the future. It still didn't seem real. Perhaps it would, in time.

'Cancer?' Gemma sounded incredulous.

Jess tried to imagine if this situation was the other way around. If she'd been summoned to Gemma's house, and Gemma had told her that she had cancer. She imagined her reaction would be pretty similar.

'Breast cancer,' she confirmed.

'Are you sure?'

Jess almost laughed. Gemma had asked her the same thing when she'd told her she was pregnant, but it had made sense in that context. People got that wrong, sometimes. People thought it was true and then found that it wasn't. But cancer didn't work like that.

'Of course I'm sure. I'm having surgery tomorrow and I need to pack, and I don't know what I'm supposed to take, because when I went to hospital to have Edie, there were loads of lists online telling me what I needed, and I was hoping you might be able to help me, because I can't ask Mum. She's pretending she's okay, but she keeps disappearing to her bedroom and I've heard her crying, and I don't want to make it worse for her…'

Jess stopped talking because Gemma had crossed the short space between them and caught Jess in her arms, and she was squeezing her so tight that Jess felt like she could hardly breathe, but it was the most wonderful feeling. Why hadn't her mum done that? She tried to remember whether her mum had hugged her, since the news. She wasn't sure.

Edie started to cry, a jerking sort of noise, and Gemma let go of Jess and kneeled down on the floor before picking Edie up.

'This is fucked up,' she said. 'And I'm so, so sorry it's happening to you.'

Jess felt as though something was unlatching in her chest, something that had been shut tight, and she let herself cry. She sank down on the floor next to her friend and reached her arms out for her daughter, and Gemma passed Edie across without saying a word, and Jess fed her, there on the floor of her childhood bedroom, with tears falling steadily on to Edie's warm head.

The two friends didn't say very much for ten minutes or so, and when Edie unlatched from Jess's breast, her eyes drooping, Jess laid her down gently in her Moses basket and turned to Gemma. The tears had stopped, and she thought she could trust her voice to hold.

'Will you help me?' she asked.

'Of course I will. What do you need? I'm here, Jess. Anything.'

Jess swallowed down the lump in her throat, determined not to start crying again. But Gemma's support was exactly what she needed. What she'd wanted from her mum. No difficult questions or anecdotes about people who'd died. Just pure, simple love. And the offer of help.

'I just need to pack. I can't think straight.'

Gemma told Jess to sit down on the bed. She went downstairs and made them both a cup of tea, even found some biscuits, and then she took control of the packing, pulling clothes out of drawers and getting toiletries from the bathroom. Putting in a book, and a hairbrush.

'Thank you,' Jess said, blowing on her mug of tea. 'I just couldn't do it.'

'I'm not surprised,' Gemma said. 'This is a massive shock. You are stupidly young for this, and you've just become a mum. It's not fair.'

It wasn't fair. Jess had found herself thinking that a lot. And she'd heard her mother's voice in her head each time. 'Life isn't fair'. It's what Caroline had said when Jess had complained about not having a brother or sister, about not being allowed to have a pet dog, about not getting the place at the university she'd initially set her heart on. Her mind landed on that, and she wondered whether all this would be happening if she'd gone to that university. She wouldn't have met Jake, she wouldn't have had Edie. Would she still be there, doing her final year with nothing more serious to worry about than hangovers and debt?

'Is this why you've been thinking about Jake?' Gemma asked.

'Yes.'

'And, any more thoughts on that?'

Jess pulled her phone from her pocket. 'I messaged him, and he replied. I'm going to ask to see him.'

If it wasn't for the fact that she'd just told her friend she had cancer, Jess knew that Gemma would have squealed at that, nudging her and making her smile. As it was, Gemma just nodded.

'That's good,' she said. 'I think that's the right thing.'

Jess had exchanged a couple more messages with Jake, and they'd both agreed that a meeting should take place, but they hadn't actually chosen a date or a time. It would be after the surgery, of course, and Jess had thought a lot, during Edie's night feeds, about whether he would be able to tell. She intended to tell him, but would he know, anyway? Would he see that she was no longer whole, that a part of her had been cut off, because it was poisonous? She'd decided to have reconstruction at the same time as having the mastectomy. An implant. There were longer, more complex procedures where the surgeons took tissue from your back, tummy or thighs to create a reconstructed breast, but Jess wasn't sure about that. She wanted to keep things as simple as possible. So perhaps it wouldn't be visible to an onlooker, especially when she was fully dressed. But still, Jess wondered and worried about it, about whether she might look different, changed, and whether people who knew her well would be able to tell.

'Gemma, can I ask you one more favour?' Jess asked.

'Anything.'

'Will you have Edie tomorrow when I go in for surgery so Mum can come with me.'

'Of course I will.'

Gemma went home shortly after that. She gave Jess another tight hug at the door, and Jess could see, when she pulled away, that Gemma was fighting tears. She took her friend's hand.

'It's okay,' Jess said. 'I'll be okay. Thank you.'

Gemma didn't answer that. She pulled her hand away very gently and turned and walked down Jess's front path, and Jess knew that she was crying, and she didn't want Jess to see. Probably she didn't want to set Jess off again.

Jess closed the door and leaned against it. She felt better now that Gemma knew. She felt like things were moving in the right direction. She checked her phone and saw that there was a new message from Jake.

**Jess, we're going to be in Manchester in two weeks. I could meet you somewhere on 2nd March? x**

Jess wasn't sure when they'd started adding kisses to the end of their messages. Whether she'd done it first, or he had. Trying to ignore her fears about how she'd be feeling and looking on the date he'd suggested, she sent a message back saying that would be fine, and she couldn't help smiling to herself at the thought of seeing him again.

That evening, after a quiet dinner with her mum, Jess took Edie upstairs. She knew she wouldn't sleep well, so she wanted to start trying early. She'd cleaned her teeth and got into her pyjamas and was about to give Edie a feed when her phone rang. It was Gemma. She started speaking as soon as Jess answered the call.

'Remember when we had that party at my house, and it got out of control and we had an hour before my parents were due back and the house was wrecked?'

Jess laughed. 'Of course.'

'That's the most scared I've ever been, until today. But it was okay in the end and this will be too.'

'Gemma, are you comparing us trashing your parents' house to me having cancer?' Jess asked. She kept her voice light. She wanted Gemma to know she wasn't cross.

Gemma started laughing. 'Fuck, Jess, I don't know what to say. I just want to make it all better.'

Jess climbed into bed and held the phone in place with her shoulder while she lifted Edie to her breast. 'A year ago, I was getting pissed at student nights and trying to drag myself in to uni with a hangover. And now I have a baby and I have cancer. How the hell did that happen?'

'I don't know,' Gemma said. 'I really don't. Do you want me to come with you tomorrow?'

'No, Mum's coming. I'll get her to text you when it's over.'

'Okay.'

Jess had an urge to say thank you to Gemma for all she had been to her over the years. It was stupid, she thought, but she was scared of never coming round from the anaesthetic. Part of her felt she had to have things in place, in case she didn't. But it was too hard to bring it up, so she didn't.

'Night, Gemma,' she said, instead.

'Night, Jess.'

## CHAPTER NINE

*Dear Edie,*

*I wanted you to know that friends are everything. You'll hear it a lot, that love will come and go but friends will always be there. It's a cliché because it's true. One of the things I hope most for you is that you have a friend like Gemma. Female friendship is important, perhaps even crucial. Remember that. Try not to tie yourself to one person. There are so many incredible girls and women. Let a whole crowd of them into your life. But also try to find at least one who's special and will always be there.*

*Gemma and I were at primary school together, and we were friends, but not best friends. It takes several years to find your feet, you know. To find out who you are and the people you want to surround yourself with. And then you go to secondary school, and everyone is separated into these groups. The sporty ones, and the popular ones, and the clever ones, and the ones that don't really fit anywhere else. There's some overlap, and the rules are so complex I'm not sure anyone really understands them. But you know about it if you end up in the wrong place.*

*And it was then that Gemma and I were first properly thrown together, and we sort of stuck. She played netball but wasn't quite in with the sporty ones, and I played the flute but didn't much like the musical ones, and we found somewhere in between and stayed there. Most of the time it was just the two of us, and that isn't great. Because if you put all your friendship eggs in one basket like that, and your friend moves away, or even if she's off for a week with the flu, you're on your own. Mum was always worried about that, always desperate for us to be part of a larger group. But three is a tricky number for friendships, too. Someone is always left out. So perhaps one number is just the same as another. There were other friends, don't get me wrong, but it was as if they were blurred and Gemma was in sharp focus. She was just my favourite. It was as simple as that.*

*The day I got my first period, Gemma came and found me in the toilets at morning break. We were in Year Eight, and my first lesson had been French while Gemma's had been Food Tech and we always met outside the Science building and sometimes we ate what she'd made that morning. But that day, as I'd got up at the end of French, I'd felt something wasn't quite right and when I'd put my hand to the back of my skirt, it had come away with blood on it. So I'd dashed out of the room, holding my bag behind me to try to cover the stain, and gone straight into the toilets opposite. I'd started carrying sanitary towels in my bag a few months before in preparation for this day, and I'd used toilet paper to soak up the blood in my pants, but what was I supposed to do about the deep red stain on the back of my skirt? I sat on the lid of the toilet, the cubicle locked and my stomach twisting with anxiety. I had ten minutes before I had to be in my Maths class. Gemma was with me for Maths.*

*And it was then that I realised Gemma would be waiting for me by the Science building, wondering where I'd got to. And then I heard her voice, calling my name. I asked whether there was anyone else in there, and she said there wasn't. I told her I'd got my period. Gemma had started hers back in Year Seven, and I'd been waiting for this day, although right then, I had no idea why. She asked me to let her into the cubicle, and I slid the latch across slowly. There wasn't really room for two in there, and our heads were bent close together as I showed her the stain. It was small, about the size of a fifty pence piece, but I knew I couldn't wear that skirt for the rest of the day and expect no one to notice. Gemma was calm. She said that there were always spare skirts in lost property in the office. She ran off to get one for me. And five minutes later, we left the toilets together arm in arm, my skirt balled up at the bottom of my bag. The skirt she'd brought me was a little bit too big, so that I spent the rest of the day hitching it up, but that was nothing. Gemma had saved me. She always did.*

*After that, if either of us had a problem, the other would say, 'Worse than period skirt?' and we'd end up laughing. Even that time I told her I was pregnant, and Jake and I had split up.*

*When we were about fifteen, my mum and her dad started to let us go into town on our own. We used to say we were going on an adventure. And it always was, as silly as that sounds. We'd just go on the bus or the train and mooch about the shops a bit and have lunch in McDonalds, but the new-found freedom was so exciting, and we'd always end up talking to boys or hunting out free samples and if nothing at all happened, we'd just spend the time making up a story to tell the others at school, and then it would seem as if it had been an adventure after all. One day, when I picked Gemma up on the way to the bus stop, she handed me a one-pound coin, and said she had one for herself, and she said we had to buy the biggest thing we could with it. Later that afternoon, we struggled on to the bus with an enormous cardboard box that someone had given Gemma for free and that she said she was going to turn into a playhouse for her baby cousin, the pounds forgotten. I've never laughed quite the way I laughed with Gemma. She was just always more fun to be around than anyone else, and that's why all the other girls faded into the background for me. Why she chose me above anyone else, I've never really understood.*

*I hope you have adventures with the friends you make. I hope you turn grey, drizzly school days bright. I hope you laugh that way, the way that sort of hurts and that makes you cry and that you think will never stop. I don't know whether everyone does. Growing up is complicated, and girls can be mean and difficult. Find the right ones and hold tight to them. They'll be worth it.*

*I remember the day I told Gemma I was going to university. She'd already decided she wasn't going to apply, and she'd talked about us finding a job somewhere together, in a restaurant or a bar or a shop. She'd talked about us saving up and getting a flat, and all the time, I was looking up courses and downloading prospectuses in secret. You see, I wanted all the things Gemma talked about. I found myself getting swept up when I was with her, agreeing to things I knew I couldn't possibly deliver on, because I wanted something else first. And I was scared that while I was away for three years, reading and writing essays and learning about who I was, she would replace me with someone else. Why wouldn't she? I didn't think I was worth waiting around for.*

*So by the time I got up the courage, I'd already had offers to study English Literature from three universities. In my mind, I was already gone. It was exam time and it was hot, and everyone was irritable and stressed. I found Gemma in the common room and sank into the chair next to her. There were other people scattered about the room, but no one close enough to listen in. The radio was on, and a boy we'd known since primary school, Mark something, was singing along to every song that came on, every word correct. There was a little crowd around him, waiting for him to slip up.*

*Gemma turned her head to face me, and I just came out with it. I watched her expression change. I thought she'd be angry, but she wasn't. She was sad. I told her that I wouldn't be going too far, just to Manchester. But she said it wouldn't be the same, and she was right, so I didn't argue. I remember her saying that when I came back, if I came back, I wouldn't want to hang out with her any more. That I'd have new friends, clever friends, and I wouldn't need her. I wanted to tell her that I'd always need her. That she was different to anyone else I knew. More sparkling. More alive. I laughed and said that I was worried about the same thing, about her not needing me. About her replacing me, while I was gone. I said that I would definitely come back, and that I would definitely need her just the same as I always had. I brought up period skirt, and she smiled. I said that no one else had ever been to me quite what she was, and she hugged me. We both had tears in our eyes.*

*Just then, the song 'Bad Romance' came on the radio, and that Mark guy was still doing his thing, and then Gemma started singing along, and then I did, and then at the same time we both stood up and started to dance. We were laughing, and people were looking at us, but we didn't care, and I knew right then that it would always be like this between us. That time and distance wouldn't matter. That she was my best friend and she always would be.*

*I wanted you to know that friends are everything. It's truly magical, to love someone like that, and be loved right back. You'll know it when you see it, Edie. And when you do, cling on.*

*With love,*

*Mum*

# CHAPTER TEN

Jess opened her eyes and looked around her. She was on a hospital ward, in the bed she'd been on before they took her down to the operating theatre. Her mum was in the chair beside her, reading a magazine. Jess watched her, unobserved, for a moment, and saw that her mum's eyes weren't moving. She was just staring at a page. Then Caroline noticed Jess's gaze and she dropped the magazine to her lap.

'Jess! How are you feeling?'

Jess sat up slowly, noticing that her chest felt tender and bruised. And then she knew she was going to be sick, and she reached across for the cardboard sick bowl on her tray table, and the action pulled something inside her and she felt a stab of pain. But then she was retching and there was nothing in her stomach but liquid, and it burned her throat as it came up.

'Where's Edie?' Jess managed to ask.

Caroline looked bewildered. 'She's with Gemma, darling. Don't you remember asking her to babysit?'

Jess did, but at that moment, she wanted her baby to be right there at her side. She knew it wasn't logical, and that it wouldn't have made sense to bring Edie here, to this place, but that didn't stop Jess from missing her.

'Can we call her?'

Jess spotted her phone on the tray table and reached for it, but then another wave of nausea hit, and she retched into the cardboard bowl again. Caroline stood up and took a couple of steps closer to Jess, put a cool hand on her daughter's forehead.

'Love, just wait a little while. You've only just come round. Give yourself a few minutes.'

Jess tried a weak smile and nodded. She looked down at her hospital gown, tugged at the neckline. Beneath it, there were bandages covering her chest. She wondered what she looked like underneath them. How uneven her breasts would be, how disfigured.

Just as Gemma had got her period first, she'd grown breasts before Jess too. One Friday, she'd told Jess that her mum was taking her shopping to buy some bras, and Jess had burned with jealousy. She knew her own mum would laugh if she asked for a bra of her own. There was no pretending she needed one, not yet. Jess clearly remembered seeing the straps of Gemma's new white bras beneath her school shirts and feeling childish whenever she put her shirt on in the mornings.

And then, six months or so later, Jess's breasts had appeared, almost overnight. She was a C cup. She'd known it was silly to feel proud of something she hadn't had any hand in, but she did, all the same. She'd seen how it made people look at her differently. How it made boys look at her. And she'd liked it. How would she have felt then, if she'd known she would only have those breasts for a handful of years? Jess felt tears pricking at her eyes, but she didn't let them fall. She concentrated hard on swallowing down the lump in her throat and blinking the tears away, and then she turned to her mum.

'Do you know how it went? Did they say? How long have I been here?'

Caroline gave her a sad smile. 'They brought you up from recovery about half an hour ago. They said you were starting to come round, but it would take a while. They didn't really say anything about how it went. I'm sure they want to talk to you about it, not me. Now, are you hungry? Or thirsty?'

Jess knew that her stomach was empty. She'd been told she couldn't eat anything that day and she hadn't gone into the operating theatre until early afternoon. Now, it was almost six o'clock. But she didn't feel hungry. She just wanted to clean her teeth, to get the taste of vomit out of her mouth. She told her mum this and Caroline rummaged in Jess's overnight bag for her toothpaste and toothbrush, and then called a nurse who helped Jess get out of bed and over to the toilet.

'Will you be okay in there on your own?' the nurse asked. 'I'll wait out here to help you back to bed.'

'I'll be fine,' Jess said. Once the door was locked, she took a deep breath and looked in the mirror. She looked tired and a little puffy, and the hospital gown she was wearing washed her out. But she'd got through it. The first step.

Jess brushed her teeth slowly and carefully, worried that sudden movements would make her sick again. And then she splashed her face with water. And when she left that tiny room, she felt a lot more human. The nurse helped her back into bed. She was a big, middle-aged woman with streaks of blue in her blonde hair.

'What can I get you to eat, Jessica? Some toast?' she asked.

Jess shook her head. 'No thanks. I don't really feel like anything.'

The nurse frowned. 'Are you sure you can't manage anything? You need to get your strength back.'

Jess nodded, defeated. 'Okay. Just dry toast, please. And maybe a cup of tea?'

The nurse beamed, then. 'Coming right up.'

There were four other women in the bay with Jess, and all of them were at least as old as her mother. When they'd arrived that morning, Jess had known they all assumed it was her mother who was here for surgery. There'd been a few double takes when Jess had changed into her gown, and even now, she could feel the women's eyes on her. It made her cross, because she was trying so hard not to focus on the unfairness of it all. She was trying not to be bitter about why this had happened to her, right now, when she was just starting out and she had a baby who needed her.

Once she'd forced down a piece of toast, Jess sent Gemma a message asking if they could have a quick video call. Almost immediately, Jess's phone started ringing.

'How has she been?' Jess asked.

'Edie? She's fine. Not massively keen on drinking from a bottle, but we got there in the end. She's asleep at the moment. How are you?'

Jess looked at her friend's face, at the concern etched on it. 'I'm okay,' she said. 'It's done. It's gone.'

And without warning, she felt tears start to spill from her eyes, and she wished that Gemma was in the room with her and could give her one of her healing, bone-crushing hugs.

'Hey,' Gemma said, 'it's okay. You are amazing. Really. You're amazing. It's all going to be okay.'

Jess didn't say anything for a minute or two. She couldn't. She didn't look over at her mum, but, at some point, her mum reached out and took hold of Jess's hand, and Jess wished it had been her mum who'd said those words. But at the same time, she knew it just wasn't in her mum's nature to gush about her like that, and it was pointless wishing otherwise. When she'd gathered herself a little, she asked if she could see Edie, and Gemma turned the camera around and pointed it in the direction of the Moses basket. Edie was fast asleep, her eyelids fluttering a little. She looked cosy and content, and Jess was so grateful to Gemma for taking care of her, and so desperate to hold her baby girl.

'I'll bring her in to see you tomorrow,' Gemma said.

Jess ached to be at home, then, but she'd been told she'd have to stay in hospital for at least one night and possibly two. She wanted to be in her own bed and to have Edie at her side. It surprised her, that need. She'd only been a mother for a few months, and yet it felt completely wrong to be away from her daughter. Just before she ended the call, Gemma leant in close to the screen and said something else.

'Cancer can fuck off, Jess. I have so many plans for the future, and you're in all of them.'

'Adventures?' Jess asked.

'You'd better believe it.'

And Jess smiled, glad that she had Gemma on her side.

# CHAPTER ELEVEN

*Dear Edie,*

*I wanted you to know how scared I am of leaving you. You are so helpless, grown in my body and fed from my body. I know that, in time, you won't need me in quite the same way that you need me now, but that's the future, and this is now. I've been told I will have to stop breastfeeding soon, because I'm starting chemo and the drugs will be in my milk. So when I was away from you having the surgery, we tested that out. First step, expressed breast milk in bottles. For days, I'd been pumping milk in between feeds to make sure there was enough. Stashing it in the freezer. Still, I was terrified that you would cry the whole time I was gone and eat nothing, that you wouldn't be able to cope without me. And now, I know that you can. That you are okay. And I don't know whether that's better or worse.*

*When Gemma brought you in to see me the day after my surgery, I felt like I'd been away from you for days. I felt like I was a different person from the one who'd dropped you off the previous morning, kissing your head and trying not to cry. Gemma pulled me into a hug, and I told her to be gentle, because I was sore. And then she held the car seat up for me to see you, and I asked her to get you out. I couldn't wait to hold you. The warmth of your body and the scent of you were overpowering. I held you against my bruised chest and inhaled deeply. And you nuzzled, your downy hair tickling my neck, and I knew that deep, racking sobs weren't far away, but I held them in.*

*I asked Gemma to stay all afternoon, and she did. I felt, somehow, as if you were going to heal me. And you did, in a way. Not medically. But you were my reason for getting better; my reason for being. You were the first thing I asked about when I came round from the surgery. I'd been so terrified, you see, of losing you. Of leaving you. You only have one parent and I feel like that's my fault, so it's more important than anything that I don't disappear. That afternoon, while I was watching you, I was thinking about your dad and whether it's time to stop pretending I don't need anyone and ask him to be in our lives. Whether we need him to be here, in case I can't be. But as far as I know, the cancer has gone, and the immediate worry is over. I will meet him though, as planned. I will show him photos of you and talk about the things you do, and I will see in his eyes whether he's ready to be a father.*

*I wanted to talk to you about my pregnancy with you. One day, you might find yourself pregnant or wanting to be, and it's important that you know what to expect. I was sick every morning, right through the nine months. I would wake up hot and confused, that cold feeling inside my mouth, and run to the toilet. After a few weeks, I got an old mixing bowl from the cupboard that we never used, and it was my sick bowl. I slept with it by my bed and reached for it every morning. And then I would wash it out, trying not to retch.*

*Other than that, though, I felt fine. They say that pregnancy is easier on a younger body, and I can believe it. Once I'd got some breakfast inside me, the nausea stopped, and it only returned if I didn't eat frequently. If I went out anywhere, I'd take little packages of biscuits wrapped in clingfilm so I would never be caught without anything to eat. Between the meals Mum and I made, I'd spread honey or jam thickly on toast or peel a banana or tip cereal into a bowl.*

*At the first scan, I nodded my head and didn't say a word when the sonographer asked if I was there on my own. Mum had wanted to come, but she couldn't get the time off work. Gemma, too. I held my breath as I waited for the sonographer to locate you. And then you were there, on the screen, all big-bellied and shadowy. I watched as you stretched out a leg and then moved back into your curled position, and I couldn't believe that it was all going on inside me and I couldn't feel it happening. I'd had the odd flutter, but nothing more concrete than that. I felt tears filling my eyes and I blinked them away. I wished I had a hand to hold.*

*It wasn't long after that that I started showing. I was slim and it seemed like my belly popped out overnight. People I hadn't told began to guess, and still I was vomiting into that bowl every morning when I first woke up. It felt like time sped up after that. Before long, I could feel you turning and stretching, and I was thinking about names and buying tiny clothes and I read a couple of books about pregnancy and birth, because I felt helpless and out of control, and I wanted to do something practical.*

*Mum asked whether I'd thought about names. She said she liked Charlotte for a girl, Robert for a boy. I pulled a face. There was nothing wrong with those names, but they weren't right for you. Somehow, I knew you were a girl. I said I was thinking about Edie. My grandmother, my mum's mum, had been called Edith, and I'd loved her more than anyone when I was a little girl. She'd had bright, sparkly eyes and she was quick to laugh, and she always had a new story to tell me about her life. She was everything I thought a woman should be, and I'd always dreamed of naming my own daughter after her.*

*Mum said it was nice, and when I looked at her, I could see that she was far away, perhaps remembering her mother, who'd died young. I was only ten and my mother was just a little over thirty and she, Edith, must only have been in her fifties. I'd never really thought about how young she was before, because I knew other friends who'd lost a grandparent, and just took it in my stride the way children do. But perhaps Mum was damaged by it. Of course she was damaged by it.*

*A few days later, I was lying on my bed with Gemma. We were side by side, just talking about a man she'd started seeing and a friend from school I'd run into, nothing to do with you, and you gave such a hefty kick that I instinctively reached for Gemma's hand and pulled it across to rest it on my belly. Gemma went quiet, and you went quiet too, staying still for a moment. And then another kick just like the first, and Gemma pulled her hand away in shock and said, 'Fuck!' and I couldn't stop smiling.*

*The last few weeks were tough. We had a lot of rain and I was terrified of slipping over, of damaging you. It was bizarre, I felt, to be carrying the most precious thing in your life at the front of your body, just where you might fall if you slipped. I was uncomfortable and ready for you to come. I had strange bursts of energy, and did tidying and cleaning during them, but mostly I sat with my feet up watching television. Every morning, I was sick, and I whispered to you to come out. I'd waited such a long time to meet you, and I was more than ready. The bag was packed and waiting by the front door.*

*I feel like I gave up sleep altogether those last few days. I rolled around, unable to get comfortable, too tired to read. Most nights, around midnight, I'd get out of bed and go downstairs. Sometimes I drank a cup of tea standing up in the kitchen, sometimes I read a book or a magazine. Once, I made scones, and Mum laughed and ate one for her breakfast when she surfaced. I waited. I waited for you.*

*And though I felt, through all those days and nights, that it would be so strange to be a mother at my age, that I wouldn't know what to do or how to look after you, now that we've been together for a while, I can't be without you. And I don't want you to be without me.*

*I wanted you to know how scared I am of leaving you. Please know, Edie, that I'm going to throw everything I can at this cancer. I'm going to try so hard. My hope is that, one day, when you're fifteen or so, I'll hand you these letters and tell you that I wrote them when I thought I might leave you behind, and I'm so glad that I didn't.*

*With love,*
*Mum*

# CHAPTER TWELVE

On the morning of the day Jess had arranged to meet Jake, she woke up with a dry throat. She was mostly recovered, and the night before she had taken off her dressings and stared at her body in the mirror and cried for a long time. She'd known that she would, but now it was done, and she was ready to get on with things. She wasn't meeting Jake until two in the afternoon, but she felt jumpy, on edge. After she'd showered and had breakfast, eating with one hand while Edie lay in the crook of her other arm, she wrapped them both up and went out for a walk.

She felt like she'd recovered well from the surgery. She'd spent a few days in bed, letting her mum take the strain, and then she'd slowly got herself back to normal. Or not normal, as such, but as normal as she was going to get, now. She'd been back to the hospital for some scans, and she was waiting to hear back about what they showed. But for that day, she was doing her best to put the anxiety to one side.

Walking had been her saviour since she'd had Edie. A year ago, she'd never have considered going out for a walk if it wasn't to get somewhere, but now she went out with the pram or the sling at least once a day, and rarely had a destination in mind. However fractious Edie was, however cross and tired and difficult, she was happy when she was outside, her body wrapped up and her face exposed to the late winter breeze. Jess could walk for miles, her breaths deep and clear and her legs pumping, with Edie snoozing or smiling up at her.

Jess thought about seeing Jake, about what she would say to him. The person she was now was so far removed from the person she'd been when they were together. Would he even recognise that she was the same person, somewhere inside? Would there be anything left between them? But then she caught herself and reminded herself that she wasn't meeting up with him because she wanted him back. It was all about Edie. About the cancer, and the fact that her future was so uncertain. About the fact that she couldn't really come to terms with, that he might be needed in a way she hadn't expected.

She walked down a lane and found herself beside the canal. Edie was starting to fuss but the sound of the water seemed to soothe her, and Jess checked her watch and saw that it had been almost three hours since Edie's last feed. It was time to head home. Jess had thought about taking Edie with her to see Jake, but he hadn't asked her to, so she'd arranged for her mum to have her, and Gemma had offered to be there too. Just like when she went to the hospital, she'd been pumping milk here and there so there was enough to cover her absence. Their breastfeeding days were numbered, as she was starting chemo in a week's time. So once they were home and she'd unwrapped Edie and put her to her breast, she tried to really fix the moment in her mind, so she'd remember it. That sharp tug as Edie latched on, the twinges she felt as her daughter drank her fill. She didn't want it to fade away to nothing. She'd spent so many hours doing this for the past few months, but she knew what memory was like, what it reduced things to. She looked down at Edie and kissed the top of her head. Edie wouldn't remember, of course. Jess hoped that she would.

A couple of hours later, she was ready to go. Gemma had come over and was holding Edie in her arms, and Jess had laid out the playmat with the mirror Edie liked to look in and a selection of toys for her to hold.

'Go,' Caroline said. 'We'll be fine here.'

Jess knew that her mum didn't approve of her meeting up with Jake, but now wasn't the time to go into it. She reached across and gave Edie a kiss.

'Thank you,' she said.

She was almost at the door before her mum spoke.

'You look like you've gone to a lot of trouble. I hope he's worth it.'

It was true that Jess had made an effort. To counter her self-consciousness about her altered body, she had spent a long time doing her hair and make-up. She'd chosen the black jeans that pulled in her post-baby tummy. She'd tried to make herself the girl she had been before. So when the message came through, she was angry. She'd had to rush to catch the train, and it had just pulled away when her phone beeped, and when she pulled it out of her pocket and saw Jake's name, she felt the way she had felt when they'd first met. Cut adrift, full of anticipation. But the message didn't say that he couldn't wait to see her, or he was on his way, or even that he was running a bit late. The message said he wasn't coming.

**I'm sorry, Jess. Something's come up, I can't get out of it. Can we do it another time? X**

Jess felt hot tears gathering in her eyes and she blinked

them away. How dare he do this, when she had arranged for someone to look after their child and spent all that time getting ready, and all that time nervously waiting? She wanted to throw something. She wanted to throw her phone, but she stopped herself. She looked out of the window at the rushing fields, and it all felt hopeless. Like it was too late. For her and Jake. For love. She started to compose a handful of messages and deleted them all. She wanted to tell him that she was already on the train, that he'd ruined her day, that she had been so excited about seeing him. But saying nothing was better. She didn't want him to know how much she still cared.

With nowhere to go and no baby to look after for the first time in weeks, Jess headed into Manchester as planned and wandered from shop to shop. She was aimless, drifting. A year or two ago, she'd have quite happily spent a morning or an afternoon like this, perhaps choosing a new top or a lipstick, but something had shifted, and she couldn't focus on anything. She ended up going to the café where she and Jake were supposed to meet and sitting alone with a coffee and a piece of cake. She read Jake's message again, checking for something she might have missed in his tone or the delivery. But it was impossible to know whether he'd just sent it on a whim because he was hungover and couldn't be bothered to make the effort, or whether something serious really had happened. Jess suspected the former was more likely.

Jess became aware of a shadow on the table and looked up to see a man standing there, waiting to speak to her. He looked a few years older than her, and he was tall and had hair that was a little long, and soft brown eyes that lent him an air of kindness.

'Can I sit with you?' he asked.

'Why?' Jess knew how rude that sounded, but she wanted

to know. She looked around her and saw that there were plenty of spare tables in the café. So this wasn't about space.

'You just look like you could use some company, that's all,' he said.

In the past, Jess would have smiled and said yes. She would have been flattered that this man was showing an interest in her, especially having just been let down by someone else. But Edie had changed her, and her self-esteem was no longer so tied up in what other people thought. And then the cancer had changed her again.

'I'm fine on my own,' she said. She didn't temper it with a smile, despite feeling like she should. There was a part of her that wanted to say that she had a baby and she had cancer, and was he still interested in her. But she wasn't quite brave enough for that. The man walked away, his face unreadable. He threw a comment over his shoulder. 'You're not even that hot.'

While once she might have been embarrassed, that day, all Jess felt was rage. She hadn't asked for his attention or his company. And in turning him down, she hadn't been rude or critical of him. So why did he feel it necessary to demean her like that? She was furious. With Jake and with this stranger. With herself, for believing that something good might come out of this day. She left her half-drunk coffee and untouched cake and gathered her things, and she went back to the train station.

She missed Edie. That was the truth of it. She wished, in a way, that she didn't, and that she could enjoy this time away from her, but there was no escaping it. Her breasts felt heavy and sore, and she wanted to feel the weight of her baby in her arms, to snuggle down with her on her bed or the sofa. She wanted to go home.

It was only when she was pulling her door key from her

bag that Jess wondered what she was going to tell her mum and Gemma. If she told them the truth, her mum would pretend to be sympathetic, but Jess knew she'd feel vindicated, having distrusted Jake all along. She wasn't sure she could bear it. She opened the door and her mum was standing in the hall. She must have heard her coming up the path.

'How's Edie?' Jess asked.

'She's fine. Sleeping. How was your afternoon?'

Jess felt tired and sad. She wanted to pretend, to say that she and Jake had talked, and it had been nice, but she was too weary to keep up with the lies.

'He didn't come,' she said.

Caroline took a sharp intake of breath. 'Just didn't turn up? Left you there waiting?'

'No, he told me as soon as he could, but I was already on the train.'

Jess wondered why she was defending him. She had no idea whether he'd told her as soon as he could.

'And what was his excuse?'

Excuse, not reason. Jess felt suddenly angry. Like the anger she'd felt earlier for Jake, but this time it was all directed at her mother.

'Sometimes things come up,' she said, her voice sharp. She walked past her mother, their arms briefly touching, and drained a glass of water in the kitchen before going into the lounge to see Gemma and her daughter. Edie was sleeping on her back with her arms up by her ears. Completely trusting. Gemma gave her a kind, slightly sad smile, and Jess knew she'd overheard the conversation she'd had with her mother in the hallway and also knew Gemma would never say 'I told you so'. Jess kneeled down beside Edie and leaned in close until she could feel Edie's small breaths. She matched her daughter's breathing with her own until she felt calmer. She was aware of her mum coming into the room, but she didn't say anything, and they stayed there like that, the four of them, all quiet, until Edie woke up.

It was only when Jake's second message came through that Jess realised she'd never replied to the first one.

**I'm sorry, okay? I hope you're not pissed off.**

Jess thought about all the replies she could send. Cool and calm, as if his cancellation had barely affected her day. A little indignant. Full-on anger. Her fingers began to type, and she sent the message before she had a chance to rethink it.

**I don't know why I was surprised.**

Almost immediately, his response came.

**What's that supposed to mean?**

Jess knew that there was a chance here, to step back and be the bigger person, but she was so hurt. Not just on her behalf, but on Edie's. Edie, who might need him to be there, to step up. Just like her own dad, he couldn't be bothered to do the right thing.

**It doesn't matter. Forget about it.**

Silence for a minute or two, and then his response.

**You always do that. If you're annoyed, just tell me. Don't pretend it doesn't matter. I've said I'm sorry, and I really couldn't change things today. I hope you believe that.**

Jess left it there. There were so many things she could say in response, but all of them would have led them further into an argument. She was surprised when her phone beeped again.

**Try not thinking the worst of me for once, okay?**

She was tempted to reply with something sarcastic but stopped herself. Did she really do that? Did she always think the worst of people? Or maybe just of men.

Jess wanted to talk to someone, but she wasn't sure whom. Gemma was about to leave for a shift at the bar and she knew her mum would join her in trashing Jake, but she wasn't sure that was what she wanted. And then she remembered Asha, her breast care nurse. Jess searched for Asha's number. She'd keyed it into her phone a couple of weeks before.

'Hello?'

'Is that Asha?' Jess asked.

'It is. Who's speaking?'

'This is Jess McKinley. I've seen you at the hospital a couple of times. I'm the one with the baby…'

'I remember, Jess. What can I do for you?'

Jess couldn't remember why she'd called, what she'd planned to say. She'd just hoped, hadn't she, that this woman knew the answers? Knew how she was feeling, how displaced she was.

'I don't know what to do. It's so hard. I'm just trying to keep going, but I'm so tired.'

'Jess, listen to me. You're a new mum and that makes everything you're going through that much harder. When I was a new mum, I was a mess for months. And I didn't have cancer. Give yourself a break. Be kind to yourself.'

Jess thought about that. Maybe it was just a case of doing

one thing at a time, taking one step and then another. Maybe if she did that, she would get there.

'Thank you,' she said.

'Do you want to ask me anything in particular?'

'No, I just needed to talk to someone who doesn't love me. Sorry, I know that sounds a bit mad. But everyone I see is so invested in me getting better. It's exhausting.'

'I get it, Jess. Call me anytime.'

When Jess ended the call, she ran a bath, and then she sank into it, trying to clear her head of everything. Jake, cancer, her mum. And that night, she slept a little better.

# CHAPTER THIRTEEN

Jess had an appointment at the hospital, and her mum had offered to come with her again. So they set out, Caroline, Jess and Edie, three generations of women in the same car, going to the hospital to find out how the surgery had gone and how she was healing. Jess wasn't too nervous this time. With every visit, the clinic felt a little more familiar and less oppressive. She still railed against this thing that was happening to her, but she did that in private. She felt like she'd healed well, and she had no reason to believe anything further was amiss, so she was expecting this appointment to be a fairly painless one.

But she could see, as soon as she was called through, that wasn't going to be the case. The doctor who'd first diagnosed her was there, next to Asha. They looked visibly relieved when she was followed into the room by her mum. Jess put the car seat down on the floor and sat down heavily.

'What's wrong?' she asked.

Jess's mum whipped her head around to look at her. She

mustn't have picked up on it. But to Jess, it was so obvious. That room was full of gloom and worry.

'It's not good news, I'm afraid,' the doctor said.

Jess was grateful to him, that he got straight to the heart of it. It was the waiting that killed you.

'When we did the surgery, the tumour was bigger than we'd first thought, which is why we called you back in for further scans. I'm sorry to say that the cancer has spread. It's in your bones.'

Jess's first thought was for her mother, who was sitting beside her hearing these words. No mother should have to go through that, she thought. She couldn't bear to hear these things about Edie. And then she looked down at her baby daughter, who was awake and staring back up at her, and it hit her that she'd never sit beside Edie at an appointment like this, because she wouldn't be around. If Edie had to face anything remotely like this in her future, she would do it without her mother at her side. And that was what made her gulp for air. She felt like she was being crushed, very slowly but with great force. The faces of the people in the room were swimming around her, and she couldn't keep them still. And then she closed her eyes, allowed the darkness to surround her, while she adjusted to this new and terrible truth.

And then things sharpened back into focus, and Jess saw that her mum was crying silently, tears streaming down her face. Jess put a hand to her cheek to check, but it was as she thought: she wasn't crying. She turned to her mum and put her arms around her a little awkwardly, and she thought about how many times they had comforted one another like this, and how many more there would be. How there were probably more behind them than ahead. It was strange, to think that. Jess could feel her mum's tears making the shoulder of her top wet, and she wanted to pull away, but she knew she couldn't. Eventually, the doctor cleared his throat and it was as if he'd broken a spell. Jess and her mum pulled apart and turned back to face the man who had brought this news into their lives.

'How long?' Jess asked.

'Jessica,' Caroline interrupted, 'I don't think it's always helpful to know…'

Jess turned to her mum and tried to convey with her eyes that she loved her. 'It's me who's dealing with this, Mum. I want to know how long.'

The doctor ran his hand through his hair. He was delaying it, which meant it wasn't good. Jess tried to guess. She felt like she could cope with hearing a year, just about. It would be awful, obviously, but that would be just enough time to do some of the things she wanted to do, to get things in order for Edie. Edie began to cry, and it struck Jess as weirdly funny that she, Jess, was the only one of the three of them who hadn't cried during this appointment about her future, or lack of it. So when the doctor spoke, she was in the middle of unstrapping Edie from the car seat, and she thought she must have misheard him.

'I'm sorry,' she said, arranging her clothes so that Edie could feed. 'What did you say?'

He grimaced. This must be the worst part of his job, she thought. Who would want this job, when it involved appointments like this in a sterile, draughty room?

'A few months,' he said. 'We think just a few months.'

'Will you go ahead with chemo as planned?' Jess asked.

'We think that's best. It could give you longer. But it's up to you. Are you happy to do that?'

Jess nodded. She didn't know. How could she know? All she could do was go along with what they advised.

They said very little in the car on the way home, because

Jess was still stunned, and her mum kept crying when she tried to talk about it. When they pulled up on the drive, Jess opened her door almost before her mum had stopped the car and got out to retrieve Edie.

'Love, we should talk about this…' her mum said.

'I'm going to phone Gemma,' Jess said, struggling to the front door with the car seat in the crook of her arm. Edie was getting heavier, she noted. It was getting harder to lug her around. And again, that line of thought. She wouldn't be here to see Edie grow out of this car seat and into the next one. To see her start to move about independently, to crawl and then walk. She would never see her daughter running. It didn't feel real, not yet.

She dialled Gemma's number as soon as she was in her bedroom with the door closed. Edie had fallen asleep in the car and hadn't stirred when Jess had brought her into the house. When Jess heard Gemma's voice, and Gemma's response to this news, she would know how she felt about it, she thought. And she wasn't sure why she needed it to be filtered in this way, or what that meant. All she knew was that she needed to share the worst news she'd ever been given with her best friend.

Gemma answered on the fourth ring. 'How was your appointment?' she asked.

Jess opened her mouth to speak and found that she couldn't. The words were there, ready to spill out, but she couldn't say them.

'Jess, are you there?'

'I'm here,' she managed.

She'd never heard her own voice sound quite so flat and it shocked her.

'Bad news?' Gemma asked. 'Jess, I'm here. You can tell me.'

Could she? She'd always told Gemma everything. Good

and bad. But this wasn't like anything else, was it? This was so final, and the kind of thing that belonged in the friendship of old women and not young ones.

'Gemma,' she said. 'I'm dying.'

No one had said that word. Not the doctor, not her mum. If she hadn't heard Gemma's sharp intake of breath, she might have thought her friend had gone from the other end of the line. Jess sank on to her bed and wondered where Gemma was, where she was hearing this news. Would she always associate that room, that place, with Jess? Would she go there to remember this conversation, after Jess was gone?

'No!' Gemma said. 'You're not dying, Jess. I won't fucking let you.'

Jess didn't say anything. She was finding it hard to breathe. She looked down at Edie and it steadied her. While she was looking at her baby, she knew how to go on. In, out. Just breathe. How could she die? How could she leave these people who she loved so fiercely? How could that love not be enough?

'Gemma,' she found herself saying. 'I don't know whether I can do this.'

'I'll be there in ten minutes.'

When Gemma arrived, she took charge. Caroline was wandering about downstairs from room to room, unable to settle or to relax. Gemma made cups of tea, looked after Edie, handed Jess her pyjamas and told her to go to bed. And all the time, Jess tried to keep reminding herself of the awful facts of her situation. She was twenty-one, she had a baby, she was dying of cancer. The three things didn't fit together at all. And yet they were all true, and she was going to have to face it.

## CHAPTER FOURTEEN

*Dear Edie,*

*I wanted you to know that I am not only cancer. All your life, you'll have this story and you won't have me. My mother died of cancer when I was a baby. That's what you'll tell people, and they will say how sorry they are, and it will seem like me and cancer are inextricable. But it wasn't always like that. I was diagnosed with cancer at twenty-one, and I lived for over two decades with no thought of cancer. Just because cancer was my ending, I don't want you to think it was my everything. My everything is you.*

*Up until recently, I associated cancer with old people. I knew that young people, even children, could get it, but I didn't think they died. I have been naïve and I'm glad about that, really. Because perhaps if I'd known that this is something that might happen to me, I'd have been more scared, and I wouldn't have lived as carelessly and well.*

*I remember the first time Gemma and I smoked cigarettes. She got her older brother Dan to buy them for us, a pack of ten Marlboro Lights. We were fourteen, and it was early summer. We walked back from school to her house together, and we snuck upstairs and knocked on*

*Dan's bedroom door. He was playing trance music really loud and we didn't know whether he'd heard us, so Gemma opened the door. He was lying on his bed with a girl from the year above us. They were kissing and his hand was inside her shirt. I'd had a crush on Dan for years, and as we stood there, I asked myself whether I wished it was me, lying there with his hands on me. I did, and I didn't. It frightened me a bit.*

*I thought Dan would shout at us for walking in on them, but he just reached down for his coat, pulled the cigarettes from the pocket and threw them at Gemma, and before we were out of the door, he was kissing the girl again. She didn't say anything, and I wanted to know how she felt, whether she minded the interruption or our eyes on her.*

*'Is Dan seeing that girl?' I asked.*

*'Looks like it,' she said.*

*Gemma's parents weren't at home. They were both nurses and they worked shifts. We went out into the garden. Gemma had a lighter that she'd bought from the corner shop. I was worried that Gemma's next-door neighbour would see us and tell Gemma's parents, but Gemma shrugged and said she didn't care. She was braver than me. She pulled the cellophane off the packet, took out two cigarettes and lit them both, then handed one to me. I felt self-conscious, but glad we were doing this for the first time together. I knew I would cough or just do it wrong somehow, and I didn't mind Gemma seeing that.*

*I remember the feel of the sun on my cheeks and forehead as I put the cigarette to my lips. It tasted awful, just the way you'd expect, and I didn't understand why so many people did it. I don't think either of us inhaled properly. We blew the smoke out into the warm air and raised our eyebrows at one another. I wondered how we looked, whether we looked cool, or older, or just different. We were still wearing our school uniforms, and I remember thinking that my mum would smell the smoke on mine and ask me about it. It wasn't enough to stop me from doing it. I felt a little bit sick and a little bit dizzy, but I put the cigarette to my lips again anyway.*

*Just then, the girl from Dan's room came out of the back door with nothing on her feet and asked if she could have a cigarette. Gemma shrugged and handed one to her, and she asked us if we were in Year Nine, which she must have known we were. It was too quiet, and I wanted Gemma to ask the girl some questions, and I was trying to remember whether she was called Lucy or Layla or Lauren. She'd played the flute once, in assembly, and I still had an image of it in my memory, and I didn't know why. She was probably fifteen, and she smoked more convincingly than either of us, and I was desperate to know whether she and Dan were having sex, whether they'd just had sex in the time between us going into his room and her coming outside to smoke with us. But I couldn't ask.*

*When all three of us had ground the butts out on the stones that bordered Gemma's lawn and Gemma had taken them to the outside bin, Dan came outside. He put a hand up to shade his eyes from the sun and said to the girl that he thought she was going home. She said she was, and she swept past him without touching, and he watched her go. And then I remember exactly what he said to us.*

*'You'll die of cancer if you smoke too many of those.'*

*It was unexpected and I wasn't sure whether he was joking. I'd seen him smoking plenty of times. But not recently, I thought. I could still taste the cigarette in my mouth, and I hadn't enjoyed it, but I was planning to smoke the rest of the pack with Gemma the first chance we got. In fact, I'd wondered which of us would have one less because of the one the girl had taken. We'd split the cost equally. I felt like smoking was probably something you had to practise before you were any good at it. But now what Dan had said had kind of spoiled it for me and I felt like the afternoon was over. I said that I was going to go home. Gemma shrugged and went inside. Dan was sitting on a deckchair near the back door, and when I walked past him, he touched my hand and said he'd see me later. I pulled away, flustered. I hadn't kissed anyone yet. I knew Gemma had, and I felt like I was losing ground, like she was leaving me behind. But I wasn't sure I was ready for it. And now Dan, the boy I most wanted to kiss, was flirting with me, and I was scared.*

*I walked home, crunching on Polo mints and hoping that would be enough to get rid of the smell of smoke. And it seemed to be, because Mum never said a word. I don't remember smoking the rest of that packet of cigarettes, but I suppose we must have done, and there were other packets after that. But I never became a regular smoker, and I've sometimes wondered how much of that is down to those words of Dan's. You'll die of cancer. And now, here I am, dying of cancer anyway.*

*I had my first kiss a couple of weeks after that, and it wasn't with Dan. It was with a boy from my English class who we saw in the park with some of his friends one Friday night. He led me away from Gemma and pushed me up against the ladder of the slide and pressed his fat tongue into my mouth before I was ready, and I hated it. I wished, then, that I'd been brave enough to flirt back when Dan had flirted with me. That I'd just turned up at his house one afternoon, knocked on the door. You have to take what you want when it's offered, because it won't always be offered again.*

*Dan still lives at home and I see him sometimes, when Gemma and I go out in town. He knows I have a baby. He probably knows I have cancer, too. I wonder whether he remembers that summer afternoon seven years ago. What he said about cancer, and touching my hand like that.*

*I wanted you to know that I'm not only cancer. I was a teenager, once, just ordinary and young. Desperate to get older, with no idea of what would happen when I did.*

*With love,*
*Mum*

## CHAPTER FIFTEEN

Once a few days had passed, Jess began to adjust to the new situation. She kept forgetting, though. Kept thinking about things she might do with Edie in the future, and then remembering that she wouldn't be there. She'd never noticed how much she thought about the future until she didn't have one. The remembering was hard and sharp; a slap. Caroline was trying to be as normal as possible but twice Jess had heard her crying behind her bedroom door. And then there was Edie. Unaware, and needing them both so much.

Jess had decided it would be nice to find some photographs to put aside for Edie. She thought about asking her mum where she kept all the photos, but she could hear her moving about downstairs and decided not to bother her. She felt like she was walking a tightrope, trying to keep her own despair in check and not upset her mother, and it was exhausting. She would find the photos herself. She went into her mother's bedroom. One chest of drawers was full of neatly folded clothes and the other one was for paperwork, trinkets, all sorts of bits and pieces. Jess pushed her hair out of her eyes and opened the top drawer of that chest. And that's where she found a bundle of letters with her name on the front. Jake's handwriting. Unopened.

The photographs forgotten, Jess pulled the letters out of the drawer and took them into her bedroom. Counted them, her hands shaking. Six. She looked closely at the dates and saw that the first had arrived not long after that enormous row she and Jake had had, the row that had ended everything. She opened that one first. Edie was asleep in her basket at Jess's feet, and when Jess looked down at her, she saw Jake in her daughter's eyes, in the curve of her lips.

*Jess,*

*You told me you like real letters when we were sitting in the cinema after watching that film about those lovers, separated by war, who wrote to each other for fifty years. The film had finished and everyone else had left but you'd grabbed my arm and told me to stay in my seat because you couldn't stop crying and you wanted some time to pull yourself together. So here's a letter for you. I know we can't unsay the things we both said yesterday, and you asked me not to be in touch, so I won't text or email or call you. But a letter seems a bit different. You can choose whether or not to open it, and when. If you're reading these words, I want you to know that I'm sorry. And I miss you already, and you've only been gone for a day.*

*Love, Jake x*

Jess felt paralysed. All these months, she had believed that he didn't care. That he'd chosen to remain silent. She tore open the second envelope.

*Jess,*

*It's been a few weeks since my first letter, and I haven't heard anything from you. I don't know whether you're too angry to get in touch or whether you threw the letter away. I keep thinking about you, and about our baby. You'll be about four months pregnant by now. I catch myself wondering whether the pregnancy is showing, or whether you can feel the baby move yet. And even playing my guitar doesn't take my mind off it, because all I want to do is call you and ask you all the questions that keep spinning in my head. First up: can you forgive me?*

*Love, Jake x*

Jess felt as though she'd been winded. She took the two letters that she'd torn open and read and stormed downstairs. Her mum was in the living room, vacuuming. She didn't hear Jess approach and when she finally turned around, her eyes were wild with surprise.

'What the fuck, Mum? Why did you hide these letters?'

Caroline reached to turn the vacuum cleaner off and gave Jess one of the looks she'd known since childhood. A look that meant: I am the adult and you are the child. I know what's best.

'Don't use that kind of language with me, Jessica. I'm sorry. I did what I thought was best.'

'How is it best to hide post from the person it's addressed to? That's not best, that's interfering!' Jess could feel her cheeks flaming red, her heart thumping.

'Now just hold on,' Caroline said, a hairline crack in her voice. 'Put yourself in my position. You'd just come home, pregnant and terrified and heartbroken. You told me it was over with Jake, that he didn't want anything to do with you or the baby. I did everything I could to put you back together. And when that first letter arrived, you were just starting to turn a corner. You'd decided to keep the baby and we were beginning to make plans, and I didn't want to set you back by allowing you to read whatever sorry excuses he was making.'

Jess shook her head wildly. 'That wasn't your choice to make. You had no idea what he was saying in here. Edie is his baby, Mum. His and mine. You had absolutely no right to get in between us like this.'

Without waiting for a response, Jess stormed out of the room and back upstairs. She didn't hear the vacuum cleaner come back on for a long time. And in that time, she read the rest of the letters, one after the other.

*Jess,*

*It's weeks since you left and every morning I wake up and reach my hand out for you. My body refuses to remember. You'll be halfway through the pregnancy now, and I can't quite picture you with a bump. You might know, by now, whether it's a boy or a girl. I try not to think of the baby as one or the other, but when I think of you holding it, I always picture a girl. When I read a book or watch TV, I think about the characters' names and whether they'd make a good name for our baby. Fuck, Jess. I know I got it all wrong that day you told me. And I know there might be no going back. But I don't want this life I have now, always on the road and no one to talk to. I want the life I had, with you.*

*Love, Jake x*

*Jess,*

*I don't know whether you're reading these, or whether you want to hear about what I'm doing, but I have to imagine you're there because I feel so lost otherwise. We're playing five or six gigs a week in tiny pubs and clubs. It's hard work, and most of the time people aren't listening. But I feel like we have this one chance and we have to put everything into it. Tom and I are writing loads of new material, too. The other day, we were in Brighton and this girl came backstage and we kissed, but it felt all wrong. I asked her to leave, and she seemed upset and I felt awful, but I was wishing she was you, and it wouldn't have been fair.*

*Love, Jake x*

*Jess,*

*It's killing me that I don't know whether you've had the baby, whether the two of you are okay. I've thought about calling your house so many times. It seems like whenever I have the TV on, there's a baby on the screen and it kills me that I don't even know whether I have a son or a daughter. This must be hard on you, doing it on your own. I know you have your mum, but I wish you had me. I decided after the last letter that I wouldn't write again, but today I forgot that decision and found myself writing this letter. I don't know how to make you understand how sorry I am. If there's any chance of us being a family, I don't want to give up on that.*

*Love, Jake x*

*Jess,*

*Okay, this is my last shot. I can't keep doing this to myself. After I send a letter, I spend a couple of days wondering whether it's arrived and thinking about you opening it, reading it, and how you'll respond. And then for about a week afterwards, I call my parents every day to ask whether there's any post, and I check my phone constantly. It's not doing me any good. I think you've made yourself clear with your silence. You'll definitely have had the baby by now, and I'll always wonder how you're both doing, what you've called him or her, whether you think about me. But I can't keep shouting into a void. I'm always here, if you change your mind or want to talk.*

*Love, Jake x*

Edie woke just as Jess was finishing the last letter, and she didn't realise she was crying until she picked up her daughter and her tears began to fall on Edie's soft, downy head. She put Edie to her breast, hoping she had enough milk to satisfy her. Since the operation, she'd been feeding from one breast, and she'd had to supplement with bottles of formula despite pumping milk every chance she got. Jess knew that her medical team thought she was being stubborn. She would have to give up feeding entirely when she started chemo, and everyone thought she should just call it a day. But she couldn't, somehow. There was something so special about feeling Edie get what she needed from Jess's body, and Jess wanted to carry on with it as long as she possibly could. It was the only thing that her body was doing right, and she wanted to hold on to that.

She thought back to the message she'd sent to Jake asking if they could meet up. Everything looked different now that she'd read the letters, as if she'd changed the lens on a camera and could suddenly see everything in focus. Jake had assumed she knew what his life on tour was like, because as far as he was concerned, he'd told her about it. And when he'd had to cancel their meeting with no explanation, he'd thought she would understand, that that was just what things were like on the road. The anger Jess felt towards her mother was still boiling away, but she was trying not to be consumed by it, because there was something more important at stake here. Jake wanted to meet up, had wanted it for a long time, and she hadn't known. And now she had more reason than ever to get hold of him.

Edie pulled away from Jess's breast, milk-drunk and apparently satisfied, but within a couple of minutes, she was opening and closing her mouth as if trying to latch on again, and Jess knew she was still expecting to be fed by a second breast. She rearranged her clothes and carried Edie downstairs to make up a bottle. She didn't want to face her mum again so soon after her outburst earlier, but she had no choice. She was spooning the milk powder into a bottle, Edie squirming and crying on her shoulder, when her mum came into the room. She reached for Edie and Jess let her take her, because she was struggling, and she wasn't too proud to accept help. Not yet.

'I'm sorry,' Caroline said.

Jess was surprised. It wasn't a word her mum used very often, and Jess knew how hard it would have been for her to say it.

'I didn't want you to get hurt. I didn't want Edie to get hurt. I thought he might come back on the scene and then disappear again. That's what men do.'

Jess whirled around. 'Not all men, Mum. That's what Dad did. But you can't keep treating Jake like he's the same person Dad was.'

Caroline smiled, but it was bitter. 'I've lived a lot longer than you have, sweetheart, and you can trust me on this one.'

She stopped quite abruptly, and Jess knew that she'd realised what she had said. 'I've lived a lot longer than you have'. Longer than I ever will, Jess added, silently.

'Look,' Caroline went on. 'None of us know what to do here. This situation is heart breaking, and no one could have predicted it. Would I have done things differently with the letters if I'd known where we'd be right now, with the cancer? Perhaps. I can't say for sure. But we are where we are, and if you want to get Jake involved, I won't stand in your way...'

'Oh, that's big of you!' Jess couldn't hold her fury in any longer. 'It's absolutely none of your business whether I get in touch with him or not. He is Edie's dad, in case you've forgotten that, and she's going to need a dad because she isn't going to have a mum for very much longer...'

Jess broke off, unable to go on. She was sobbing, and she

still hadn't finished making the bottle, and Edie's cries were getting more and more insistent. Caroline was rocking her gently, making soothing sounds and trying to distract her. She was a good grandmother, Jess couldn't and wouldn't deny that. Jess wouldn't have been able to do it without her. But surely that didn't give her the right to behave like this, to treat Jess like a child who couldn't make her own decisions about her life and her daughter's future.

When the bottle was ready, Jess handed it to her mum in silence and left the room. She knew without asking that Caroline would feed Edie and settle her, so she went upstairs and crawled into bed and let herself cry. It was such a mess, and it wasn't fair, and she didn't know how to make any of it work. She reached for her phone and typed a message to Jake.

**I just read your letters for the first time. Mum kept them hidden from me. I had no idea you wanted to be in touch.**

She looked over it again before sending. Did that capture it? There was so much she wanted to say. Part of her wanted to pick up the phone and just call him, but she didn't trust herself to not let it all out, the cancer and everything, in one terrified rush. She pressed send and put her phone on the floor beside the bed to stop herself from checking continuously for a response.

Jess must have fallen asleep because the next thing she knew, her mum was sitting on the edge of her bed with Edie in her arms.

'Love,' Caroline said, 'how are you feeling?'

Jess sat up and reached for Edie. 'I'm okay. I didn't mean to go to sleep. Sorry to leave her with you.'

Jess stopped, aware that what she was saying was ridiculous when the likelihood was that in a few weeks or months, Jess would be leaving Edie with her mum forever.

'What am I going to do?' she asked, then. 'I mean, when I can't look after her. When I'm too ill, tired from the treatment, all of that.'

'We'll work it out,' Caroline said. 'I mostly work in the daytime and Gemma works at night. She's offered to help out as much as she possibly can. We'll rope your dad in if we need to…'

'And Jake?' Jess asked.

She looked at her mother's face, took in the worry that was etched there.

'I guess that's up to you,' she said.

It was a victory, of sorts, but it didn't feel like one. Jess laid Edie down next to her on the bed and snuggled down beside her. Perhaps if she just stayed close to Edie for as many hours as possible, she would somehow imprint herself on her daughter's memory. Perhaps Edie would remember feeling safe and loved, even if she didn't remember Jess's face or the sound of her voice.

Caroline stood to leave the room, then turned back. 'Is there anything you want?'

Jess tried to swallow down the lump in her throat. There were so many things she wanted, but unlike when she was a child, her mum couldn't fix everything. 'I'm okay,' she said.

Jake's response came through just after the door closed behind her mum.

**Are you serious? I've spent months thinking you hate me. Why would she do that?**

Jess was surprised by the sharpness of his tone, especially

having read his six sweet and heartfelt letters in one sitting. She didn't know what to think. She typed a reply quickly.

**I promise it's true. I really need to talk to you about something. Can we rearrange our meeting?**

Meeting didn't seem like the right word. It felt too cold and business-like, but she couldn't think of an alternative, so she pressed send. And then she waited, lying beside her daughter, for a reply that didn't come.

# CHAPTER SIXTEEN

*Dear Edie,*

*I wanted you to know how your dad and I broke up. The pregnancy had knocked us both a bit. That must be hard to read, and I'm sorry, but I want to tell you the whole truth. I don't want to sugar-coat anything. We were young and we had big plans for the future and we'd never talked about having children, certainly not yet, and so we were thrown, and we didn't really know what to do. I'd been walking around in a daze since finding out, and I hadn't told anyone other than your dad. Not Mum, not Gemma. I carried you around like a secret.*

*Then one day, a few weeks after I'd found out, I went to see your dad and I could tell that something had happened. Something exciting. He kept moving around, couldn't keep still, but every time I asked him what was going on, he said it was nothing. So we spent an hour or two together, talking about things other than the pregnancy, both of us trying to pretend that nothing had changed between us and we were still just a young couple in love, with no ties and no responsibilities. Then, while we were sitting on the sofa watching TV, your dad got a text, and his phone was on the arm of the sofa next to me, and I looked over and I saw what it said. It was from his friend Tom and it read: Have you made a decision yet? He reached for his phone, read the message, and then put it in his pocket without replying. He knew I'd seen it, and I waited for him to say something about it, but he didn't. For a minute or two, I watched him as he watched the screen, and it was as if I wasn't there. So I stood up and picked up the remote control and turned the TV off, and I stood in front of him with my arms folded and waited for him to say or do something.*

*'What?' he said.*

*I'm pretty calm most of the time but I'd had enough. I exploded.*

*'What do you mean, what? I came here today hoping we could talk more about what we're going to do, about this baby, and instead I find that something's going on with you, but you won't tell me what it is. You're all jumpy and odd. I've been trying to ignore it and just be with you, but then you got that weird text from Tom and pretended it wasn't happening. You need to tell me what's going on, right now!'*

*Halfway through my little speech, Jake had lifted his hands to either side of his head, as if in surrender.*

*'Calm down, Jess. All right, I'll tell you. Will you just sit down?'*

*I sat down on the sofa next to him. I thought about all the times we'd sat here together, watching films or just talking. Usually entwined, legs and arms wrapped around each other. But then, we were sitting a few inches apart and I wanted to cross the distance with my hand, but I knew I needed to hear what he had to say first.*

*'It's the band. Tom's had this guy get in touch from a record company. They like us. They want us to do this massive tour of pubs and clubs, try to get a bit of a following.'*

*I felt my stomach drop. I was going to lose him. I knew, in that second, that it was over. I asked him loads of questions, like whether the record company were actually signing them and whether they'd be getting paid while they were doing this tour, and all the time I was thinking that the answers didn't really matter, because I could see how much he wanted to do this, and how much he'd grow to resent me if I asked him not to.*

*I asked whether he'd told Tom about the pregnancy, and he shook his head. And I thought that told me, that he wasn't prepared to move his life around to make room for you. He pulled me towards him then, with both his hands in my hair, and he kissed me on the forehead. And it felt like he was saying goodbye. How awful that it was this incredible opportunity that had brought it all to a head. An opportunity that I would have been cheering and celebrating at any other time. It was a step towards the thing he really wanted, a thing so many people wanted and most of them didn't get, and I desperately didn't want to stand in his way. And yet, things had changed, because of you.*

*He nodded towards my abdomen and asked whether I'd decided what I wanted to do. That sealed it. Before, we'd always talked in terms of an us, talked about what we would do. But now, I was on my own. It couldn't have been clearer. I stood up, hoping he couldn't see that my heart was breaking inside me, and I tried to be strong. I told him I was going to have you. It was the first time I'd said it out loud, but as soon as I did, I knew it was true. I said I was going to go home and live with my mum, and he nodded. I was letting him go. 'What will happen after I get back?' he asked. He hadn't said, until that point, that he was definitely going to go.*

*I wasn't sure what he was asking. Did he want to know if we could still be together, if I still wanted him? I thought about him going from town to town, playing his guitar and singing those sweet, sweet songs he and Tom had written, and I knew there would be other girls. I couldn't keep hold of him. It just wouldn't work. I wanted to be adult about it, but I was so hurt, and that hurt just came spilling out.*

*'You can't be in our lives,' I said. 'Not mine or the baby's. It's not fair. This is it, for us.'*

*Jake looked confused, and I wondered what he'd expected. Had he thought I might say that he should go away for months on end and I would have our baby, and then he could come home and play Dad, and everything would be okay? I couldn't say that. Perhaps some women could, but not me. He looked sad and he looked angry, but he never once said he would stay. That we could make it work, him and me and you. If he'd said that, I would have backed down. I would have clung to him.*

*It was time to go. There was nothing left to say. I gathered the things I'd left scattered about: my jacket, my keys, my phone. And I thought about when I'd arrived here, a few hours earlier, how casually I'd removed that jacket, not knowing that when I put it back on again, my great love would be over. I wanted to kiss him, to remind myself, but I knew it was impossible. He asked me not to leave with things like this between us, but it was a feeble request. He knew it was done. We both knew.*

*When I was at the door, he called my name. He asked whether I would keep in touch, tell him when I'd had the baby, let him know that everything was okay. I stopped, my hand on the door handle, and the tears started to come. Somehow, I held my voice steady.*

*'No,' I said. 'It's over, Jake. None of that is your business anymore.'*

*And I walked out of the door and squinted in the bright sun, and I cried all the way home. I wanted you to know how your dad and I broke up. It was messy, and sad, and I believed it was final.*

*Love,*

*Mum*

# CHAPTER SEVENTEEN

Gemma scrolled through her phone and then attached it to the cable in her car.

'You made a chemo playlist? Really?' Jess found herself laughing softly, on this day when she hadn't expected to be able to. She had Gemma to thank for that.

'Of course! I make a playlist for everything, you know that.'

It was true. Through their teenage years, Gemma had made playlists for every party they'd been to or trip they'd been on. Every crush, every boy. Jess thought about the Jake playlist Gemma had sent her just after they'd got together, and then the breakup one she'd sent after Jess turned up back at home, single and pregnant.

Jess expected the chemo playlist to be sombre, so she was astonished when the first few notes burst out of the car's speakers. 'Titanium'. She found herself smiling. Of course. It wasn't about being sad, or ill. It was about being empowered. She should have known that Gemma wouldn't drag her down on a day like today.

Gemma sang all the way to the hospital, her voice loud and

off-key. She'd always loved to sing, despite knowing her voice was terrible. Jess had hung back more. Refusing to join in at karaoke nights, only really letting loose when she was in the shower. But now, she decided that that was stupid, pointless. She put her window down and sang loud along with 'Roar' as her hair whipped against her face.

'Wow, you can really sing! Who knew?' Gemma shouted over the music.

Jess didn't know whether it was true or another attempt to lift her spirits. But again, it didn't matter. Gemma's words made her feel good, and she carried on singing with a smile on her face. When Gemma pulled into a parking space and turned off the engine, the music stopped abruptly and Jess felt exposed, somehow.

Gemma reached across the space between them and put her hand on Jess's knee briefly. 'We've got this,' she said.

Jess had read a bit about what to expect. She wasn't scared of needles or of hospitals in general, so the process itself wasn't the frightening bit, for her. It was afterwards. The sickness, the hair loss, the never-ending list of side effects she'd read. And to do all that, knowing that she didn't have long anyway. Was it even worth it?

When she was called in, she glanced around the room. Eight or nine other people hooked up to machines, tubes coming out of their veins. A mixture of men and women, a range of ages. But no one as young as her. And moving around between the patients, three nurses, their faces friendly, their hands quick and sure. Jess was taken to a free seat, and Gemma was given the visitor's chair beside it. Every time Jess looked over at her friend, Gemma flashed her a smile that wasn't quite straight. How would she feel, she wondered, if it were Gemma going through this, and she was in the role of supportive friend? She'd feel wretched, she knew. Tearful and angry and scared. She smiled back at Gemma, trying to convey that she didn't have to be strong every single minute. That it was okay to be scared, to cry.

The nurse looking after Jess was called Kia. She was young, maybe a handful of years older than Jess. She talked them through everything, and Jess nodded, just keen to get it under way now. Kia seemed to sense this and acted quickly and efficiently. Perhaps that was just her way, Jess thought, but regardless, she was grateful for it.

Once they'd found a vein and the treatment had started, Jess felt a tiny bit lighter. She'd worried that she would instantly feel sick, had even asked Kia for one of those cardboard sick bowls, just in case. But she didn't feel anything, not really. Kia had said it would take three hours or so, and Gemma had packed a bag full of snacks, books and magazines. She delved into it and pulled out a book of crossword puzzles, held it up for Jess to see and raised her eyebrows. Jess shook her head and felt like she might cry because of the care Gemma had taken. She blinked the tears away and gave Gemma the brightest smile she could manage.

'I just want to sit here, and talk,' Jess said. 'Can we pretend we're out for lunch or something? Or in the common room at school between lessons?'

Gemma looked so sad for a moment. But then she overcame it, somehow, or at least hid it, and started talking about her brother Dan and his mates, about a holiday they'd recently come back from and how Dan had returned with a dodgy tattoo of a pair of lips on his right hip. And then, with no pause whatsoever, she launched into a story about a girl called Esther they'd both known a little at school who'd come into the bar where Gemma worked the night before on a blind date. How she'd sat at the bar chatting to Gemma while she waited for him to arrive, and when he had, it had been Mr Matthews, their French teacher from Year Eight, and Esther had asked Gemma to create a diversion while she snuck out of the bar, unseen. Gemma had always had stories, had always swooped and dived from one to another, making Jess laugh like no one else. She couldn't imagine anyone else she'd rather have by her side on this difficult day.

Jess closed her eyes.

'Do you want me to shut up?' Gemma asked. 'You only have to say.'

'No, no, please don't. I'm just trying to pretend we're somewhere else.'

It felt a little like old times, better times.

Gemma had brought sandwiches wrapped in clingfilm, and when it got to midday, she pulled them out and passed one of the packages to Jess. Jess imagined her making them that morning, or possibly the night before, after a late shift. She pictured her friend, tired, her feet aching, carrying out this task with love. The sandwiches were a little squashed, but they were tuna and cucumber, Jess's favourite, and Jess closed her eyes while she ate them and was transported back to the little bench the two of them used to sit on in all weathers to eat their packed lunches at school. When she'd finished, Gemma held up an apple in one hand and a bag of Hula Hoops in the other, and Jess pointed to the crisps. Jess barely noticed the other patients, just as she'd barely noticed the other kids at school. Gemma was in technicolour, and Jess hoped she would be able to come with her to every one of these weekly sessions.

So when the nurse came to say that it was done, Jess was a little surprised. It had been nothing like she'd imagined, although she knew the worst could be yet to come. She'd been talked through the side effects, she was expecting to lose her hair and to feel tired and sick. They got back into Gemma's car.

'Playlist?' Gemma asked.

'Why not?'

Gemma nodded and started the playlist at the beginning, and Jess thought it felt a long time since they'd been listening to these same songs on their way in to the hospital. When her phone buzzed, she took it out of her pocket, expecting it to be her mum, checking up on how it had gone. So she was surprised to see Jake's name come up. It had been two days since she'd pleaded with him to meet up with her again, and the previous day, she'd checked her phone obsessively. But she'd been distracted, that day, by the chemo, and the sight of his name caught her off guard.

**I can't meet for another three weeks or so. We're down south until then. I'll be in touch when I know more about dates.**

Jess looked out of the window at the houses rushing past. Three weeks. What could she expect to look like after three more sessions of chemo? Would she have any hair left? She remembered when they first met and she'd worried about him only seeing her in her supermarket uniform, which was unflattering and stripped her face of colour. Here she was, just a couple of years later, with worries that were so much weightier. She tried to push it out of her mind. She needed to see him, and that was the bottom line. She needed to talk to him about Edie. It was too much to think about. She typed a one-word reply.

**Okay.**

Before sending, she added 'Please don't forget' to the end, then removed it.

When Gemma pulled up outside her house, Jess felt a sudden wave of exhaustion. Was it the chemo kicking in? Or perhaps it was just the stress of it all. The constant worrying and thinking and planning.

'Want me to come inside?' Gemma asked.

'No, that's okay. I've had enough of you today.'

Gemma smiled and Jess knew her friend was pleased she was up to making jokes. She reached across and gave Gemma a hug that was slightly awkward because of the gearstick being in the way.

'Call me, okay? Whenever.'

Jess nodded and got out of the car. She waved as Gemma pulled away. There was a part of her that didn't want to go inside. She knew her mum would have lots of questions, and all she wanted to do was lie down and try to sleep for a while. But she couldn't just stay outside, so she made her way to the front door and let herself in. The first thing she heard was Edie wailing. She followed the sound to the living room, where her mum was trying to feed her.

'She doesn't seem to want it,' Caroline said, twisting to face Jess. 'She took one earlier, no problem.'

'Maybe she's not hungry,' Jess said, moving over to the sofa and reaching for her daughter.

'It's been three hours, and she was rooting.' Caroline gestured to her breasts. 'No milk here, sorry!'

Jess wanted, more than anything, to put her baby to her breast. Edie started snuffling, opening and closing her mouth. She looked up at Jess, confused. Unable to understand why her mother wasn't lifting her top, like usual, and offering her breast. Jess felt like crying.

'I'm sorry, baby,' she whispered. 'I can't.'

Jess took the bottle from her mum and tried to sneak the teat into Edie's mouth, but she wouldn't take it. She was getting more and more red in the face, hungry and angry and lost. It wasn't fair, Jess thought. It wasn't fair. None of it was her fault and none of it was Edie's. She wanted to scream, then, and she didn't think she could do it.

'Can you take her?' she asked, looking up pleadingly at her mum. 'I'm sorry. I know you've had her all day. I just...'

'It's fine,' Caroline said, coming over and giving Jess's arm a quick stroke before taking Edie from her. 'It's fine, darling.'

Jess could hear her daughter's cries as she went upstairs, could hear them when she went into her bedroom and shut the door behind her. She let the tears fall, then, and they were fast and hot on her face and she felt like a little girl again, curling up on her bed and feeling like the world was ending.

# CHAPTER EIGHTEEN

Jess didn't realise she'd fallen asleep in her clothes until she woke in them the next morning. Still lying on top of her covers, but with a blanket covering her. Her mouth felt grim because she hadn't cleaned her teeth, and it was the first night she'd spent at home without Edie beside her, so she felt an odd sort of panic. But now that she couldn't feed Edie anymore, it wasn't only Jess who could look after her. There was a strange lifting feeling connected to that which Jess wasn't ready to explore.

There was a soft knock on the door and her mum came into the room with a mug of tea in her hand.

'Morning,' she said. 'How are you feeling?'

Jess wanted to answer honestly, so she gave herself a quick check. She didn't feel sick or massively tired. She felt okay. She told her mum, and her mum looked at her closely to check she was telling the truth. Jess was grateful for that care.

'Where's Edie?' Jess asked.

'She's fast asleep. We had a bit of a night of it, she and I. But she's taking bottles better, for now at least.'

'Thank you for taking her.'

Jess wanted to say that she felt like she was failing her baby, but she knew her mum would tell her not to be silly or something like that. And even though she knew, deep down, that it wasn't her fault, it was still something she felt, and she wanted someone to acknowledge it, to understand.

'You know,' Caroline said, coming further into the room and sitting down on the edge of Jess's bed. 'I didn't breastfeed you for long at all.'

Jess didn't know this, and she wondered why she'd never asked.

'It was difficult, and painful, and people kept telling me it would get easier if I gave you a bottle. So I did.'

Jess tried to read her mum's face. Why was she telling her this? Did she feel guilty about this decision? She seemed quite matter-of-fact about it.

'I'm just saying,' Caroline continued, 'I know you had to stop for a very specific reason, but you're not alone in stopping, or never even starting, and feeling bad about that.'

'Why did you feel bad?' Jess asked. She was tentative. She felt like something in the dynamic between her and her mother had changed, opened up, and she was scared to say the wrong thing in case it slammed shut again.

'There is endless guilt involved in being a mother,' Caroline said. 'Whatever choice you make, you always wonder about the other ones, and whether they might have been better. It's part of what makes parenting so exhausting.'

Jess thought about that, about how her experience of being a mother had been so overshadowed by cancer that she didn't know what was normal. It was possible that some of the things she blamed her illness for might have been part of it all regardless. It didn't make her feel better or worse to acknowledge that, and she'd never know for sure, but it felt like something worth exploring.

She thought, too, about her mother, how she'd been young when she became a mother as well, and how she'd been quite alone. She felt a rush of gratitude for the support her mum was offering. And then it hit her like a slap to the face that she would not get the opportunity to play this role for Edie. And the injustice of it caught in her throat.

Jess heard the sound of Edie stirring, then, and got out of bed and went through to her mum's bedroom to see her daughter. Other than when she'd had her surgery, this was the longest she'd been away from her, these few hours she'd just slept. She'd missed her. Edie was wide awake but not making much noise. When she saw Jess, she raised both her arms towards her mother, and Jess was overwhelmed with love for her. There was raging anger in there too, but it didn't outshadow the love; not yet. Jess picked Edie up and held her to her chest, and her heartbeat seemed to slow a little, and she felt calm, as if this was where she was meant to be.

They went downstairs, the three of them, and Jess took the first of her cocktail of pills and they drank tea and ate toast. Jess realised, at some point, that her mum was shifting a bit uncomfortably and knew she had something to say. She hoped it wasn't something that would make her angry or upset. She was enjoying this peace.

'So,' Caroline eventually said, 'I've taken some time off work. I want to be here for you and Edie, and I know you're both going to need me.'

'Can you afford that?' Jess asked.

'I've got some money put by. It will be fine. And I know your dad will help out financially if I ask him to. God knows, he hasn't helped much over the years. He owes you.'

'When you say some time off, how long are we talking?'

'Six months. It's a sabbatical.'

Silence hung between them and Jess knew they were both thinking about where they might be in six months' time. Caroline might have full-time care of a baby by then. Jess might be gone. She knew it was true and yet it all felt like a fiction to her, like something they were pretending. She realised how far she was from being ready to give up on life.

'Thank you,' Jess said. 'I don't know what to say, it doesn't seem like enough. But I don't know how I'd do it without you.'

'Well,' Caroline said, sitting up a little straighter. 'You don't have to think about it, do you? Because I'm here, and I'm not going anywhere.'

They hadn't always had the easiest of relationships, but this was their biggest test, and her mum was doing brilliantly. Jess reminded herself to keep that in mind when little things her mum did nagged at her, and she felt like snapping.

'But what about…?' Jess couldn't quite bring herself to say the words. And then she took a deep breath and forced herself to, because it was happening, and she couldn't pretend it wasn't. 'What about after? When I'm gone?'

Jess wouldn't have thought she'd be the type to hover around a topic like this. She'd always been quite direct. She remembered when her mum had tried to talk to her about sex, and she'd muttered words like 'down there' and Jess had said, 'Do you mean my vagina, Mum?' But even she couldn't bring herself to say the phrase 'when I'm dead'.

Caroline didn't answer for a moment and when Jess looked up to see why, her mum was crying. She hadn't seen her mum cry much, over the years, and she wasn't really sure what to do. She had cried endless times, of course, as a child and teenager. Her mum had always pulled her in tight to her chest and stroked her hair, and she'd usually felt reassured. Jess stood and moved around the table to where her mum was sitting. She stood behind her, put her arms around her mum's neck, and felt hot tears fall on to her wrists.

'I can't talk about after,' Caroline said, at last. 'Not yet.' She looked over at Edie, who was in her bouncy chair, happily batting at the plastic shapes in front of her. 'You're my baby, just like she's yours.'

Jess tried to put herself in her mum's position, tried to imagine if it was Edie who was facing this, but it was too hard. She pulled away from it almost straight away. She knew she'd much rather do it herself than see it happen to her baby. She would have to remember that, when her mum annoyed her, and she felt like screaming. There were so many angles to this, and it was hard for everyone.

'I know,' Jess said. She didn't move for a while, just stood there, comforting her mum, watching her daughter. Wondering how it would work when a link in this chain was broken.

Later, she called Gemma. She was in her bedroom with the door closed, and she could hear the radio downstairs so she knew she wouldn't be overheard.

'How are you?' Gemma asked.

'I'm pretty okay, chemo-wise,' Jess said. 'But there's stuff I need to talk about. Stuff I can't say to Mum.'

Gemma went quiet for a moment. 'What kind of stuff?'

Had Jess imagined it or was there a slight crack in her friend's voice? She needed to talk to someone about this stuff, and Gemma was the only one for the job.

'About dying,' she said. 'Mum can't handle it, and I'm not sure whether I can either, but I need to. I need to tell someone what I want and don't want. Can we meet up?'

She heard Gemma's deep sigh. 'Of course we can. Where and when?'

An hour later, Jess was walking to the park where she and

Gemma had met up for years. As pre-teens, just to get out of the house and complain about their parents and talk about the boys they liked. And then as teenagers, to drink and smoke and kiss the boys they liked. Jess felt slightly odd walking without Edie's pram, as if she'd forgotten something, but her mum had insisted on her leaving Edie at home, and Jess hadn't put up a fight. She knew she needed this.

She got to the park and found it empty. She sat down on the bench she and Gemma had shared many times and looked around. Usually, she would pull out her phone and look at Instagram or Twitter to pass the time, but she made herself just sit there quietly. It wasn't long until Gemma arrived. Jess enjoyed watching her approach. She was sitting up, taking notice of things. If only it wasn't almost too late to do so.

'Is this conversation going to break me?' Gemma asked, as soon as she was close enough for Jess to hear her.

'I don't know, but I have to have it.'

Gemma nodded and sat down on the bench next to Jess. It was a good way for them to sit while they talked, Jess thought, because they didn't have to look at one another. She wasn't sure she could say the things she needed to say while looking into her friend's eyes.

'I'm just going to start,' Jess said. 'I hope that's okay.'

'It's okay.'

'Mum can't hear this stuff, I don't think, so I need you to know it. It's important to me. First, I want to donate my organs, if any of them are any use. I'm young, so in theory they should be in good shape, but I'm also dying of cancer. Anyway, if any of it is any use to anyone, I want them to take them.'

Out of the corner of her eye, Jess saw her friend give a tight little nod.

'I don't want any mention of religion at my funeral. I don't want it to be in a church. I don't believe in god and even if I did, fuck him, or fuck her. Who would want to believe in a god who'd let this happen to them? No. Mum's oddly traditional at times, so I can imagine her railing against this, but I need you to be firm.'

'I don't fancy arguing with your mum over this stuff, Jess,' Gemma said.

Jess turned her head to look at her friend. They were both crying, but it wasn't overwhelming, not yet. Just single tears tracking down their cheeks, one after another.

'I'll write this all down too,' Jess said. 'So you can show it to her. But today I need to say it out loud.'

'Okay. What else?'

'I don't want to be buried. The idea of it terrifies me. Let them burn me. Then keep the ashes and let Edie decide what to do with them, when she's old enough. Or don't, if you don't think she can handle that. You can scatter them, or Mum. I don't really mind where. I don't believe that anything comes after, so it doesn't really matter to me.'

Jess didn't speak for a minute or two, because she couldn't, and while she was gathering herself, Gemma spoke in a small voice.

'I just can't even imagine...'

'I can't either. Maybe I will start to, when I feel more ill. I'm guessing that's coming.'

Gemma stood up, then, and reached for Jess's hand. When Jess gave it to her, her friend pulled her up so they were standing side by side, in front of the bench. The park was empty but there were a few cars going by outside, the odd pedestrian.

'FUCK YOU, CANCER!' Gemma shouted.

Jess jumped. She hadn't expected it. And then she started laughing and she couldn't stop.

'Try it,' Gemma said. 'It made me feel better.'

Jess took a deep breath and stopped giggling. 'FUCK YOU, CANCER!' Her voice wasn't as loud as Gemma's, or as strong, but there was definitely something freeing about it. She looked across to the park gate and saw that a woman walking by with her dog was looking at them with disdain. She didn't care.

'What about the funeral?' Gemma asked, sitting down again.

'I can't decide,' Jess said. 'I've been thinking about it. But it's all been done, hasn't it? Asking people to wear brightly coloured clothes, making it into more of a party. I like the sound of all that, but I don't want to be a cliché.'

'I'll do a playlist,' Gemma said quietly.

And that set Jess off again. The thought of her best friend in the world sitting in front of her computer, compiling her a playlist for the last time.

'Will you make playlists for Edie?' Jess asked. She hadn't thought of it before, but suddenly it seemed crucial. 'I want her to have someone in her life who cares enough to do things like that.'

'Of course I will,' Gemma said. 'First day of school playlist, first time she has her heart broken, best friend playlist.'

'I just can't believe I'm going to miss it all,' Jess said.

'No.'

'I've been writing letters for her, for Edie,' Jess said. 'If I give them to you, will you pass them on when you think she's old enough?'

'Yes. How will I know? Do you want me to read them?'

'No, they're just for her. It's just all the things I can think of, to tell her. About what I believe and what I know and answers to all the questions I can imagine her asking as she grows up. I tell her about her dad and about my pregnancy and how I feel about the cancer. All of it.'

Jess turned to Gemma and pulled her friend in for a hug. 'You'll know. I trust you. It might not be until she's eighteen, but it might be earlier. And if you're not going to be in her life for any reason, you can pass them on to my mum and ask her to do it…'

'Why wouldn't I be in her life?' Gemma asked, her voice a little higher than usual.

'I don't know, Gemma. I don't know what's going to happen in the next ten or twenty years. You might decide you want to go and live in Australia, or you might fall out with my mum about something. None of us know.'

Gemma stroked the top of Jess's head, over and over. It was comforting.

'Listen, Jess. You're right in some ways. We can't know where life will take us all. But I promise you – I absolutely promise – I will be in Edie's life. I will do everything I can for that girl. Okay?'

Jess couldn't answer that, because she was crying too much, but she nodded her head against Gemma's chest and allowed herself to be comforted.

# CHAPTER NINETEEN

*Dear Edie,*

*I wanted you to know that death, in itself, isn't scary. It's who and what you're leaving behind. I can't promise I would have been the best mum in the world. No one can promise that. Chances are, there would have been times when I would have acted unreasonably, when I would have shouted at you or been unfair. Chances are there would have been lots of those. I would have done my best, Edie. Know that.*

*I'm sitting here, trying to think about the times when I've most needed my own mum. I want to share those times with you, because these are the stories I would have shared with you if you'd come to me with your problems. I hope these letters can be something of a comfort to you, even though I'm gone. And I hope you can turn to them, as well as turning to Nanna and Gemma, when you're feeling down.*

*So here goes. When I was about seven, I had this best friend called Alana. You don't choose your friends according to having mutual interests or being similar when you're really little. You just end up being best friends with whoever you happen to be sitting next to in your class, or the child of your mum's friend. I don't remember how Alana and I were thrown together. We weren't a great match, but I didn't know that at the time. So sometimes she'd say that I was boring, and she was going to play with this other girl called Lucy instead, and it broke my heart. I would sit in the corner of the playground, watching them play the games Alana and I usually played together, and I would feel like I was going to be alone for the rest of my life. I know how dramatic that sounds, but it doesn't mean it isn't true.*

*Another time, when I was thirteen, there was a boy I liked at school and the feelings I had for him were so intense. I couldn't eat, and my mum was really worried and pretty much dragged it out of me. When I told her it was about a boy, I expected her to be dismissive or play it down, but she was so understanding. She told me stories about her own first love, and looking back, I'm so pleased she called him her first love and not her first crush, because those feelings are so strong and devastating at the time. She told me that she fell in love with this boy who went to the boys' school down the road from her girls' school, and when the two schools got together for a disco, she was determined to tell him how she felt, but she ended up tripping and falling down a set of stairs and being laughed at by all the boys, including him, and then she was too hurt to do anything. Hearing this story unlocked something in me, and I told her everything, about how I was in the same class as this boy I liked for Science and Geography, and I waited all week for those lessons to come around. In Science, I sat at the desk in front of his, and in Geography, I was a bit behind and to the right, and I would miss most of the lessons because I'd be looking at him, hoping that something would happen to make us speak. Mum listened to it all, she didn't laugh or downplay my emotions, and I was so thankful for that.*

*I guess what I'm trying to say, Edie, is that I hope Nanna and Gemma and anyone else who's significant in your life has helped guide you through these complicated things. I'm sorry it wasn't me. I would have given anything for it to have been me. I don't believe in heaven so I can't tell you I'm looking down on you, watching out for you, or anything like that. I'm simply not there, and it's so unfair I want to scream.*

*I hope that my death hasn't made you fearful of death. I could understand how it might have done. But no child or teenager should be thinking too much about their own mortality. You should feel free to do all the reckless things young people do. You should feel invincible. You should smoke, and drink too much, and experiment with things that aren't right for you. I suppose it's easy for me to say that, knowing that I won't be the one who has to pick up the pieces and lead you back to the right path, but I really believe it. You can't get everything right first time. Make mistakes and enjoy making them. It's part of what being young is about.*

*With love,*

*Mum*

# CHAPTER TWENTY

A couple of days after the second round of chemotherapy, Jess was running her hand through her hair and a small clump of it came away in her fingers. She couldn't work out why she was so astonished. She'd been expecting this. Everyone had told her this would happen. And yet, it was more brutal than she could have imagined. She stood in front of the full-length mirror in her bedroom, the place where she'd assessed how she looked countless mornings before school, and before every party she'd ever attended, and she looked hard at her thick, dark hair. For reasons she couldn't fathom, the loss of it made her feel that time was running out. It was harder to take, in a way, than the diagnosis. She felt shallow for even thinking that way, but it was just so noticeable, and such a common sign of sickness. Up to that point, she'd been in control of who knew, and how she told them.

She felt, out of nowhere, that she must do something brave and significant before she looked like a typical cancer patient. Jess took a step forward, looked really closely at her face in the mirror. She looked a little tired, but make-up could fix that.

She pulled a low-cut black top from her wardrobe and put it on over her favourite bra. Slipped into her favourite skinny jeans. All the time, she was wondering about the unevenness of her breasts. The wound had healed, and she didn't feel any pain, just a numbness that she had begun to get used to. No one had seen her undressed since the operation. Sometimes she stood in front of the bathroom mirror and imagined what it would be like, for someone else to see her. And now, perhaps, someone would.

Jess went downstairs and into the living room, where her mum was with Edie on the playmat, stacking up cups and letting Edie knock them over. Edie was lying on her tummy, holding her head up. Jess couldn't see her face, but she knew that every time the cups fell, she was grinning.

'Do you mind if I go out for an hour or so?' Jess asked.

Caroline looked up at her, and Jess pleaded silently for her not to ask where she was going.

'No, that's fine,' Caroline said, and Jess let out a deep breath.

She went over to the playmat and crouched down, her long hair falling over Edie's head as she kissed her daughter on the forehead.

'Be good for Nanna,' she said. 'I love you.'

Jess wasn't sure whether she'd always told Edie she loved her when they were going to be apart for any length of time, but she did now. Her mum had started doing it with her, too. It was as if none of them trusted that they wouldn't be torn apart, unexpectedly.

Outside, it was warmer than Jess had anticipated, and she enjoyed the feeling of the spring sunshine on her arms as she walked to Gemma's house. A thought crowded in: This is the last summer you'll have. It was true, of course, unless some kind of miracle happened, but she pushed it to one side. Today wasn't a day for that kind of thinking. She didn't have a plan, not really. She knew that Gemma was at work and was pretty sure Gemma's parents would be too. She'd seen Dan post something on Facebook about spending the day in the garden, and she was banking on him being alone.

She felt a flutter of nerves when she rang the doorbell, but she ignored them. Who was this new person she'd become, if only for today? Dan answered within seconds, almost as if he'd been standing by the door waiting for her. He was wearing jeans and a crumpled white T-shirt, and his hair was messy. He looked like he'd just got out of bed and the thought of that excited her a little.

'Jess,' he said. 'Gemma's not here.'

'I know.'

Dan frowned, looked unsure what to do or say next.

'Can I come in?' she asked. There was a small shake to her voice, but she hoped it wasn't noticeable to him.

Dan took a step backwards, as if inviting her inside, but he also looked confused. Jess stepped closer to him. Their bodies were close, and when she looked at him, she could hear that his breathing had changed a little. Jess dared herself to look up and meet his eye, and when she did, he leaned in and kissed her, as she'd been hoping he would. Jess hadn't kissed anyone since Jake, all those months before. And that had been a goodbye kiss, of sorts, before the argument but when they'd both really known that it was over. This was nothing like that, and nothing like the more familiar kisses with Jake she was used to. It was like a release, a door opened. In an instant, she was fourteen again, and her dream was coming true. Dan put both of his hands in her hair and something in Jess jolted. Would he feel it coming out? Would he see? It was so unfair. She just wanted this one thing. This one day to feel normal before she resigned herself to being a cancer patient. To dying.

Gently, she reached up and took hold of his hands, and she guided them to her waist. Safer. Dan didn't seem to mind.

They kissed the way you kissed someone you'd wanted to kiss for a long time. Deep and long and breathlessly, never pulling apart. When Dan stopped, it was to look at her properly.

'Are you sure about this?' he asked. 'Are you… okay?'

Jess wanted to have this moment, wanted to be normal for a little while. She felt a burst of anger, and yet, he was just making sure she was doing this for the right reasons, wasn't he? He was trying to be kind. And she didn't have a backup plan, anyway.

'I'm fine,' she said.

It was a lie, but it didn't matter, it was a one-off thing. She was doing this for the fourteen-year-old girl who never dared to.

'Good,' Dan said, and moved to kiss her again.

Jess put her hands on his broad back and for a second, an image of Jake came to mind. Jake's body was much narrower. He was slim-hipped but strong. She pushed aside the part of her that wished she was with Jake right now and led Dan up the stairs by the hand.

When they were in Dan's bedroom and the door was closed, Jess really could believe she was the teenager she'd been. His room had barely changed. It was still littered with clothes and plates and mugs, still the room of that messy almost-man. She closed her eyes and let herself forget everything, let Dan touch her and start to undress her. A couple of times, he asked if she was sure, and she shushed him, urging him to understand, that she needed him to let her lose herself in the moment. She needed to be fourteen for this to work. Not a mum, not a cancer patient. Not that she would have done this at fourteen, she thought, as his hand slid up her side and round the back to unhook her bra. Jess made herself forget about her scar, her stomach that had never been as flat as it was before she had Edie. She tried to feel and not think, and for a while, it worked.

It was her who put a stop to it in the end, though. They were naked, tangled up, his sheets half covering their bodies. She sat up.

'I can't,' she said.

Dan made a sort of groaning noise, but he pulled his hands away, sat up beside her and just looked at her, a question in his eyes. Jess felt vulnerable and wished fervently that she wasn't entirely naked. She leaned out of the bed to reach for her underwear, but it was too far away.

'I'm sorry,' she said.

'You don't have to be sorry, Jess.'

'I thought I could do it. I really thought I could.'

'But why?' Dan said, stepping on to the floor and handing her clothes back to her a piece at a time after pulling his own boxers back on. 'Why did you want to? You've never been interested in me.'

Jess laughed. 'Are you serious?'

Dan sat down on the edge of the bed and reached for Jess's face. She let him stroke her cheek with his thumb. It felt good. It felt right.

'I remember one day Gemma brought you home,' he said. 'I was fifteen, I think. Maybe fourteen. I'd never noticed you before. You were too young, but I knew how beautiful you were going to be. I could see. And then you were a bit older and I wondered whether you'd ever have a thing for me, but it never happened.'

'Dan,' Jess said, her voice full of laughter, 'I always had a thing for you. Always.'

Dan brought the base of his palm to his forehead. 'Really?

Why didn't you ever say anything? Gemma told me you would never look twice at me, and then you moved away. Next thing I heard, you were back, and you were pregnant. And now...'

He didn't need to finish that sentence. And now, she was dying. Jess secretly cursed Gemma for telling Dan she didn't like him. It made sense, she supposed. Nobody wanted their best friend to get together with their brother. But still, it stung a little. It shouldn't have done, given that she'd loved someone else and had a baby since it happened, but it did.

She thought about telling him that she was scared. There was something refreshing about the idea of telling someone she wouldn't usually talk to about this stuff. But she'd come here trying to seduce him, and it felt wrong to open up like that, to turn him from her teenage crush into her confidante.

'I think I should go home,' she said.

Dan didn't say anything, but he nodded. Jess was dressed again by this time, and Dan had pulled on his T-shirt and jeans. She looked down at his tanned feet, then back up at his serious face. Part of her was giddy. Part of her wanted to tell her past self that this had happened, that she had had this chance.

'What?' he asked.

She hadn't realised she was smiling. She stood and kissed him, and it was a lazy kiss, the kind you might have lying on a blanket in a park, the grass tickling your toes. It wasn't a kiss that promised to lead to anything more. But it was perfect, in its way.

'Thank you,' she said. And then she slipped out of his room before she could change her mind and lie back down on his bed.

At home, she found her mum giving Edie a bottle. Edie looked peaceful and still, and Jess felt a twinge in her breasts, like an echo of a want.

'Did you get sorted out?' Caroline asked.

Jess wasn't sure how to answer. She said she thought so, and her mum smiled, content with that response. When Edie finished her bottle and lay back, satisfied and sleepy, Caroline passed her carefully to Jess and Jess sat down on the sofa. She felt like a different person from the one who'd been in Dan's bedroom. The weight of her daughter in her arms was a physical reminder of the weight of responsibility she carried now.

'Mum?' she spoke tentatively, slightly unsure of what she was going to ask and what she expected the answer to be.

'Hmmm?' Her mum had picked up a book and was putting her reading glasses on.

'When Dad left, was it because he didn't think you should have me?'

'I think he would have preferred it if I hadn't gone through with the pregnancy, yes.'

'Thanks,' Jess said.

'What for?'

'For telling me the truth.'

It wasn't the same as what had happened between Jess and Jake, nothing like. But it was enough to make Jess feel angry about the fact of being a woman. Being born into this gender, which was the downtrodden one. The one which stayed at home and raised the children. The one which was left. But then she looked down at Edie and felt differently again. How could she complain about being the one who got to raise this perfect, tiny person? And then the memory, like an unexpected punch, that she wouldn't get to raise Edie at all. It all came back to that, every time.

Jess went upstairs and looked at herself in the bathroom mirror. Really looked at her thinning hair. She thought about meeting Jake that first time in the supermarket, how he'd said later that it was her hair he'd first noticed. And then she took a pair of scissors from the bathroom cabinet and hacked at it, letting it slip off her shoulders and on to the cream tiles. She'd bought some clippers in preparation for this day, and she went to fetch them from under the bed, where she'd hidden them, hoping the time would never actually come.

She wanted to get it done before she changed her mind. She ran the clippers up the back of her head and touched the stubble they left behind. It was necessary, she told herself. It was the only way. She spent a long time looking at herself in the mirror when she'd finished. Her head was a perfect oval, her ears small and neat. It wasn't as bad as she'd feared. She thought about the time when she'd had her hair cut into a bob, at fourteen, and it had looked awful, too thick and wavy to hang right, and she'd tied it back as soon as she could and grown it and sworn she'd never cut it short again. She thought about a boy she'd kissed when she was sixteen, who'd put his hands right into her long hair and held on to it. She thought about the photos she'd seen from her childhood, the way her fringe was often a little too short or not quite straight, cut in the garden by her mother. She thought about Edie, and what her hair might be like, and hoped she would never know how this felt.

When she was ready, Jess went back downstairs. Her mum did a double take when she saw her, and Jess watched her try to arrange her features into a neutral expression.

'Is it awful?' Jess asked. 'You don't have to pretend.'

'It's just a shock,' Caroline said. 'Come here.'

She held out her arms and Jess went to her, allowed herself to be pulled into a hug. She could feel her mum's heartbeat against her ear, and it was a comfort. It was done. It was over.

## CHAPTER TWENTY-ONE

Jess stood at her father's door and pressed the bell hard with her finger, trying to talk herself out of changing her mind. She thought back to when she'd last seen him. Before. Definitely before the diagnosis, though her mum had called him to let him know. He'd sent a card and not visited, despite living a short drive away. When he appeared at the door, he looked a bit like he'd just woken up. It was a little after nine on a Sunday morning, so it was possible that he had.

'Jessica?' He made the word into a question, and she didn't know how to answer it.

He was the only person who consistently used her full name. She took it as an acknowledgement from him that he didn't deserve to shorten it. That it was too intimate for someone who should have been central to her life but was actually little more than an acquaintance. Jess saw her dad noticing her headscarf and, a little flustered, she put her hand to it to check it was still in place.

'Can I come in?' she asked.

He stood back and waved her inside with his arm, but his

expression was conflicted, and for a dreadful moment she wondered whether there was someone else here. A woman. There had never been anyone else, as far as she knew. She was so used to her father living and being alone that finding him in the company of someone else would have thrown her. But there didn't seem to be anyone else in the house. It was just her who set him on edge. Her illness.

'Cup of tea?' he asked.

Jess nodded weakly and he disappeared off into the kitchen, leaving her in the living room. She'd toyed over bringing Edie with her, but her mum had insisted on having her so that they could talk. But now, Jess wished she had Edie as a distraction, because it's hard for things to be awkward when there's a baby to fuss over. She pushed a newspaper and a small pile of books to one side and sat down in the armchair. When her dad reappeared, he put two mugs down on the coffee table and sat down opposite her, and Jess tried to hastily order words in her head. She wanted to ask him things, but she didn't want to get angry.

'I was talking to Mum, last night, about how your relationship ended.'

Her dad cleared his throat and shifted a little in his seat. He wouldn't meet her eye.

'How do you make a decision like that? To leave someone when they're pregnant with your child.'

'It wasn't only my decision, Jessica.'

Jess felt reprimanded. It was true to an extent, of course. It was never all down to one person when a relationship ended. She thought of her and Jake on that final day, when he was asking about being a part of her life, and the baby's, and she was saying no.

'I understand that,' Jess said, 'but that's basically what happened, isn't it?'

He opened his mouth to speak and then closed it again, and she wondered whether this was hard for him, and decided that she didn't really care.

'Look,' he said, 'I don't know what it is you're trying to do. I know you're going through something truly terrible, but I really don't see how dragging up the past is going to help...'

'I don't think you know the half of it,' Jess said. The words had burst out of her. She hadn't meant to be so hard. But once she'd started, it seemed hard to stop. 'I am twenty-one years old, Dad. Look at me. I'm a new mum and I am dying of cancer. I don't have years ahead of me, I might not even have many months. If I want to find out the truth about my past and where I came from, would you really deny me that, now?'

Jess was standing and she couldn't remember getting up. Her legs felt shaky, and she sat back down, feeling a bit silly.

'But why? That's what I don't understand. What use is this information to you?'

Jess thought about that. 'It's for Edie,' she said, at last. 'I'm trying to leave her as much as I possibly can. Family, friends. Possibly a father. I want to know who she can and can't rely on.'

'You know I'll help out where I can,' he said.

Did she know that? He hadn't been there for her, had he? Why should she expect that it would be different with his granddaughter? She tried to count the number of times her dad and Edie had met. He had turned up with a gift a couple of weeks after she was born. And then a week or so after that, Jess had gone to his house, much like she had today, and insisted on him coming out for a walk with them. Beyond that, there had been two or three sporadic visits. It didn't amount to much. It didn't make a grandfather.

'Here's what it is,' Jess said. 'I want to know what it was that scared you so much about becoming a father. That made you leave before you'd even seen me, before you'd tried it. I want to know for my sake, and for Edie's. Because I'm not going to be around to see her grow up, and I need to work out whether or not it's in her interests for me to get her dad involved.'

When she stopped speaking, she felt oddly raw and as though she'd revealed too much of herself.

'Jessica,' he said, his eyes glistening. Was he close to tears? 'I think you're asking the wrong person. I think it sounds like you need to have this conversation with Jake. I'm not him. My reasons aren't his reasons. But for what it's worth, I was stupid and young, and I felt like I wasn't ready to settle. Your mum and me were okay, we had this relationship that wasn't great and wasn't terrible, and I thought there must be more out there. I didn't want to say that this was it, for me. And having a baby was the furthest thing from my mind. So when your mum told me she was pregnant, and that she was keeping it, I ran away. And then I've never fully involved myself in your life because I haven't felt like it's my right to do so, when she's the one who chose to have you and did all the hard work.'

Jess felt like there was a heavy weight on her chest, and it was beginning to lift a little. 'Really? That's why you weren't around? Not because you didn't care?' She knew that her voice sounded thin and needy, and she didn't much care. She didn't have much left to lose.

'I always cared, Jessica. But I can't pretend I'm something I'm not. I'm stuck in my ways, I'm very used to being on my own. I was wrong about there being something better around the corner, you see. If I'd known I had a lifetime of loneliness ahead, I might have chosen differently. But the past is what it is. I haven't been the father I could or should have been, regardless of whether or not your mother and I were together. You deserved better than me.'

Jess was close to saying he was wrong, that he'd done okay. That was her natural reaction, when someone criticised themselves. But this was important, and his absence from her life really hadn't been all right, so she didn't pretend. She felt like this was the most honest and open conversation they'd ever had, and it had taken this — her dying — to make it happen.

There was a long silence, and when Jess's dad broke it, she was surprised by what he said.

'I'm sorry you're going through this.'

'I'm not going through it, Dad,' she said. 'Going through it implies that I will eventually come out the other side. I'm not coming out of this. You do know that?'

He nodded, and then she saw that he was crying. She wasn't sure whether she had it in her to move across the space between them and give him a hug. Where had he been when she'd been lost and lonely, as a child? When she thought there were monsters under her bed? When her friendships fell apart and she felt like she was losing everything that mattered to her? And even now, it was her that was facing this. She shouldn't have to be the one to offer comfort.

'I never thought this would be my only chance to be a father,' he said, faltering. 'I was your age when your mum got pregnant. I thought there would be so many roads ahead. I didn't want to tie myself down. And now look. My only child, and I'm losing you.'

You never had me, Dad, Jess thought. You never had me to begin with.

She left soon after that, and on the drive home, she thought about the things her dad had said. Jess felt confused and tired. It didn't seem fair that she was having to navigate all this right now, when she had so little time left. Her phone buzzed, and when she pulled up on the driveway, she checked it. Jake.

**I can meet tomorrow if you're free. Sorry for the short notice. Same time and place as before? x**

At home, Edie was sitting in the highchair while Caroline busied herself at the hob. Jess had bought the highchair in preparation for weaning, but Edie was still a few weeks away from six months and Jess had never thought of putting her in it. Jess stood in the doorway and watched as Caroline scooped something soup-like into a bowl and then held a spoonful out to Edie.

'What the hell are you doing?' she asked.

Caroline and Edie both turned to face her, and Jess crossed the distance between them and lunged for the bowl in her mother's hand. She meant to take it, but instead she knocked it, and the orange mush splattered all over the floor, and the highchair, and the three of them. Her mum grabbed hold of the wipes and started to attack the mess.

'She's ready, Jess. I had a bit of time and I thought I'd try her on some sweet potato and see how she got on.'

Jess looked at Edie, at the food that was around her mouth, at her mouth opening for more. She had a splatter of sweet potato across her cheek.

'She's too young! The health visitor said to wait until she was six months…'

'Things like this change all the time,' Caroline interrupted. 'It was always four months when you were little. Babies haven't changed, just the rules have.'

'Yes, and have you wondered why they would change their advice? They don't just do it on a whim. It's because they've found out some new information or some baby has died. Anyway, none of that is the point. The point is that you should have asked me. She's my baby!'

Jess waited for her mum to make eye contact with her, but

she didn't. She kept on wiping, the floor, the legs of the high-chair, her jumper. Jess had known, when she'd made the decision to raise Edie here at home, with her mother as her support, that they would have clashes like this. But she hadn't known how helpless she would feel, knowing that someday soon all these choices would be out of her hands.

When Caroline had finished clearing up, she threw the handful of wipes in the bin and leaned back against the kitchen counter. Jess unstrapped Edie from the chair and took her in her arms, still waiting for her mum to look at her.

'You know,' Caroline said, at last, 'I would never do anything to upset you. I'm just doing my best, like you are. I'm just trying to help and be a support and make things a little easier for you. And it's hard for me too.'

Jess had heard her mum getting up in the night more often recently. When Jess was up with Edie, she often heard the toilet flush, the creak of her mum's door, the kettle boiling. She tried to see all of this from her mum's perspective. But she was too caught up in her own devastation to be able to fully see anyone else's.

'I'm still here,' Jess said. 'I know I won't always be, but I am now. I just don't want everything to be taken away from me.'

Caroline moved across the room then and put her arms around Jess. Edie was between them, her cheek resting on Jess's neck, and Jess expected her to object to this, but she didn't. She was content. The only one of the three of them who could find any peace, and that was only because she had no idea what was happening.

## CHAPTER TWENTY-TWO

*Dear Edie,*

*I wanted you to know that I never fell out of love with your dad. I know how hard it is to come from a 'broken home'. I hate that phrase. My home never felt broken just because it didn't have a dad in it. But I remember hearing mum telling people that it was just me and her, and the look they'd give her. Sometimes sympathy, sometimes mistrust. As if any woman without a husband might be trying to grab hold of theirs.*

*I always knew that my mum and dad didn't like each other much. It was hard to imagine that they'd ever been together, much less that they'd managed to create a life. I even asked Mum, once, if she was sure he was my dad. She just laughed and put her arm around me and said, 'I'm afraid so'. But I want you to understand that it isn't like that with Jake and me. We loved each other. I loved him. I still do. I'm sorry that we couldn't make it work, for you. I think we were too young. I think if we'd met later, things might have been different. But then we wouldn't have had you, of course. And there isn't going to be much 'later' for me.*

*Your dad has never met you. He doesn't know your name. He*

*doesn't know that you have a rough circle of freckles on your lower back and rolls of fat on your arms and legs. He doesn't know that you laugh whenever I call you 'Ediesaurus' and stomp around the room like a dinosaur. He doesn't know how it feels to hold you against my chest and breathe in the scent from the top of your head. He doesn't know you had blue eyes, like mine, when you were born, but they changed to be brown, like his. He doesn't know you. He's missed so much.*

*And I want you to know that that isn't because he doesn't care. When we split up, while I felt like I was ripping in two, I said I didn't want to hear from him ever again. I said he'd given up his right to be any sort of a father. I said that you were mine, and not ours, and that he'd better not try to sneak into either of our lives. So you see, it's my fault that you don't have him, that you haven't had him up until now.*

*This afternoon, I will meet him for the first time since we went our separate ways, our hearts in shreds. I will tell him about you, show him photos. I will tell him that cancer has come into our lives like a thief, and that it's taking me. I will go back on everything I said, because I was wrong back then, thinking only of me and not of you, and because everything has changed, too. I'm trying to ask myself, honestly, what I hope will happen when we see each other. It's so hard not to be selfish. I hope he says he's been miserable without me. But how likely is that, when his dreams of being a musician are coming true? I hope he's interested in you, Edie. How could he not be? You are so perfect and, while I think of you as wholly mine, I know you are half his. I know that your long toes and your beautifully olive skin and your elegant nose are his. I hope he will see that.*

*Edie, I've talked to all sorts of people about the relationships they've had and here's what I believe. Sometimes a relationship fizzles out. The people in it stop caring enough about one another to be together. Sometimes it just becomes too hard. The differences between the two people start to get in the way, and there are argu-*

*ments and it is tiring and futile and they give up. Sometimes the couple realise they never liked each other enough in the first place. They were swept along by lust or excitement or hope. None of these things is what happened to your dad and me.*

*I'd had a couple of boyfriends before him and they'd been okay. But when I met Jake, I felt like I couldn't breathe. No, that's not right. I felt like I could only breathe properly when we were together. When he touched my face, I felt like I was on fire. When he kissed me, it was almost scary. All that pleasure, and my insides wound tight like a ball of wool, and I knew that one tug would unravel me. Sensation is a circle, and pleasure sits at the top, right next to pain. What I'm trying to tell you is that we were good together. And when it ended, it wasn't because we'd stopped being good. It was because we didn't agree about what should happen next. About you.*

*I imagine you reading this. I don't know how old you are. You might be fifteen, you might be older. You might have a boyfriend. You might know a little of what I'm trying to explain to you. If you've felt that kind of longing, burned like fire at someone's touch, I hope you're with that person now. I hope you've clung on. I hope that your dad is in your life, that he's been a dad.*

*I hope that you can't imagine your life without him, or with me, or any different to how it's been. I hope you're happy.*

*I wanted you to know that I never fell out of love with your dad. And that I wish we had tried harder to make it work, for you.*

*With love,*

*Mum*

# CHAPTER TWENTY-THREE

Jess sat at the same table she'd sat at last time with a latte in front of her. No book, no magazine. No distractions. She'd had a text from Jake to say that he was on his way. She felt turned inside-out at the thought of seeing his face. She remembered walking away, both of them crying, and how she'd had to stop herself from turning back, from saying she was wrong, she was sorry. How her pride had stopped her. She was having good and bad days, on chemo. On bad days, she stayed in bed and her mum or Gemma brought her soup and snacks and sometimes laid Edie down beside her for cuddles. Luckily, this was a good day. She'd bought a wig that looked better than her old hair, and Gemma had done her make-up.

'This isn't about getting him back,' her mum had said. A statement and not a question.

'Of course it isn't,' Gemma said. 'But there's no harm in showing him what he's missing.'

Jess had stood in front of the full-length mirror before leaving the house. You couldn't tell, when she was dressed, that her breast had been removed and replaced with a piece of silicone. And with the wig on, it looked like she had full, shiny hair. It was all tricks and angles, being a woman, she thought.

She looked up at the door just as he came in. He looked the same. His hair was a little longer, and he hadn't shaved recently. He was wearing a black jumper that she had often worn when they were together. She remembered the way it had hung over her hands. He caught her eye and smiled, and she had a sudden memory of the way he smelled, and she knew that if he went to hug her, she'd be lost.

But he didn't do that. He pulled out the seat opposite her and sat down, then asked her if she wanted anything, stood up again and went to the counter to order a drink. Jess wondered whether he was nervous. He'd never struck her as the nervous type, but everyone had their limits, didn't they? For the first time, she wondered whether he had any idea what this meeting was about, whether he'd guessed that she was in trouble.

'How is the tour?' she asked, when he was sitting opposite her again.

His face broke into a smile and she felt a flash of jealousy that he was living the life he'd dreamed of, while she was putting her affairs in order.

'It's like a whirlwind,' he said. 'I never know where we are. We're always playing the same handful of songs, answering the same questions on these tiny local radio stations. But it's brilliant.'

Jess felt close to tears. She had wanted this for him, but it was hard to hear it, too. She blinked a few times, bit the inside of her lip. Willed herself to hold it together.

'That's so wonderful,' she said.

'So, how are you?' Jake asked. 'Can I ask about... the baby?'

It was so strange, Jess thought, that the last time they'd

seen each other, Edie had barely existed. She'd been a collection of cells growing inside Jess, and now she was a baby girl. And Jess couldn't quite remember what it was like not to have her.

'She's a girl,' Jess said. 'Her name is Edie.'

'After your grandmother?' Jake said.

Jess was caught off-guard. She hadn't remembered telling Jake about her beloved maternal grandmother. But she must have told him, and he had remembered. She nodded.

'I wanted to call you so many times. I sent those letters and I just hoped one day you'd get in touch. You told me not to call and I didn't want to ignore that.'

Jake put his hand on the table and reached for Jess's, and she picked up her drink, knowing that if he touched her, something would shift, and she wouldn't be able to do this.

'Do you want to see a photo of her?' Jess asked.

If Jake noticed the shake in her voice, he didn't say anything. 'Yes,' he said. 'Please.'

Jess pulled out her phone and scrolled through the recent photos she'd taken. Almost all of them were of Edie. Edie clapping, her face a picture of pure delight. Edie sleeping, her eyelashes long and her hair in disarray. Edie sitting up, surrounded by cushions. She chose one that showed the cheeky smile Edie did when she was being playful, and she watched Jake's face closely as she handed the phone to him. She watched his face change from neutral to joyful in a second.

'Can I?' he asked, motioning scrolling through the photos with his finger.

'Yes.'

Jess kept her eyes on him as he uncovered all the moments she'd lived through with Edie in one go. It was magical, seeing him discover her, but at the same time, she wanted to scream.

Where had he been when Edie had that raging temperature that wouldn't settle, and she was terrified? When she'd been up all night breastfeeding and needed someone to take care of her? When she questioned every tiny decision she made as a new mother, feeling like she was going mad? But it wasn't fair to ask him those things. She was the one who had told him to stay away. But why had he listened?

'She's so beautiful,' Jake said, handing the phone back to her.

There was a beat of silence and Jess knew that it was time to explain why she'd asked to see him.

'I have cancer,' she said.

And again, she watched his face. He'd always been easy to read. She'd liked that about him. He didn't hide what he felt. At that moment, it was confusion she saw in his eyes. Not sadness, not yet. He didn't quite believe it.

'What?'

'I have cancer. That's why I wanted to see you.'

Jess remembered that Jake's grandmother had died of breast cancer shortly after they'd started seeing each other. Perhaps that was when she had told him about her own grandmother. He reached for her hand again, then, and she didn't stop him, although she knew that she should. His hand was warm from holding his coffee, and she felt that old spark she'd always felt when he touched her, but she didn't allow herself to dwell on it.

'Is it bad?'

Cancer was always bad, wasn't it? But she knew what he meant. Was she going to die? It was what everyone wanted to know, in the end.

'It's breast cancer. And it's spread to my bones. They're hoping that chemo will stabilise it, but they think I might only have a few months.'

Jess had got used to delivering this news. It didn't break her. But she could never make herself say 'a few months to live'. Jake closed his eyes, as if to shut it all out, and for a moment she felt sorry for him. It was a lot to process, a lot to take in.

'I'm sorry, I know it's a shock. Listen, I want another drink. Do you want one?'

He nodded and pushed his cup towards her, and Jess went and stood in the queue to give him a few minutes to process what she'd said. When she got back to the table, Jess could see that he was desperate to speak. He did this, she remembered. Took a couple of minutes to take things in, and then started throwing out solutions left and right. She asked herself what she wanted him to say, or to offer. What her ideal scenario was. But nothing was ideal about this, and she felt ridiculous even asking herself, so she just sat down and started stirring sugar into her drink while he spoke.

'I can help,' Jake said. 'I'll move in with you and your mum for a while, help with Edie...'

'You haven't even met her!' Jess hadn't meant to raise her voice, and a few people in the café turned to look at her before the general buzz of chatter started up again.

'I know that,' Jake said. 'But you told me not to get in touch with you. I didn't want to ignore what you'd asked by phoning you. I wrote those letters because I thought it was the least intrusive way to get in touch. You could ignore them altogether if you wanted to. Which you did...'

'I told you,' Jess said, her voice quieter but no less fraught, 'my mum hid them from me. I only found them the other day.'

'What do you want?' Jake asked. 'I knew that whatever I said, it wouldn't be right.'

Jess felt a familiar twisting in her stomach. It was the way she always felt when they argued. It bothered her for days.

'Look,' Jess said, 'I said I would raise Edie on my own, that we didn't need anything from you, but that was before I knew that I wouldn't be around for her. Everything has changed. She's not going to have a mum, she won't even remember me, and so I thought it was only right that I let you know that, in case you wanted to be involved…'

Jess hadn't quite finished what she wanted to say, but sobs had overtaken her. It was so hard to face up to it, to talk about exactly what was going to happen, and what it meant for Edie. Jess hated to think of her, lost and orphaned, not having anyone to talk to about the things that mattered to her. If she could change one thing, it would be that. It wasn't about her own pain or missing out on things, it was all about leaving Edie without a mum.

Jake pulled his chair closer, so that they were sitting side by side rather than opposite each other. He put an arm around Jess's shoulder and pulled her into him, until she was crying all over his jumper. It was so comforting, to be so close to him again and be able to breathe him in. Out of nowhere, and for the first time, Jess imagined the two of them sitting like this with Edie in the space between them. Imagined them as a family.

'Yes,' Jake said. 'Yes, I want to be involved. I want to help. You're not very good at letting people help you, you know?'

Was that true? Jess wasn't sure, and she didn't think that now was the time to analyse it. He leaned forward, reached out to touch her hair, and Jess pulled back so quickly he looked like she'd slapped him.

'I just don't want you to promise the world,' Jess said. 'You don't know you can deliver it. Until about an hour ago, you didn't even know whether you had a son or a daughter, and now you're offering to throw away your career to move in with us and help out, and it's too much.'

Jake pulled back so he could look at her eyes. His were red and puffy, and she saw that he'd cried when she left him alone at the table. Of course he had. That, in itself, didn't prove that she still meant something to him, that she was still important. But she wondered, whether she might be. He was still so important to her. A flame of hope burned in her heart, and then she remembered that there was no point in looking to her own future, since she didn't have one. All of this was about Edie.

'I feel like nothing I do is right,' Jake said. 'I'm so sorry this is happening to you. I'll do anything I can to make it better. But I can't be doubted at every stage because you don't trust me. I need you to decide what you want and tell me, so I can get it right.'

Jess was so busy trying to determine whether she'd heard a crack in his voice that she didn't notice straight away that he was standing up, gathering his things together. She was so tempted to ask him to stay. To say that she was sorry, and she was grateful for his kindness, to say that his hand on hers had made it feel like everything could be okay for a minute or two. But she let him go, instead. Was that right, what he'd said about her mistrusting him? Probably. When he was almost at the door, he turned.

'Please call me, Jess,' he said. And then he was gone.

## CHAPTER TWENTY-FOUR

Jess ordered the drinks and pushed back through the crowd to where Gemma was waiting.

'Are you sure you're okay?' Gemma asked.

Jess didn't tell her friend that she was feeling slightly woozy, that her vision was a bit blurred. She had been craving a night out since seeing Jake and this was the first day she'd felt well enough. They were in the bar where Gemma worked, and it was Jess's birthday, and she wanted to pretend for one evening that she was an ordinary twenty-two-year-old girl. She rolled her eyes at Gemma and handed her friend one of the two brightly coloured cocktails she'd ordered.

'What's in it?' Gemma asked.

'I don't know, you work here.'

'They all look more or less the same. Listen, this is my last question. Are you definitely allowed to drink on chemo?'

'Yes,' Jess said. She was pretty sure she'd been told that one or two was okay. 'Now stop trying to ruin everything. Can we just pretend I don't have cancer for one night?'

She was talking loudly to be heard over the music, and

when she said the word 'cancer', two girls standing nearby turned to look at her. Jess wanted to call them out on it, to say that cancer wasn't catching, that they didn't need to shuffle away from her, that she was sorry if her dying was putting a dampener on their evening. But she stopped herself. Took a sip of her drink. Tried to pretend that she wasn't feeling tired. That her limbs weren't aching.

After that, Gemma did what she'd asked and dropped the cancer talk. For about an hour or so, it felt like old times. They pointed out men they thought the other would like, they gossiped about people they'd gone to school with. Jess told Gemma what had happened with Dan, and Gemma put her hands over her face.

'He's my brother! God, I thought I'd nipped that in the bud years ago. Dan, for god's sake?'

Jess laughed. 'Well, nothing really happened in the end. It wasn't my finest moment. I just felt like I wanted to do something for the fourteen-year-old inside me who really liked him and never got to kiss him.'

Gemma pulled a face, as if she couldn't believe that anyone could find her brother attractive. And then Gemma's face went in and out of focus, and Jess felt like she needed to sit down. She looked around for a table, but they were all occupied. Instinctively, she reached out a hand and took hold of Gemma's arm.

'Jess, are you okay?' Gemma's face was a picture of worry.

'I'm not sure, I feel...'

Jess couldn't think of the words she needed. They'd had three cocktails and she felt so tired and as if she wasn't quite there. And then she fell.

It was as if she blinked and when she opened her eyes, she was in hospital and a doctor she didn't know was looking down at her. Jess scanned the room. Gemma was there, and her mum.

'Where's Edie?' she asked, panicked.

'Your dad is looking after her. I didn't want to wake her up.'

Jess thought about whether her dad was up to the job of looking after her sleeping daughter. Had he ever been left alone to look after a baby? She didn't think so. And then she realised, as she always did, that these things were going to be beyond her control very soon, and she needed to start trusting the people who were helping her.

'What happened to me?' Jess looked from her mum to Gemma. She could see that there was some tension between them. Her mum wouldn't meet her eye, didn't speak. It was Gemma who broke the silence.

'You collapsed in the bar,' she said. 'It was terrifying. You said you were okay to drink!'

Jess looked from Gemma to her mum to the doctor and didn't say anything. They were all looking at her with their own personal brand of disapproval. She wanted to whine and say that it wasn't fair, but she could sense that it wasn't the time.

'I'm Dr Lowdon,' the doctor said. 'I'm the on-call doctor. We're going to do a CT scan. Your friend says you'd had three drinks, and while that isn't really advisable, it shouldn't have been enough to cause you to collapse like this. Are you having any problems with your vision?'

'I'm not now,' Jess said, 'but before it happened, things were getting fuzzy.'

'Why didn't you tell me?' Gemma asked.

Jess didn't reply. She knew, then, that that night out she'd just had with Gemma would probably be her last. None of them would trust her again. They'd all be keeping a close eye on her, telling her it was probably for the best if they just stayed in and watched a film. She was so frustrated she wanted to cry. It hadn't seemed like too much to ask, to have a night out on her birthday.

Dr Lowdon came back into the room less than an hour after the scan, and Jess knew that the news wasn't good.

'Tell me,' she said.

She wished it was Dr Singh. One of the things she liked most about her oncologist was that she didn't pretend. She told it straight, every time. It wasn't always easy to take, but Jess preferred that to someone beating around the bush when there was life-changing news to impart. Thankfully, Dr Lowdon had a similar style.

'There's a new tumour, in your brain,' he said. He was holding a clipboard, but Jess noticed that there was a slight shake to his hands. From the corner of the room, Jess's mum made a low groaning sound, and when Jess looked round, she saw that Gemma was crying.

'The chemo isn't working. I'm sorry, Jessica. We can try another type, there are options. Or we can stop using medication and let you enjoy the time you have as much as possible. I can talk you through these options, and what they mean. But I'll give you a bit of time.'

He retreated from the room, closing the door behind him, and Jess looked down at the sheet covering her body, trying to decide what she could possibly say. She wished that Edie was there, to hold against her chest, and then she felt selfish for wishing that, when it was late and Edie was fast asleep and safe, away from this noisy place where her mother was being told she was edging closer and closer to death.

'Are you up for trying another type of chemo?' Gemma asked.

Jess thought about that. About the tiredness that hit like a truck the day after chemo, the nausea and the sweats and the constipation and the clumps of hair on the pillow in the morning, and she wanted to say no. To say that she would do as the doctor said, stop with the poisonous medication and just enjoy the time she had left with her baby. But then, Edie. Didn't she owe it to Edie to fight this with everything she had in her? Hadn't she promised her daughter that?

'Yes,' she said. 'Whatever they can try.' She looked over at her mum, who was still sitting on the chair in the corner of the room, silent. 'Do you think they'll let us go home today?'

'I don't know,' Caroline said. 'I hope so, love.'

'Maybe now's the time to let Jake help out,' Jess said.

She saw her mum's mouth tighten into a thin line.

'What?' she asked.

'I just don't know why you think you need him. You've got me, you've got Gemma. We're coping okay, aren't we?'

Jess felt frustrated. It wasn't a case of Jake coming on the scene and pushing her mother out, was it? Surely it was time for all hands on deck.

'And right now,' she said, 'all three of us are in the same room, and you've had to rope someone else in to look after Edie. So how can you say we don't need an extra pair of hands?'

'She's with your father, not some random person off the street,' Caroline snapped.

'Yes, and I'm suggesting she spend some time with *her* father. I don't understand why you have such a problem with that.'

There was the sound of a throat being cleared, and Jess and her mum both turned their heads to see that Dr Lowdon had just come back into the room.

'Everything okay in here?' he asked.

Jess nodded.

'You know, I know it's difficult, but it's really not going to help you to get stressed like this.'

Jess felt tears prick her eyes and brushed them away as they began to fall. She knew there was a very real possibility of her starting to cry and not being able to stop. It just all felt so unfair. That her mother was being difficult when she most needed her support. That she was being told off by this doctor for getting het up about the care of her baby daughter.

'Can I go home?' she asked.

Dr Lowdon smiled. 'You can, as soon as we've decided how we're moving forward with your treatment.'

'I'd like to try another type of chemo,' Jess said, her voice flat.

'Are you sure?'

'Yes. I'm sure.'

'Okay then, come in on Monday as usual, and Dr Singh will take it from there.'

Caroline drove the three of them home, and nobody spoke much in the car. When they pulled up outside the house, Jess was desperate to get inside, to check on Edie. She opened the front door, listening out for sounds that would let her know which room they were in, but it was quiet. She looked at her watch. It was a little after six in the morning. In one way, it felt like the hours spent in that hospital bed had whizzed past, but in another, it felt like more than a night had gone by since she was last in this house. She strode through the rooms, starting to worry. She climbed the stairs. She found them in her bedroom, her dad lying on top of the covers, his chest rising and falling with heavy sleep. Edie was curled in his arms, her eyes closed and her thumb in her mouth.

Jess stood in the doorway. She and Edie slept like this, sometimes, on the nights when Edie wouldn't return to her cot after a feed without screaming. Somehow, Jess always felt like she was doing it wrong when she ended up placing Edie on the bed beside her. But looking down at this scene, it looked perfect. Edie was sleeping so soundly. When she was alone in her cot, she fidgeted constantly. Jess vowed to sleep like this with Edie more often, to spend as much time as possible beside her daughter, breathing her in. And then the pain of knowing she would die made her double over, and suddenly Gemma was behind her, holding her up and asking if she needed to go back to the hospital, and her father was waking up, a confused look in his eyes.

'Go back to sleep,' Jess said, tears streaming down her face. She pulled the door closed. 'I'm okay,' she told Gemma. 'I'm okay.'

They went back downstairs, and Gemma made them all tea, and they sat drinking it in silence.

'I'm amazed at how tidy the place is,' Caroline said when she finally spoke. She gestured around the room, at the washed bottle on the draining board and the pile of folded muslins that Jess's dad must have taken out of the dryer.

'No offence,' Gemma said, 'but you two have the worst expectations of men. They're not all so bad, you know.'

Jess smiled, and she felt like Gemma's comment might have the power to reunite the three of them again, but Caroline didn't react. She just kept looking around, as if she wasn't quite sure where she was, or what was happening.

# CHAPTER TWENTY-FIVE

Jess spent the next few days in bed. She drifted in and out of sleep, her curtains closed, never quite sure what time of the day or night it was. Sometimes she would look at her phone and see that it was the middle of the afternoon, and Edie would be lying asleep beside her, and then she'd blink, and the room would be much darker, and it would be nearly midnight, and Edie would be gone. It was a confusing time. Her mum had bought a small TV for her room, but Jess couldn't concentrate on anything. Couldn't read a book. Couldn't even scroll through Instagram. There was a stack of magazines and puzzle books lying, unopened, on her bedside table.

So it was hardly surprising that she didn't notice for a while that Edie was gone. She had no idea how long she'd been awake, didn't know what day it was or when she'd last eaten. There was a knock on her bedroom door and when she called out, Gemma slipped inside.

'Hey,' she said. 'Do you know where your mum and Edie are?'

Gemma had a key so she could come and go when she was helping, which was more and more.

'No idea,' Jess said. 'Maybe they've gone for a walk.'

'The pushchair is in the hall,' Gemma said.

'Is the car on the drive?'

'No.'

'Supermarket then, maybe.'

It struck Jess that she should be more involved than this in her family's life. That she should know where her daughter was at all times. But she didn't, and she couldn't, and there was nothing to be done about it. Gemma asked if she wanted anything. It was lunchtime, a Friday. Gemma was free until her shift at seven. Jess asked her for some chicken soup, and Gemma went away to prepare it.

They passed the afternoon together, Gemma sitting on the empty side of Jess's double bed, bringing Jess drinks when she wanted them. By four, Jess had called her mum several times and got no response.

'She never hears her mobile,' she said to Gemma, after the fourth attempt. 'She keeps it in her bag on silent.'

Jess wasn't worried. Not yet. At six, Gemma asked if she should call her manager and say she wasn't coming in.

'No,' Jess said. 'I don't need someone here all the time. I'm fine, really. Besides, they'll be back soon. It's nearly Edie's bedtime.'

So Gemma left to get ready for work, and Jess lay in bed, looking up at the ceiling and listening out for the door. She got up and went downstairs for the first time that day on wobbly legs. In the kitchen, Gemma had left her a salad covered with clingfilm. Jess took it through to the lounge and picked at it. She put the TV on and turned it to a reality TV show about celebrity couples, but she couldn't even follow it. All the women looked the same.

Every evening, at six, Jess or her mum, or often both of them, would take Edie upstairs for her bath. She loved the water. Even if she was getting tired and fractious, she'd start splashing and laughing the minute they put her in. Jess had found bath-time quite stressful when Edie couldn't sit up and she'd had to cradle her head the whole time, but now it was fun. Then after the bath, they read stories and gave her a bottle of milk and rubbed cream into her dry skin and sang songs until seven, when they put her in her cot and left her to go to sleep. So when it got to half seven, Jess was worried. She called her mum again and left a voicemail.

'Mum, I don't know where you are or what you're doing but Edie needs to come home. It's bedtime. She'll be tired and she'll wonder where I am. Please call me. Please come home.'

She paced up and down for a bit, but it made her feel tired, and she didn't want to fall asleep until Edie was home, in her arms. So she settled back into the armchair, checking her phone every minute or so, listening out for the sound of the door opening. A message came through when it was nearly nine, and she jumped at the sound. She'd long since turned the TV off and the room was silent. She reached for her phone, willing the message to be from her mum, but it was Gemma.

**Everything okay? Did your mum and Edie get back?**

She typed a quick reply.

**No, still not here. I'm really worried. Can you come over when you finish?**

It struck Jess that she was in the middle of a crisis, and she didn't know how to react to it. She didn't know whether she was overreacting or underreacting. She remembered a documentary she'd seen once, about a child abduction, and how the mother had said she didn't know when to start shouting and making a scene. But this wasn't like that, was it? Edie wasn't with some unknown stranger.

**What the fuck? I'll come as soon as I can, but it might be close to midnight.**

*Thank you,* Jess replied. The next time Jess's phone buzzed, it was coming up to eleven. She saw the word Mum on the screen and fumbled to enter her password to see the message.

**We're safe, love. You know I wouldn't do anything to hurt her.**

Jess phoned her mum's number, half expecting to get no reply. So when her mum picked up after four rings, she didn't have her words ready. In the end, it was her mum who spoke first.

'Jess, I just needed to get away and clear my head.'

'What? Why did you take Edie? Where the hell are you?'

Jess could hear the screech of fear in her voice.

'You can't look after her on your own at the minute. Only I can do that.'

All Jess's fear turned into rage, then. Trying to get her head around leaving Edie motherless was one thing, but to have her taken away like this? And by her own mother?

'I'm dying of cancer, Mum! That's why I can't look after her without help! That doesn't give you the right to take her without telling me!'

She stopped abruptly, because she'd heard her daughter's cry in the background.

'Is she okay? Why is she crying? I need to see her!'

There was silence on the other end and Jess wondered whether they'd been disconnected, but then her mum's voice came back on the line, loud and clear.

'Of course she's okay. She's with me. You don't need to worry.'

'Bring her back,' Jess said, as clearly and calmly as she could. 'Please, Mum.'

And then the line went dead, and Jess burst into furious tears and threw her phone at the wall. The next thing she was aware of was the scrape of a key in the lock, and she hoped it would be her mum, while knowing it would be Gemma. Gemma came into the room and swooped over to where Jess was curled up, and it was only when Gemma took Jess in her arms that Jess realised how much weight she must have lost. She felt tiny, suddenly, next to her oldest friend.

'What's happened? Have you heard anything?'

'She's taken her,' Jess said. 'I don't know what the hell is going on, but she's taken her. It's because of Jake, I think. She's scared she's going to lose us both.'

'Fuck,' Gemma said. 'And you know this for sure? You've actually spoken to her?'

Jess filled Gemma in. She was so tired by this point that she could barely keep her eyes open, and Gemma persuaded her to go back to bed, promising she would stay up and watch over Jess's phone for any news. Jess wasn't keen, but she knew she didn't have a choice.

'Do you want me to call the police?' Gemma asked, when Jess was in bed and she was standing by the door, Jess's phone in her hand.

'Will they take me seriously if I say my mum has taken my baby?'

'I don't know. Let's wait until morning and see if we know any more by then.'

Jess nodded, and Gemma blew her a kiss before closing the door. She felt like she couldn't cry any more, but she did, when she thought of Edie sleeping somewhere unfamiliar without her usual things around her, and without her mum. She wanted Jake, she realised. She wanted to talk to Jake about it. She reached for her phone instinctively, meaning to send him a message, and then remembered that Gemma had it. She would text him when Edie was back, she decided. Tell him she wanted him to meet Edie, that she wanted him to be involved. She didn't care what her mum thought, not after this. And she didn't remember thinking anything else, because she fell asleep, and when she woke again, the house was full of noise and shouting.

Jess shot out of bed and down the stairs. She could hear Gemma's voice, and her mum's, and they were arguing. Gemma was telling her what she'd done was unforgivable and her mum was saying it was none of Gemma's business. But she couldn't hear Edie. She burst into the kitchen, where the two women were standing a little too close to one another.

'Where is she?' she demanded.

Her mum and Gemma both turned to face her, and she burst into tears.

'What's happened? Where is she?'

Gemma crossed the room and put her arm on Jess's shoulder.

'It's okay, Jess. She's in the lounge, in her car seat. She's fast asleep.'

Jess went through to the lounge to confirm this. It wasn't that she didn't trust what Gemma had said, but she needed to see for herself. And there she was. Edie. Her lips smacking slightly, her eyes shut tight. Jess leaned down and picked her up, couldn't help herself. She stroked Edie's hair rhythmically, over and over.

'I'm here, baby, I'm here. It's Mummy.'

Her mum and Gemma had followed her into the room. Jess took in how exhausted Gemma looked. She'd worked a shift and then stayed up all night, waiting for Jess's baby to come home. She would thank her, Jess thought. She would let her know how much that meant. Her mum looked tired too. Jess wondered where they had passed the night. The fury rose in her again, like bile.

Without saying a word, Jess took Edie back to bed with her. She wasn't sure how to face her mother. If she could, she would have stormed out, taking Edie with her, saying that they couldn't live in that house with her any more after what she'd done. But she couldn't do that, could she? She had no money and nowhere else to live and she was completely reliant on her mum's help with childcare. Edie was looking at her, eyes wide. Jess knew that it was ridiculous, but she felt as though Edie understood. As though she was trying to tell Jess she would be okay.

It was so hard, all of this. Jess had been writing Edie these letters, trying to get things in place for her, and now the cancer was taking over her and she felt like she was going to leave Edie in the middle of a huge mess. With no mother, no father to speak of and a grandmother who seemed to have lost all sense of reason.

Just then, as if summoned, Caroline appeared in the doorway. She had the good grace to look sheepish, Jess noticed. She looked like she hadn't slept either, and Jess felt a familiar tug of concern. But then it was replaced by another wave of anger.

'Before you say anything,' Caroline said, 'I was acting in her interests.'

'It's not acting in her interests to take her somewhere away from her mother, without telling anyone! Where the hell were you, anyway?'

Caroline shook her head, as if batting the question away. 'I don't think you're thinking straight...'

'*I'm* not thinking straight! Mum, you kidnapped her. Gemma and I were on the verge of calling the police.'

'There's no need for anything like that, Jess...'

'How dare you! It's not for you to say what I can and can't do when my baby is missing...'

Jess was sitting up in bed, now, with Edie held against her chest. Her heart was beating furiously, and Edie was starting to wriggle, and she hated that she was putting her through more stress.

'Please go,' Jess said, her voice quiet but steely. 'I can't talk to you. You know how much we need you right now and you do something like this. It's unforgiveable.'

Jess had never known her mum to back down from a fight. But this time, she did. She stepped out of the room, and a few minutes later, Jess heard the car pulling out of the drive and speeding away. And part of her was glad, and part of her wanted her mum. She lay back down with Edie, whispering promises in her baby's ear.

'You are safe, Edie, and I love you. I will never let anything happen to you.'

# CHAPTER TWENTY-SIX

*Dear Edie,*

*I wanted you to know that being a mum is the hardest thing I've ever done, and I often feel like I'm getting it wrong.*

*I wanted to make things as straightforward and neat for you as possible, before I have to go, and now things are more of a mess than ever. I just wanted to bring your dad into your world, so that you might have one parent, but the idea of that seems to have tipped something in Mum, and now we're in this strange no-man's-land and I don't know what's going to happen. It's so scary, not knowing how long you might have left. If I started to go downhill today, and couldn't sort any of this out, I'd feel like I'd failed you.*

*This morning, I sent a message to your dad with two photos attached. One of you, wearing a navy blue cotton sundress and my sunglasses, sitting up with a wooden block in each hand. And one of the two of us, on a blanket in the garden, my eyes on the camera and your eyes on me. I love that one. That look you're giving me. Like I'm the whole world.*

*After ten minutes, your dad sent a message back. Just four words. Can I meet her? I put the phone down to stop myself from replying straight away, because what is the answer to that question? I want him to come, to be here with us, to see you, to know you. I want it so badly. But if Mum reacted like that to the suggestion of him coming, then I don't know what she'd do if he actually appeared.*

*Of course, you don't know what has happened. Yesterday, Mum took you and I didn't know where you were for hours on end. It sounds less dramatic, when I sum it up in a sentence like that, but perhaps one day you'll have children (wow, that hurts to think about) and you'll understand the terror I felt during that absence. We haven't spoken this morning, despite passing in the kitchen. We live in the same house, and she's my main source of help. I don't know where we go from here.*

*I think that being a mother makes you do these crazy things, sometimes. I try to remind myself, regularly, that I am to her what you are to me. That while I'm having to face up to dying, and to leaving you, she is dealing with losing her baby. I know I have to give her some leeway, but I don't know how much.*

*Here's a story for you. When you were four days old, we were still in hospital because you were jaundiced, and you had to go under these special lights until you were better. I was fed up and tearful and I felt like I'd somehow done something wrong, because I'd seen all the other mums and their babies pack up and go home. Also, I was the only mum who didn't have a partner coming in every day bringing chocolate and changes of clothes and holding up their baby with a look of pure adoration in their eyes. That day, when Mum had gone home to get some rest and bring in some more nappies and sleepsuits, I burst into tears and one of the nurses put her arms around me and pulled me into her body and I could smell the fabric conditioner she used on her stiff blue uniform.*

*'Day four is hard for everyone,' she said.*

*I thought she was making it up. I didn't know anyone else who'd had a baby, other than Mum, and she'd never said anything about that. But here was a woman who dealt with women who were about to give birth and who'd just given birth every single day.*

*'It's true,' she said, seeing the mistrust in my eyes.*

*And then she released me and went off to check the blood pressure of the woman in the next bed.*

*When Mum came in later that afternoon, I was trying to get you to latch on to my breast, and it was toe-curlingly painful, and I had my teeth gritted and my eyes screwed shut.*

*'Mum,' I said, my voice like a toddler's, 'have I made a huge mistake here? Please tell me it gets easier.'*

*She sat down on the edge of my bed and took hold of one of my hands, the one that wasn't supporting your head. She said that it didn't necessarily get easier, but that you learned how to manage it, and that she would do everything in her power to help both of us. I asked her if she'd heard about this day four thing, and she nodded.*

*'I spent all day in tears four days after having you. I thought I was such a failure, that I wasn't up to being a mum. It's hormonal. It's to do with your milk coming in. It will pass. And if it doesn't, and you need some help, we'll get that for you.'*

*I didn't know anything about post-natal depression then, but I guess that's what she was alluding to. I had no idea what was in store, did I? I had no idea that things were going to get so much more unbearable than those early days of breastfeeding. And neither did she. But I'm not sure how we've got to this place, where we're fighting one another over what's best for you, and barely speaking. I don't know how we've got from there to here in a few short months.*

*Edie, I have no idea what your relationship with your grandmother will be like by the time you read these letters. I don't know whether she'll have been, to all intents and purposes, your mum, and whether you'll love her wholeheartedly and hate me for saying anything negative about her. Part of me hopes so. But know this: all of this tension is because we both love you so much and are battling it out to see who knows what is best for you. And it's better to be loved too much, by too many people, than too little, by too few. I'm trying to pour all the love I have for you into the cuddles we have, and hoping it will be enough; that somehow, your body will remember.*

*I wanted you to know that being a mum is the hardest thing I've ever done. But it's the best, too.*

*With love,*

*Mum*

## CHAPTER TWENTY-SEVEN

Jess felt like she spent as much time at the hospital as she did at home. There was her weekly chemo, and there were always blood tests and checks to be done. Since Caroline had taken Edie that day, Jess hadn't wanted to ask her for help, so she was visiting the hospital with Gemma more and more. Edie in the backseat, then carried in in her car seat. So that was the arrangement on the day when Jess was told things were getting worse yet again.

'Can you say it again?' Gemma asked. She looked across to Jess. 'I mean, I'm sorry, I just want to make sure we've got it right.'

Jess looked down at Edie, asleep in her car seat as she had been for so many of these appointments. She couldn't bear it, all of a sudden, that Edie had spent so much of her early months in hospitals and clinics. She knew she wouldn't remember, but that was no comfort, because it only served a reminder that Edie wouldn't remember her at all. Perhaps when she was older, an adult, she would walk into a hospital and something about the smell and the sounds would make her think of Jess. And that was enough to make Jess want to weep.

'I'm sorry we don't have better news,' Dr Singh said. 'The cancer is spreading faster than we can control it. I'm surprised at how well you seem.'

'But if she seems better than you'd expect, maybe that's a good thing?' Gemma asked. 'Maybe she's fighting it better than you think.'

The doctor shook her head slightly, and Gemma hung her head. It had been a long shot, Jess thought, but she loved Gemma for taking it. Of course these people, with their medical degrees and their years of experience, knew what was going on better than she or her friend did. If they said it was nearly over, then it was.

Asha was in the room, sitting on a chair in the corner, and Jess glanced over at her and they exchanged sorry looks.

'Can you say how long?' Jess asked, through tears.

'We can never say that for definite. But I think we're looking at weeks now, Jess. I'm so sorry.'

Jess couldn't look her in the eye, couldn't say it was okay, because it wasn't. Things were falling apart, and while it had been happening in slow motion, it had felt manageable. She had been trying to do all the things she needed to do, to secure her daughter's future, and that had helped take her mind off the fact of it, and the pain that was probably on its way. There was no slow motion now. Things were caving, quick and heavy, and how could she stop them? She couldn't hold up a roof on her own. She was just one person.

'Let's go home,' Jess said, standing up.

She could hear the change in her own voice. She sounded like she was beaten.

'Is there anything else we need to know? Anything she should or shouldn't do?'

'Not really, at this stage. Do whatever makes you happy, Jess. And think about how you want it to be, at the end...'

Jess snapped her head up. This sounded important, like something she needed to be fully present for, and properly take in.

'Some people want to stay at home with their family,' the doctor continued. 'Others go into a hospice for the last few weeks. There are no right or wrong answers, and we can guide you through any decisions you might want to make.'

'Okay,' Jess said. That was enough, for now. She felt like she was a jug and the oncologist's words were water and she was full, and the water was spilling out.

'Remember you can call me,' Asha said, and Jess nodded.

On the way home, Jess and Gemma barely spoke. Jess said things like 'Don't forget it's left here' and 'Do you mind if I put the cold air on?' and Gemma just nodded and drove. When they were halfway back, Edie woke up and started to cry, and Jess was glad because the silence in the car had been stifling.

'I don't know how to tell Mum,' Jess said, when they were nearly at the house. It was easier to say it to a background of Edie's hungry wails.

'Do you want me to tell her?' Gemma asked.

'No, that doesn't seem right.'

'What do you need me to do?'

'I need you to make me a death playlist.'

Jess expected Gemma to laugh, but she didn't.

'I need to just do it,' Jess said, opening the car door and stepping out.

'Do you want me to come with you?'

'No, go home. You've got work in a bit. I'll text you to let you know how it went.' Jess lifted Edie's car seat out of the car and spoke to her indignant daughter. 'I know, baby, we're going inside now. I'll feed you, I promise.'

Jess stood on the pavement while Gemma pulled away. She wondered whether Gemma would cry, when she got home. Whether she'd tell her mum, or Dan. What they would say. And later, at work, if she was quiet, would she tell her colleagues that her friend was dying? As in, really dying, in the next few weeks. Jess tried to put herself in Gemma's place and Gemma in hers. How would it be for her, if Gemma was the one who was dying? It was impossible to know.

She let herself in and busied herself with making a bottle for Edie, whose cries were getting louder by the minute. When her mum came through to the kitchen from the lounge, Edie was drinking hungrily, and the room was quiet and still. Jess could see dust particles floating in the air between them. Something so small and insignificant, but it made her feel that she wasn't done with this life, with this world. Where dust can dance in the sunlight.

'Cup of tea?' Caroline asked.

She wants to make amends, Jess thought. She often did that with tea. Jess wondered whether her mum knew that she'd been at the hospital. Probably. She marked all her appointments on the calendar her mum kept hanging on the inside of one of the kitchen cupboards. Plus, it was really the only place she went these days.

'Yes please,' said Jess, and there was a slight crack in her voice. She swallowed thickly. 'Bad news,' she said. She took the empty bottle from Edie's slack mouth and placed her daughter in her bouncy chair on the floor.

Caroline was standing by the kettle, but she turned, fast. Raised her eyebrows.

'It's spreading fast. Just a few weeks now, they think.'

Jess didn't remember, afterwards, seeing her mum cross the room. But the next thing she knew, she was in her arms and they were both crying at the waste of her short life.

'So what now?' her mum asked, a minute or so after the kettle had boiled, and the silence had come back into the room.

Jess shrugged. 'Nothing. It just… is. We just wait.'

Caroline turned away and made the drinks, and Jess wondered at people's ability to just go on. Hers included. Shouldn't she be planning an insane trip somewhere she'd always wanted to go? Or behaving inappropriately for no reason? Shouldn't she be breaking down? Breaking apart? But there were no rules, were there? It was just something you muddled through. So she would sit in the kitchen and have a cup of tea with her mum while her baby daughter slept. That was her way.

Jess drank her mug of tea and ate two shortbread biscuits before she worked up the courage to ask her mum the question she wanted to.

'Why did you do it, Mum? Why did you take her?'

She made sure her voice wasn't too shrill or too loud. She stayed calm. Enough time had passed now that she could manage that. Her mum didn't say anything at first, and Jess kept her eyes trained on her mum, to show her that, while she wasn't as angry anymore, she really did want this question answered. It took a while to realise that her mum was crying. When she spoke, Jess could hear it in her voice.

'I was so scared, Jess. I still am. I'm terrified of losing both of you. I don't think I could cope if I did.'

'But what makes you think you'll lose her?' Jess asked.

'I thought Jake was going to come back on the scene and take her. I thought…'

She trailed off, but Jess understood there was more to come, and she waited for it, her eyes fixed on her mum's.

'I thought he and his family would look after her. His parents are together and they all live close to one another, don't they? They have this solid family set-up that I can't offer her.'

Another pause. Jess's mind was whirring, and she longed to speak but she felt she owed it to her mum to hear her out.

'If she stays here, it's just me,' Caroline finished.

Jess could see how hard it was for her mum to acknowledge that she would no longer be around. Instinctively, she put a hand over her mum's, on the table, to let her know that it was okay. She hadn't thought about these things. She'd thought about Jake being involved, yes, but not about him taking Edie and bringing her up with his family. No one had even mentioned that. How had her mum got there? She thought about the times she'd heard her mum getting up in the night, the times she'd gone to the toilet after feeding Edie and seen a dim light on in her mum's bedroom. She wasn't sleeping well, Jess knew that. And was it this stuff that was circling her mind in the dead of night, when she felt alone and lost? It seemed likely.

'I think you're getting ahead of things, Mum,' Jess said, as gently as she could. 'It's not only you, here. There's Gemma, and there's Dad, I guess. We might not be a conventional family, but we pull together when we need to.'

Idly, Jess thought that at some point she would have to stop talking about 'we' when it came to Edie's childcare team and start saying 'you'. She wasn't going to be a part of it. She'd been the central part, but that wouldn't count for anything when she was in bed, too ill to lend a hand.

Jess moved to pull her hand away from her mum's. Edie had dozed off in the bouncy chair and she wanted to have a shower, to try to wash away some of the fear and sadness of that last appointment. But her mum grabbed hold of her fingers.

'Please, Jess, sit down.'

Jess did so, aware that her mum needed to tell her something. She hoped it wasn't something bad, didn't think she could take more bad news today. She felt clammy, uncomfortably hot.

'I lost a baby,' Caroline said.

Jess was taken aback. She had so many questions, but the one that came out first was a single word. 'When?'

'Before I had you. Not with your dad. I had this boyfriend, Sean, I might have told you about him. We were together for a year, and he was a few years older than me, and ready to settle down. He kept on about having a baby, and I knew I wasn't ready, but I didn't want to lose him. So I agreed, in the end, and I got pregnant the first month of trying. I remember taking that test, knowing what the result was going to be. My breasts felt tender and I had this churning in my guts. And I'd gone off tea. Just one day, out of nowhere, I couldn't face it. So I knew it was going to be positive, and we were in the bathroom together waiting to turn it over and see, and Sean was holding my hand, and I could see how excited he was, and I didn't know how to tell him that I'd changed my mind. I didn't want it, any of it. I wanted to rewind time, hold my ground, say no.'

Jess was so caught up in her mum's story that when Edie began to cry, she wasn't sure where the sound was coming from. And then she looked down, saw her daughter with both arms up, asking to be held, and she unclipped her from the seat and sat her on her knee. 'Go on,' she said.

'Well, it was positive, as I'd expected, and I was too scared to say anything about the way I felt. I pretended it was good news. Went through the motions. We decided we wouldn't tell anyone until I'd got to twelve weeks, and the next few weeks were a kind of hell for me. Every day, I'd decide I was going to tell him. I'd made an awful mistake and I just couldn't go through with it and I was going to have an abortion. And then every evening, I'd see him, and he'd start talking about his plans and his ideas for names and whether or not we should get married, and I couldn't say it. He was very controlling, and if I'm honest, I was scared of him. And then one day, about a week before the scan, I started having these cramps. I went to the toilet and I was bleeding, so I went home from work and just lay in bed, knowing what was happening. I was scared to tell him that, too. But a big part of me was relieved, and I've never really forgiven myself for that.'

'How awful,' Jess said. It didn't seem enough, but what could she do? She couldn't change anything, couldn't turn back time and be there for her lost and scared teenage mother. For a second, she thought that if that baby had lived, she would probably never have been born. And perhaps her mum would have a child that she wasn't losing now.

'I think that's why I took Edie,' Caroline said, her voice hitching as if caught on a nail. 'It's no excuse. I know it was the wrong thing to do. I knew it then. I had a part of my brain telling me that it was inexcusable, that I couldn't do it, and another part refusing to back down. But I think it all comes down to what I've lost, and what I'm about to lose, and how frightened I am of all that.'

Jess wanted to tell her mother that she forgave her, but the words got stuck. It would be the best thing, and the right thing, wouldn't it? To forgive and forget, to end her life on good terms with as many people as possible. But she wasn't gone yet, and what her mother had done had terrified her, and she wasn't okay with brushing it under the carpet, because what if her mum took that to mean it was okay to do it again?

'I think we're all frightened,' she said, eventually. 'Except Edie, who has no idea what's going on. The lucky thing.'

Edie was still on Jess's lap, trying to fit her whole hand in her mouth and dribbling. Jess pulled her a little closer and Edie squawked in response. She wanted a bit of freedom, these days. She was getting on to her hands and knees, rocking a little. Getting ready to crawl. She was moving away from them. Becoming more independent. Jess squinted and imagined Edie's fuzzy dark hair grown longer, brushed out of her eyes and secured with brightly coloured clips. Imagined her toddling on unsteady feet, falling on her nappy-cushioned bum every few steps. She felt her eyes begin to fill and blinked the tears away.

'Thanks for telling me that, Mum,' she said. She meant it. It was a piece to store in the puzzle of her mother's past. It explained certain things. It wasn't too late, was it, to understand the people in her life a little better?

'Well,' her mum said. 'I just wanted you to know.'

# CHAPTER TWENTY-EIGHT

*Dear Edie,*

*I wanted you to know how to deal with cancer. Don't get me wrong, I hope that you'll never need this information; of course I do. But sometimes these things run in families, and I never want you to face a cancer diagnosis and wish you had me around to talk to about this stuff. So I want to tell you everything I've learned. I know that medicine will have moved on in the intervening years, and I hope that you can laugh at these things, safe in the knowledge that there's a better solution for you. Like chemo. When I first heard I would be having chemo, I thought I'd be vomiting day and night. That's the visual I get when I think of chemo. But it hasn't been like that at all, for me. I have some nausea, sure, but I haven't vomited once. I hope that, if you ever need to know about cancer, things will have changed so much that you just have to take a pill every day or every week or every month to fight it.*

*The main thing is that it's tiring as hell to have cancer. The medication makes you tired, and all the worry makes you tired too. The constant fretting and questioning, it all takes it out of you. Now, you might have heard that having a baby makes you pretty tired too, and I can confirm this, so I definitely wouldn't recommend doing the two things at the same time. But surely that won't happen to you. I know that lightning can strike twice, but that would be ridiculous. Anyway, the point is that you must ask for help, and accept help, and not try to be a hero. You can be a hero later, when you've got through it.*

*Because that's important to know, too. If you're facing this, don't ever think that you won't get through it because I didn't. I've been unlucky, but my story is not everyone's story. Not by any means. There are many more people who come out the other side of this than those who don't. So although you're bound to be scared, try not to be terrified.*

*If you're reading this and you have cancer, you could be my age, or you could be forty, or you could be seventy. God, I hope you're seventy, Edie. I hope you're wrinkled and getting tired with life. I hope you've done plenty of the things you always wanted to and known enormous amounts of love. I hope you're a mother, and a grandmother. I hope you are surrounded by friends and loved ones. I hope you have plenty of hands to hold. I can't help but laugh at the thought of twenty-two-year-old me giving advice to a seventy-year-old you. But I'm still your mum, Edie. I'm still allowed to boss you around.*

*Try to trust in your team. There have been times when I've wanted to throw things at my oncologist, but I know, I really know, that she knows best. She doesn't want me to die. It isn't her that's killing me. She is doing her utmost to keep it at bay, and she has more experience with this than me, or my friends and family, or anyone else I know. I will do whatever she tells me to do. It's so hard when the news isn't good. But it just can't be, for everyone.*

*I'm not sure what all that amounts to, really. But the thing I'd really like to do is be there to hold your hand, and I can't be, so this letter will have to do instead. I know you're scared. I know you want and need and deserve to have your mum at your side. I hope you have a crowd of people to take my place.*

*I wanted you to know how to deal with cancer. But I hope with everything in me that you never need to.*

*With love,*

*Mum*

## CHAPTER TWENTY-NINE

Several weeks had passed since Jess had seen Jake, since he'd asked her to call. She hadn't. There had been too much going on. But it didn't mean she hadn't been thinking about him. At least once a day, she'd found his number in her phone and thought about pressing the button to connect to him. And he'd sent a few messages, here and there. Asking how she was, how Edie was. It was so confusing. Jess wanted to ask if his interest was purely about their shared daughter, if he would be getting in touch at all if there was no Edie. But that wasn't the kind of thing you could say, and what did it matter anyway? She didn't have a future to consider.

She'd started spending a lot of her time in bed. She was feeling weaker, more tired. She believed what they said about her not having much time left. Sometimes, her mum would bring her a ham sandwich and it seemed so strange to her to be eating something so mundane when her remaining meals were numbered, and she didn't need to worry about her weight or her health. But she didn't have much of an appetite anyway.

Jess was lying in bed with a book when Jake got in touch again. She saw his name flash up on her phone and for a minute or two, she allowed herself to imagine that he was telling her he loved her. That he wanted her back. And then she opened the message.

**How are things?**

She wanted to ask him what he meant. How were things with her, or how were things with Edie? How were things with her mum, who was just about holding it all together? She typed a long reply, filling him in on the latest prognosis, telling him that she felt like her body was quietly but determinedly shutting down, that she was scared. She told him that Edie was trying more and more solid foods, that after the argument over her mum starting her too early, Jess had been at the forefront of her daughter's weaning, coming downstairs to watch Edie's first tastes of butternut squash, and apple, and fingers of toast and cucumber. She told him about the faces Edie had pulled, not unhappy but so surprised at the world of tastes that awaited her beyond her love affair with milk. And then she deleted it all and sent a message that read,

**We're okay, thanks. Are you?**

And then she threw her phone gently towards the other end of the bed and vowed not to lie there waiting for his response.

When there was a knock on the door, she expected it to be Gemma or her mum, so she called for them to come in. She was taken aback when Dan's head appeared around the door. He was holding Edie awkwardly, and she was wriggling. Jess's hands went to her head, to check her scarf was in place. When

Edie saw Jess, she reached her arms out towards her mum and, for a terrible moment, Jess thought Dan was going to drop her, but he managed to make it to the side of her bed and passed Edie into her arms.

'Gemma's been keeping me up to date,' he said, by way of an explanation. 'I just wanted to say…'

Jess was trying to get Edie into a comfortable position. She didn't want to be held, it seemed. She wanted to sit on the bed beside Jess and play a game of peekaboo with a muslin she'd found. So Jess didn't notice at first when Dan's voice trailed off uncomfortably. When she did look up, he was staring at her.

'You're so good with her,' he said. 'Your mum passed her to me and asked me to bring her up here and I didn't even know how to hold her.'

'I'm her mum,' Jess said. 'I've had quite a bit of practice over the last few months.'

'Yes of course, but I just can't see myself being like that with a baby. So comfortable and right.'

'You will be,' Jess said.

Before she'd had Edie, she hadn't known anything much about babies. She had no siblings, and there had been no babies in the family when she was growing up. She remembered looking down at her hard, swollen belly and wondering who the little person inside her was. What he or she might look like, and what they would want from her. And then Edie had been born and made it so clear what she wanted at all times: milk and cuddles. And in a more abstract way, she wanted what everyone wanted. To be made to feel loved, and safe. To be protected. To be put first.

She tried to imagine Dan with a family of his own. She couldn't. He would always be that boy she'd liked, her friend's cooler older brother. If she was going to live, she would see him adjust, gradually, and her perception of him would adjust, too. One day, he would probably be a middle-aged man with a little too much weight around his middle and a couple of kids kicking a ball at his feet. But she wouldn't be around to see it, and it was too far away to picture it properly now.

'Are you glad you had her? Even now, with everything that's going on?'

'Now I'm dying, you mean? It's okay, you can say it.'

Dan looked down, his neck reddening. He'd sat on the edge of the bed, but he was facing the door, turning towards her when he spoke. It was as if he couldn't fully commit to having this conversation and wanted to be ready to leave at a moment's notice. Jess thought about his question. No one else had asked that. When she was pregnant, several people had asked whether she was sure about having the baby, but the whole matter was dropped when Edie arrived. You couldn't regret having a child, could you? You certainly couldn't talk about it.

'I can't imagine not having her,' she said. It was the truth. She could try to picture herself back at university, in her final year, nothing more pressing to worry about than deadlines and overdue library books. She could try to see herself going out drinking with her friends when she should be doing reading for the next day's tutorial, or lying in until early afternoon, skipping lectures, drinking coffee with her friends and talking about abstract issues and the books they were half-heartedly reading. She would be worrying about her finals by now, looking into career options. And this girl, this tiny, perfect human with her eyelashes that brushed her cheeks when she looked down and her hands that were learning to hold smaller and smaller items, she wouldn't exist.

'I know she's going to have to grow up without me, and it's awful. But it doesn't make me wish I hadn't had her at all.

Maybe it's selfish, but I feel like I'm leaving a little part of me behind, with her. And I won't be there when she falls over and needs a cuddle or when she gets her first job or finds out what it's like to fall in love, but she'll do all those things anyway.'

'And you'll be watching over her?' Dan asked, his face more serious than she'd ever seen it.

'No, I don't believe that. I wish I did. It's like, she'll do those things and more, and she'll do them for me. She'll do the things I'm not going to have time to do. Travelling, and getting married, and having grandchildren. All that. I can't but hopefully she will.'

Dan nodded. 'I just can't believe how well you're handling it,' he said. 'I'd be falling apart.'

Jess thought about telling him that she'd done her fair share of falling apart. That turning up on his doorstep and trying to seduce him was one example of her falling apart. But for once, she decided to just take the compliment and thank him for it.

'You know,' Dan said, 'all those people we went to school with, and it ends up being you. Why couldn't it have been one of those kids who had nothing to offer the world, who were always angry and causing fights. Remember Simon Jackson? Why couldn't it be someone like him? He used to pick on Gemma, you know, and then he punched me in the face when I tried to defend her.'

'His mum died,' Jess said, suddenly remembering. She hadn't thought about Simon Jackson for years. And Dan was right, he'd always been this bundle of fury and everyone had pretty much kept out of his way because you never knew when he was going to explode. But Jess had a vague memory of his mum standing at the school gates in a headscarf. Her face pale and drawn. And she remembered her mum telling her that Simon's mum had died, when they were about eight, and that she should be kind to him. Jess had shrugged that advice off – who was going to be kind to Simon Jackson? You'd have to get near to him first.

Jess and Dan both looked at Edie, then. It was hard to imagine that she might be that person when she was at school, full of fury and fear. But you just didn't know, did you, what losing a mother might do to a child? Jess reminded herself that the only thing she could do was set Edie up with a support network. And that was what she'd been doing. She felt the familiar panic rising in her chest, but she knew the only way to deal with that was by taking deep breaths, so she did that, one after another, until she felt calmer.

'Thanks for coming,' she said.

Dan shrugged. He looked embarrassed.

'What are you going to do?' Jess asked. 'I don't get to stick around to see, so it feels like I have the right to ask. You're not going to live at your mum's house forever, are you?'

'I hope not. I'm not clever like you, though. University was never on the cards. I'm looking at jobs in Manchester. I'd like to live there, move in with some friends.'

'What kind of jobs?'

'I want to get into illustration. I've been doing this evening class at the college. Eventually, I'd like to illustrate children's books.'

Jess was taken aback. She half remembered Dan being reasonably good at art, could picture him sketching in the garden when she and Gemma were lying on a blanket, gossiping. But she couldn't have imagined he was holding an ambition like that. She felt privileged, having that information. She suspected he hadn't told anyone else.

'I hope you do that,' she said.

She felt exposed, and she could tell that he did, too. More so than when they'd been half naked in his bed. While they'd been talking, Edie had settled back on the pillows and gone to sleep. To detract from the intensity in the room, Jess stroked her daughter's hair away from her forehead, slightly adjusted her wrinkled clothes.

'I'd better go,' Dan said, standing. He rubbed a hand across the back of his hair, and Jess could tell he was trying to decide whether to say something. She wondered whether it would be the last time she'd see him. She didn't want him to have regrets.

'Say it,' she said.

'I'm just so fucking sorry. I see you here, with Edie, and you should have it all ahead. She should have a mum, and you should get to have a life, and it just isn't fair. I know you know that. I just want you to know how much I wish it could be different. That I'd take your place, if I could.'

Jess didn't know what to say. Dan was crying, his face red and ugly. She got out of bed, aware that she was only wearing a pair of thin pyjamas, and she hugged him, pressing her cheek into his chest.

'Thank you,' she said.

And then he was gone, the heels of his hand pressing into his eyes as if he thought he could push the tears back inside. And Jess sat back down on her bed, feeling as if she'd been punched. This is what it's going to be like, now, she thought. Goodbye after goodbye after goodbye.

# CHAPTER THIRTY

Jess spent the next couple of days waiting for a reply from Jake that never came. She pictured him, sending that message asking how things were and then going into rehearsals, seeing her reply when he was busy with other things and meaning to get back to her, and then forgetting. That was the crux of it. He had a busy, full life and she did not. It was horribly unfair, and if she thought about it too much, she got angry, but she knew it wasn't his fault. It didn't mean that he didn't care as much, necessarily, but she and Edie were just one of the things on his mind as he tried to get his career going and travelled around and met new people. He wasn't lying in a bed, waiting. And because of that, the evenness that had existed as part of their relationship was gone for good.

One afternoon, while her mum was out seeing a friend and Gemma was taking care of Jess and Edie, Jess decided it was time to take action.

'You know those letters I told you about?' she asked.

Gemma was kneeling on the floor beside Jess's bed. She'd laid out Edie's playmat there and was driving cars across the mat and helping her build towers of blocks. 'The letters for Edie?' she asked, looking up.

'Yes, those. I've changed my mind about them.'

'What do you mean? You don't want me to take them anymore?'

'I'm going to get rid of them. They were a mistake.'

Gemma frowned. 'Why the change of heart? They sounded like a good idea. It sounded like a nice way for Edie to have something of you.'

Jess pushed the covers back and swung her legs round to get out of bed. She felt a little dizzy, doing so, but didn't say anything about it because she knew Gemma would make her lie back down if she admitted to feeling unwell. She was in pain most of the time, now. She took medication to control it, but it was always in the background.

'I wanted her to have a dad,' Jess said, aware that she was on the verge of crying and determined to hold back the tears. 'But I don't think that's going to happen now.'

'Has something happened, with Jake?' Gemma picked Edie up and sat down with her on the edge of the bed, where Jess was still sitting, gathering her strength.

'No, that's just it. Nothing's happened. He knows what's going on and he's too busy to come here and meet his daughter…'

'Hold on. Didn't he ask to meet her?'

Jess wasn't sure why Gemma was defending Jake. She wanted Gemma to be unequivocally on her side. She was her best friend. It wasn't her job to make excuses for him.

'It's just too hard,' Jess said, quietly.

'For Edie? Or for you?'

Jess said nothing. She stood up, her legs wobbly from her days in bed. She didn't want an argument, she just wanted to get rid of the letters and maybe, if there was time, write some new ones that didn't involve Jake. She went to the drawer where she kept them and pulled them out. It was quite a stack, now. She hadn't realised. She thought about asking Gemma to get rid of them for her, but she knew she was going to have to do it herself, to be sure. Gemma seemed to be on Jake's side, for one thing. Jess stuffed the letters under her arm and headed for the door, ignoring the dizziness she felt.

'Wait, Jess!' Gemma followed Jess out of the room, Edie in her arms, and tried to catch hold of Jess's hand to stop her. 'Your mum said you'd been told to stay in bed. She'll kill me if she finds out I let you start wandering around…'

Jess couldn't believe it had come to this. Her best friend trying to stop her from doing something as simple as going downstairs in her own house. She felt trapped and angry. She pulled away from Gemma's grip and continued down the landing. She started to go down the stairs, then lost her footing and slid from the middle of the staircase to the bottom. She heard Gemma shout out her name, and she let go of the letters so that they fell all around her. She was shocked, at first, so she didn't notice the pain in her hip and her leg. Gemma rushed down the stairs as quickly as she could while still holding Edie, and then offered Jess a hand to help her get up.

'Are you okay?' she asked.

There was so much worry in her eyes, Jess noticed. They were clouded with it. And it was all Jess's fault. Until a few months ago, Gemma had been a carefree young woman. Working in a bar, spending time with her friends. Jess thought about the lives that had been affected by her cancer. The ripples it had caused.

'I'm sorry,' she said. She put her head in her hands and cried. She wanted to gather up the letters, but she didn't have the strength to stand and pick them up.

'Don't be silly,' Gemma said.

It was then that Edie started to cry. Jess wondered whether it was a coincidence, whether she was just hungry, or whether she, too, was saddened by how things were turning out. How bad things were looking. When the doorbell rang, Gemma looked at Jess intently.

'Do you want me to answer it?' she asked.

Jess shrugged and nodded. It would be the postman, she thought. She watched Gemma walk to the door, picking her way through the fallen letters, Edie on her hip. And she watched her open it, watched Jake's face slowly appear in front of her, her mouth open. It was too late to change her mind, too late to ask Gemma to ignore it. Jake looked inside, took in Gemma and the baby, then Jess, sitting at the bottom of the stairs in her pyjamas, her bald head uncovered.

'Can I come in?' he asked.

And just the sight of him, and his voice, was enough to make Jess want to weep for everything she'd lost.

'Er, sure,' Gemma said, opening the door wider and stepping to one side.

'Is this her?' Jake asked, looking from Jess to Edie and back again. 'Is this Edie?'

Jess wanted to say that of course it was. Couldn't he see that she was a perfect mixture of the two of them? Didn't he feel connected to her, feel deep inside that she was his? And how could he bear to be there, in the same house as her, and not reach out his arms for her?

'Yes,' she said, standing. It was painful, but she managed it. 'This is Edie.'

'Are you okay?' he asked, then.

'Yes,' Gemma said, 'are you?' She turned to Jake. 'She just fell down the stairs.'

'Shit, I'm sorry. Do you need some help?'

Jess shot Gemma an angry look. Wasn't it bad enough, this situation, without Gemma making it worse by filling Jake in on the series of disasters that had preceded his arrival? Gemma seemed to understand and flashed her an apology of sorts with her eyes. And it was then that Jess took in what Jake had just said. She felt like she was being treated as either a small child or a very old woman. Someone who needed assistance with every little thing. She remembered the way she and Jake had been when they were together. The way they'd laughed and pushed one another, joked and fought and held each other. And now here he was, offering to help her back to bed. It was humiliating.

'Listen,' Gemma said, 'I'm going to let you guys catch up. I'll be in the kitchen. Do you want me to take Edie, or...'

'No,' Jake said. 'Can I?'

He looked at Jess for permission, raised his eyebrows, and she nodded. It was what she'd wanted, for him to care, and to meet Edie and to fall in love with her. She knew he would. But it was heart breaking, too, that it was happening like this, when she was slowly fading out of the picture.

Jess watched Gemma pass Edie to Jake, and she saw that he was a little awkward, not knowing how to hold her, and she wanted to step in and show him what to do, but she stopped herself. He would work it out. There wasn't so much to it, really. She started to climb the stairs, wincing at the pain the fall had caused, determined not to let Jake see it. And he followed her, Edie wriggling in his arms, his face lined with concentration.

When she was back in bed, Jess felt a little better. She thought briefly about the letters, about the fact that she'd left them scattered all over the hallway and the stairs, and they contained her most private thoughts about everything, and then she decided to just let it go. There were bigger things to worry about.

'I didn't know things were this bad,' Jake said.

Jess thought she heard a slight wobble in his voice, and she looked up. He'd lowered himself on to the edge of the bed, where Gemma had been sitting just a short while ago, and he kept looking from her to Edie, as if he couldn't quite believe they were there.

'I didn't know how to tell you,' she said. 'It's not going to be long now. Weeks.'

She saw the shock in Jake's eyes. She wondered how she looked to him. She'd lost weight, although she wasn't sure how much, and she hadn't worn make-up for weeks. Did he even see the girl he'd loved when he looked at her, or was she too far removed?

'I don't know what to say,' Jake said. 'Fuck.'

'What about her?' Jess said, nodding towards their daughter. 'She's pretty great, right?'

When she'd been in the hospital after having Edie, and since, too, this is what Jess had missed. Someone to talk to about every little thing Edie did, every change Jess noticed. She knew that her mum loved Edie, but it wasn't quite the same. She believed that only the other person who'd had a hand in making this little being would really want to talk endlessly about her, the way Jess did.

Jake held Edie away from his body, as if appraising her. 'I can't believe her,' he said. 'She's too perfect.'

Jess forgot everything she'd felt that morning, then, about wanting to get rid of the letters and feeling that perhaps Edie would be better off without Jake in her life, if he was going to be flaky and non-committal. Now that he was here, Jess could see that she needed him. That Edie needed him. She was so grateful that she'd got to see them meeting for the first time.

'You know, you can trust me, Jess. I think you can't let yourself, and I think it's because of your mum. But just try.'

Jess bit her lip to stop herself from crying.

'Can I do anything?' Jake asked, his eyes serious and fixed on her. 'Right now, I mean?'

Jess thought about all the things she could ask him. To stand up to her mother over what Edie did and didn't need. To ask her father to do more. To move here, give up the band and his life and be here until the end, and then raise Edie for both of them.

'Can you just lie here with me?' she asked.

She reached out and he passed Edie to her, and Jess laid her down in the middle of the double bed. And then she gestured for Jake to lie down on the other side, and he did, his head on the pillow a few inches from hers. Edie giggled and grabbed hold of her feet and rocked backwards and forwards, and both of them reached down at the same time to touch her, Jess stroking her hair and Jake taking hold of one of her hands. And for a minute or two, Jess allowed herself to pretend they were a normal family.

# CHAPTER THIRTY-ONE

*Dear Edie*

*I wanted you to know about love. You will fall in love and you will have your heart broken. I don't think anyone misses out on those things. You might be lucky and meet someone when you're young who you want to stay with as you get old. But it's much more likely that you'll have some missteps and false starts, and that you'll have a few nights of crying yourself to sleep because the boy or girl you want to be with doesn't want to be with you. It's so hard. It's one of the hardest things.*

*Edie, it is so painful for me to think of you hurting and know that I won't be there to wipe your tears and make you laugh and listen to what's making you sad. Know that I would be right there doing all those things if I possibly could. If it helps, try talking to me. I don't believe that I'll be able to hear you, but I've found that sometimes just saying things out loud (or writing them down) makes them a little less awful. It diminishes them, somehow.*

*Your dad told me that he thinks I have problems trusting men because of my mum, and I think he's right. I couldn't see it before. You grow up thinking that what goes on in your family is absolutely normal, and then you look at it from a bit of a distance once you're older and understand a bit more about family dynamics, and you realise that some of the things you learned weren't quite right. You'll see what I mean, I know you will. I remember going to Gemma's house for the first time and being surprised that Gemma and Dan were expected to do a lot of the things that Mum did for me at home, like washing and cooking. I'd taken her for granted. I hadn't seen the things she did in the background.*

*And this trust thing was the hardest of all to see. But I suppose I grew up without a dad, and with a mum who had been hurt, and I absorbed her mistrust of men, as if by osmosis. So that when I met Jake, we were already doomed before we started, in a way. I was already looking ahead to the day when he'd let me down, and so it became a self-fulfilling prophecy. When I found out I was pregnant with you, and he didn't immediately drop everything he'd been working towards, I walked away. We walked away. Because you were curled up inside me, building me a future full of love.*

*I hope you'll break the mould, do things differently. I hope you'll fall in love hard and give your whole heart to someone. I hope he or she will keep it safe. I hope you'll have learned, from not having me, that life can be unfairly short, and love should always win out. Maybe that's one good thing that will come from all of this.*

*Let me tell you something. For me, there have only ever been two boys. All through secondary school, it was Dan. And afterwards, it was Jake. And in the past few weeks, I've learned that I could have been with Dan instead of pining over him at home, if I'd just been a little braver and let him know how I felt. And I'm starting to wonder if perhaps I could have stayed with Jake, if I had behaved differently when we found out about you. It's hard to write that, because it's painful to admit that all these months I've spent alone, I could have been with him. And now it's too late to do anything about it. Yes, he had this opportunity to go on tour, but we could have worked around it. I didn't have to cut him out of our lives altogether. I wish I hadn't. I wish I'd done the harder, better thing.*

*I don't know whether any of this is helpful to you, Edie. I wonder whether you're reading this, at the age of fifteen or so, feeling unable to relate to any of it. But if there is a boy or a girl that you can't stop thinking about, try to be brave and show them how you feel. They might not feel the same way, and that is hard, but they might. It's better to know. And if someone feels that way about you, and you don't want to be with them, be as kind as you can be. Kindness is king, in so many situations.*

*Time is running out now, Edie. Sometimes I feel like I've covered everything I need to in these letters, and other times I feel like there's so much more I want to tell you. I feel in my body that there won't be many more of these. I don't know what happens at the end, but I imagine it will get harder to write and harder to focus. Sometimes I gaze down at you and I wish I could ask you what you might want to know. There must be things I've learned that would be useful to you, but I feel like my brain is getting more and more crowded with cancer and I can't think straight. Know this: I love you and I'm proud and I'm sorry.*

*I wanted you to know about love. I hope you have so much of it.*

*With love,*

*Mum*

## CHAPTER THIRTY-TWO

'When is Jake coming again?' Gemma asked.

Jess shrugged. She was at the hospital, having a blood test, and Gemma was sitting beside her in the waiting room.

'Is he still touring?'

'No, they finished a few weeks ago. They've recorded an album. He's back at the supermarket while he waits to see what happens with it all.'

'Do you think they'll be famous?'

Jess thought about that. She'd heard Jake's band play a few times and they were good. He and the singer wrote catchy tunes that were somewhere between pop and indie. He had left her with a copy of the album, and she'd listened to it over and over, feeling proud. He'd done something real, and it was good. It struck her, then, that if it was Jake in this situation, rather than her, he'd be leaving something behind. Something that proved he'd been here and lived a life. But then, perhaps that's what Edie was, too. Proof of Jess's existence.

'I don't know,' she said. 'I don't know whether they even want to be. They just love playing music.'

'Do you still love him?'

Jess snapped her head up. She'd been expecting another question about Jake's career. Gemma was smiling.

'I hoped if I just slipped that in there, you might answer truthfully without really thinking about it,' she said.

Jess smiled back. And then her name was called, and she didn't have to answer the question. While the nurse was finding a vein, while Jess was trying not to imagine her oncologist telling her that things weren't looking good, that things were worse, that she had days left, she thought about Gemma's question. Did she still love Jake? Or did she love him again? Where was the line between love and affection? And if you felt like you couldn't trust someone, could you love them? Jess didn't mind having her blood taken, which was good, because it was such a regular occurrence by then, but she didn't like to watch. She'd been distracted and hadn't realised that the nurse had finished what she was doing until she put a cold, gloved hand on Jess's arm.

'All done, love,' she said.

Jess turned to her and arranged her face into a thin smile. 'Thank you.'

'You don't have to thank me, Jess.'

Jess stood up and started to say something, but the nurse was already shuffling out of the room with Jess's tubes of blood in a plastic tray. Everyone had commented on how polite she'd been, throughout. Nurses had told her that they were used to being shouted and sworn at, that they'd had things thrown at them by patients who were angry that their lives were drawing to a close just as they felt they were getting started. But Jess didn't see any sense in that. These were the people who were helping her, who cared about her future, or lack of one. She didn't know the name of this nurse who was taking her blood today, but she'd seen her a handful of times and she'd imagined her going home to her husband and telling him about the poor young woman she'd seen in clinic that day. The woman who was going to die before her daughter's first birthday. She'd imagined her brushing away a tear. And the thought of it made Jess want to reach out and hug that nurse whenever she saw her, to thank her for choosing this career, which meant long hours and pain, and little thanks.

'So?' Gemma said, when Jess had returned to the waiting room and raised her eyebrows to indicate that it was time to go.

'So what?'

'Don't think I've forgotten that you didn't answer my question about Jake. Do you still love him?'

'What does it matter, really?' Jess said. They were heading down the corridor, the soles of their shoes squeaking on the lino. They passed one of the porters pushing a wheelchair, and in it, a child of no more than six or seven, her skin white and her head bald. Jess looked away. There were things even she didn't want to see.

'Of course it matters,' Gemma said.

'Gemma, I'm going to die.'

At this, a couple of middle-aged women stopped their conversation and turned to look at the two friends, and Jess made eye contact until they broke it.

'I'm going to die. This year, maybe this month. Even if I did love Jake, and I'm not saying that I do, but even if I did, what would be the point in telling him?'

Gemma reached across and took hold of Jess's arm, forcing her to stop. They were standing in front of the sliding doors at the hospital's main entrance, and it had started to rain heavily outside, so there was a crowd of people standing around them, waiting for it to ease or stop. People were rushing inside, shaking out umbrellas, and people were deciding to risk it and dashing out, pulling up their hoods.

'Jess, I think you love him, and I think he loves you. And it makes all the difference in the world. So maybe you can't have a long and happy life together. Maybe you've only got a few weeks. But isn't that better than nothing? And isn't it worth him knowing for the rest of his life that he was loved like that, by someone as wonderful as you? Isn't that better than everyone pretending for the next few weeks, and then you dying, and those of us who are left wishing we'd done things a bit differently, or had that difficult conversation, like the one we're having now?'

When Gemma stopped talking, she was breathing heavily, as if she'd been running. Jess could see that it had cost her something to say all that, and she knew she owed it to her to take what her friend had said seriously. She looked around and saw that everyone waiting in that foyer was looking at them, their faces full of expectation and apology. Jess wanted to scream at them all that it wasn't their fault, that it was what it was, and she'd accepted it. But just looking at the sadness in those strangers' faces made something in her crack a tiny bit. It was different from seeing what this was doing to her mum, or to Gemma, or to herself when she looked in the mirror.

'Yes, it's better,' she said. 'I hadn't thought of it like that.'

Gemma broke into a big grin, and Jess realised she hadn't seen an uncomplicated smile like that on Gemma's face since this whole thing had begun, and she remembered that they'd barely stopped laughing, once upon a time. That their friendship hadn't always been like this, heavy and sombre and ending.

'I knew it!' Gemma said.

And Jess took hold of her friend's hand and pulled her

towards the door. It didn't matter that it was raining, or that they weren't wearing coats, or that the car was parked right at the other end of the hospital car park. What mattered was that she loved Jake, and she was running out of time.

'What are you doing?' Gemma shouted.

Jess had broken into a run and Gemma was keeping pace with her, her hair plastered to her face and her grin still wide.

'I'm going home,' Jess said. 'Come on!'

Once they were in the car and Gemma had chosen a playlist, Jess spoke again.

'I've been looking at everything wrong,' she said. 'I've been so selfish. I'm not going to be here but the rest of you are. And you deserve the best of me while I'm still able to give it. I love Jake, but I also love Edie and you and Mum, even though she makes some terrible decisions sometimes, and we need to make the most of what we have left.'

'I will do whatever you want,' Gemma said. 'You know that.'

'All I've been doing is checking off hospital appointments and lying in bed in between...'

'Jess,' Gemma said, 'I understand what you're saying, but I think there's a balance. I'm sure there's a way to fit more in and make everything count and all that, but you have to acknowledge that you're ill. You get tired easily, and you're often in pain. We can't push it too hard.'

Jess went quiet for a minute. Why couldn't they push it too hard? If she was going to die anyway, what difference did a few days or weeks make? What was the worst that could happen? She was tempted to snap back at her friend, but she didn't, because she knew Gemma was just thinking of her. Just being a friend.

'I'm not talking about flying to Ibiza to take a load of drugs and dance all night,' she said. 'Well, I've got the drugs covered.

I just need to feel like I'm doing something, Gem. Does that make sense?'

'Yes, it makes sense.'

When they got back to Jess's house, Gemma waved and drove away, and Jess went inside to face her mum. She found her in the kitchen, making up a bottle with Edie in her arms.

'Can we just forget about everything?' Jess asked.

Caroline turned. 'Forget about what?'

'You taking Edie and all that. I can't completely forgive it and I still don't really understand it, but I could die any time now, and I don't want it hanging over us.'

Caroline pulled Edie a little tighter into her chest. 'What did they say, at the hospital?'

'Oh, nothing. It's not about that. I just feel like I finally understand what's going to happen to me. Something's clicked into place. I always knew I was going to die, in my brain, but now I think I know it in my body. And it's okay. I mean, it's not, but there's nothing any of us can do about it. And I just don't want to spend my final weeks arguing and being stressed. That would be such a waste.'

Caroline nodded. 'Okay,' she said. 'You're in charge.'

Jess smiled and reached for Edie. Her mum had said exactly the right thing. Because everyone wanted to be in charge of something, didn't they? And so much had been taken out of her control recently. It felt good to take something back.

'How are you, Edie girl?' she whispered into her daughter's ear.

And Edie giggled as Jess's hot breath tickled her face and snuggled into her mother's neck. Jess inhaled deeply. She'd heard people talking about the smell of babies, about the top of their heads, about how that glorious scent they carried faded and disappeared. She put a hand protectively on Edie's head, marvelled, as she always did, at the softness of her fluffy hair. She pressed her lips to Edie's forehead and swallowed down a sob. Some mothers didn't even have this, she thought. Some mothers lost their babies while they were still in the womb or delivered tiny corpses. It felt absurd to think it, but she was lucky in a way.

## CHAPTER THIRTY-THREE

'Are you free?' Jess asked.

Jake was silent and Jess took the phone away from her ear to check that she hadn't lost him, but the signal was still strong, the call still connected.

'Today?' he asked, eventually.

'Yes. But it's okay if you're not. I just wanted to ask you first.'

'I'll be there in half an hour.'

'Half an hour! Aren't you in Manchester?'

'It's a long story.'

Twenty minutes later, there was a knock on the door. Jess opened it to find Jake standing there, his eyes bright and clear. Jess wanted to tell him that she'd missed him, but she didn't know how. She invited him in and took him into the kitchen where she put the kettle on.

'Are you feeling better?' he asked. 'I mean, last time I was here, you were in bed...'

Jess had had a shower that morning and dressed in jeans and one of her favourite tops. She hadn't realised how much weight she'd lost until she pulled those clothes on for the first time in weeks. She'd been living in pyjamas and jogging bottoms, and it was a shock to feel the jeans that had once been a little too tight threatening to slip over her hips.

'I'm going out,' she said. 'I'm taking Mum for afternoon tea.'

Jake looked confused. 'So why am I here?' he asked.

'Because we need you to look after Edie.'

Jess watched surprise and fear and joy chase one another across her ex-boyfriend's face.

'I didn't tell you on the phone because I thought you might make an excuse. I knew you'd be scared. But I've written down everything, and I can show you anything you want, because we don't have to leave for another two hours. You can say no, but I want you to think about it.'

Jess didn't pile on the pressure by adding that he needed to learn this stuff, and fast. She'd spent the night before wondering how she could get him to agree to a crash course in parenting. And at one in the morning, it had come to her. It was too much to say that she needed to teach him how to feed and care for Edie for when she was gone. An afternoon out was much more appropriate.

'Where is she?' Jake asked.

'Mum's got her upstairs. I think she might be having a nap.'

'Couldn't she have saved that for when you've left? Naps I can handle.'

Jess felt a genuine smile creep across her face and when she looked up at Jake, his expression matched hers. 'So you'll do it?'

'Of course I'll do it. She's my daughter, isn't she?'

They sat at the kitchen table and drank a cup of tea. Jess thought about all the times they'd done this before. But they'd been together, then. And there had been no Edie. She thought about reaching across the table and kissing him. Time was short, after all. But she couldn't quite bring herself to do it. What if he didn't want her, now that she was dying? And what if he went along with it anyway, out of politeness? She couldn't bear it. When Jess's mum came into the room with the baby monitor in her hand, she looked surprised to see Jake, but she didn't say anything.

'Edie's sleeping,' she said. 'She's had about an hour. I was thinking about waking her.'

'No, let her sleep,' Jess said. 'She's got an afternoon with Daddy ahead and she'll need to have her wits about her.'

'What do you mean? What's happening?'

Jess almost laughed at how worried her mum looked.

'I want to take you out for the afternoon,' she said. 'You don't have to worry, I'm going to show Jake the ropes.'

There was a cry, then, and all three of them looked at the monitor Caroline was holding in her hand.

'Can I?' Jake asked.

Jess nodded and Caroline said nothing. He disappeared upstairs and Jess counted in her head. She wondered whether she could get to ten before her mum said anything negative about Jake. One, two, three, four, five, six...

'You know, I don't know whether this is a good idea,' her mum said.

Jess laughed at her predictability.

'I don't see what's funny, this is your baby's life we're talking about.'

'Mum, what do you think he's going to do? Worst case scenario, we'll come back having had a lovely break from it all and her nappy will be on backwards and she'll have refused her bottle. She'll be okay, Mum.'

Jess wanted to bring up the fact that her mother had been the one to take Edie without permission, but she'd promised herself she would leave that alone. Her mum sighed and looked about to speak, when there was a shout from upstairs.

'I think I need some help here, guys.'

Jess ignored her mum's I-told-you-so expression and headed up the stairs and to her bedroom. Jake was kneeling on the floor and Edie was on the changing mat, laughing and trying to roll over and everything was covered in shit. Edie's vest, the changing mat, Jake's hands. He looked up at her with panic in his eyes.

'I don't know whether I can do this, Jess.'

She laughed, couldn't help it. 'Yes, you can. I'll help you.'

'But what about later, when you're out?'

'Jake, she's done this about four times in her life and I'm willing to bet it won't happen twice in one day. You should be grateful she's done it now, while I'm still here. Now, what you need is wipes. Many, many wipes.'

Jake wiped his hands and together they cleaned up Edie. Jess took the soiled vest into the bathroom and threw it in the sink to deal with once she was finished, and she chose a new outfit. While she was looking for socks to go with the leggings she'd chosen, she tried to imagine Jake doing this, being involved to this level. It was hard. But he'd only just met her. And here he was, willing to look after her alone for the afternoon. It wouldn't all come at once, but it was heading in the right direction. Five minutes later, Edie was clean and dry, and Jake was holding her in his arms. Jess could see that he was nervous, but she thought that was only because she knew him well. To anyone else, he probably looked like an older brother or a young dad who knew what he was doing.

'I cannot believe that all of that came out of her,' Jake said. 'I mean, look at her. She's so tiny and so cute, how can she get shit in her hair?'

Jess laughed. 'That was really something special. A baptism of fire.'

'We're going to be okay, Edie, aren't we?'

He didn't change his voice the way most people did when they were talking to babies, Jess noticed. But Edie was delighted by him, her gaze fixed on his as he held her on his hip and supported her with his arms.

Over the next hour, Jess showed Jake where everything was. Nappies, changes of clothes, muslins. Then she took him downstairs and showed him how to make up a bottle and watched as he fed her, making sure the angle of the bottle was right and she was comfortable and happy. It struck her, as she did it, that she had learned a lot in the past eight months. Because she'd had to learn it on the go, it hadn't really seemed like anything. But put together like this, and taught in a concentrated stint, it added up to a fair bit. It wasn't like being at university and learning about literature or being on the road with a band and learning about music and life, but it was something, nevertheless. When it was time to leave, Jess was confident that Jake would be okay for a few hours. And if he was still nervous, he did a good job of hiding it.

'One last thing,' he said, as she grabbed her bag. 'What shall we do? If she's not feeding or being changed or sleeping. What do you do with her?'

Jess could feel her mum's eyes on her, and she ignored them.

'Just play with her. Sing her songs, tell her stories. Build a tower and let her knock it down. Give her different things to hold and feel. Blow raspberries on her tummy. Show her how to clap.'

Jake nodded, but he looked unsure.

'You'll be fine,' she added. Impulsively, she went up on her tiptoes and kissed his cheek.

'Have a nice time,' he said.

And they did. Jess couldn't remember the last time it had been just the two of them and they hadn't been at a hospital appointment or looking after Edie. It was wonderful to shrug all of that off for a while and be indulged. Jess had booked a table at a fancy hotel in a nearby town, and her mum gasped when she saw where they were heading. Jess knew that, despite having lived in the same place her whole life, her mum had never gone inside this hotel. And that was a shame, Jess thought. Money was important, but it wasn't everything. Everyone deserved the odd afternoon of luxury. Perhaps her more than anyone.

Early on in the afternoon, Caroline asked a question about Jess's medication and Jess held her hand up. 'No cancer talk today.' And Caroline nodded and obeyed. At first, the conversation was a bit stilted, and Jess realised that her cancer, something that had only been in their lives for a few months, had taken over completely. It seemed that neither of them remembered what they had talked about before. But tentatively, they began to share stories of Edie, and Caroline relayed a couple of anecdotes from work, and they discussed Gemma and what a wonder she had been. And it wasn't long before they were back to their pre-cancer selves, talking easily about things that weren't so very important, and things that were.

'Will you bring Edie here one day?' Jess asked.

She saw the cloud pass over her mother's face.

'When she's older, I mean. When she's my age.'

'Yes.'

There were tears in her mum's eyes, and Jess wished she hadn't asked that. But at the same time, they all had to get used to the fact of what was happening. Her, her mum, Jake. Not Edie, because she couldn't understand. Never Edie.

'Don't cry,' she said. 'Please.'

Jess picked up a tiny pink-iced cake just as her mum put the cake in her own hand back down on the plate.

'I can't bear it, sometimes,' her mum said, her voice low and almost unrecognisable.

'You will. And you can't fall apart, because Edie needs you.'

'Does she? I feel like you have other plans for Edie.'

Jess felt the sting that she knew her mother had intended.

'Mum, even if I was going to be around, Edie would need you. You're her grandmother. The fact that Jake is going to be on the scene doesn't change that.'

'It changes everything, Jess. I don't even know what my rights are. He's the dad. You haven't told me who you're expecting to raise her.'

Jess felt so tired, at that moment, that she thought she could have put her head down on the table and slept. The afternoon had been so nice, such a great distraction, but now she'd remember this part of it over everything else. And it was almost time for her next round of medication.

'Let's go home,' she said. 'I'm tired.'

Jess stood up and the scrape of her chair sounded too loud. A waiter hurried over, and Jess asked for the bill, and then she went to the toilet because she knew she was going to cry, and she didn't want her mum to see. When had that happened? She'd cried in front of her mum so many times. As a child and a teenager, as a new mum and a cancer patient. But that day, she cried alone in a toilet cubicle. When she'd washed her face and returned to the table, the bill was gone.

'I wanted this to be my treat,' Jess said.

'It's done. Jess, I didn't mean to upset you.'

'You did, Mum. You know that thinking and talking about what's going to happen to my baby after I'm dead is upsetting. And if you don't, you should.' Jess was aware that her voice was too loud for the room, but she didn't care. She saw a few people on nearby tables turn their heads, looks of horror on their faces.

'Jess, let's go, we can talk about this on the way home.'

Jess couldn't believe that, even now, in this situation, her mum was trying to save face. Trying not to be involved in a scene. So concerned with what everyone else thought. They were both standing up, facing one another across the table where they'd laughed and chatted and eaten sandwiches and cakes. Caroline began to walk towards the door, but Jess stood her ground.

'Don't you dare walk away from me!'

Her mum turned, and Jess saw the tears streaming down her face. She didn't put a hand or a tissue to her face, to stop them. She just stood there, looking at Jess, both angry and so, so sad. There was no fight left in her, Jess saw. And yet still she was needling and picking at every decision Jess made.

'I didn't have a dad, not really, and I don't want that for Edie. You can't make me choose. It isn't you or Jake. She doesn't just need one person who loves her. She's not going to have a mother, and she needs as many people as possible to fill that gap!'

The room was silent, now, the other customers and the waiting staff either staring at Jess and her mother or bowing their heads, pretending not to hear. Jess saw a man in a suit making his way through the tables towards them. The manager, she assumed.

'We're going,' she said, as he approached. 'Don't worry, we're going.'

She followed her mother to the door, because what else could she do? She'd never been as angry with another person as she'd been with her mum at times over these past few weeks, but she'd never loved anyone else as much, either. Until Edie. And now the three of them formed a sort of triangle of love and need and devotion, and she knew it was unbreakable. This was why they could shout and scream at each other, she realised. Because neither of them would ever walk away for good.

When Jess got to the front door of the hotel, her mum already on the other side of it, but waiting for her, Jess felt someone reach for her arm. She turned, ready to unleash her anger again. It was the manager, the one who'd been trying to reach their table, the one she'd assumed was going to throw them out. He smiled at her and she saw that his eyes were kind.

'I'm sorry,' she said. 'I'm sorry we ruined everyone's afternoon.'

He shook his head. He let go of her hand but neither of them moved.

'I lost my wife a few years ago,' he said. 'Cancer?'

Jess nodded, swallowed.

'I'm sorry. I heard you say you have a baby. We didn't have children yet. Sometimes I'm grateful for that and sometimes I wish we'd got on with it sooner.'

Jess didn't know what to say. The words were pouring out of him and she felt sure he had little control over them. It made sense, in a way, for people to bring you their sad stories when they heard yours. But she didn't know what to do with them. She didn't feel like she had space for anyone else's sorrow.

'If your mum and your child want to come back here, they're always welcome. They'll be my guests. No charge.'

He pressed a stiff, thick piece of card into Jess's hand, and she saw that it was a business card. His name and title and phone number. And on the back, in pen, he had written the words 'Wishing you the very best.' Jess slid it into her pocket and muttered a thick thank you to the man, who nodded and stepped back, as if to release her. Jess stepped into the revolving door and pushed, feeling her strength and energy ebb away. Outside, her mother was standing in the street, her eyes red from crying, waiting for her. Jess didn't know what to say, but when she reached her mum's side, they started to walk back to the car in step. And though nothing had really been resolved, Jess felt a little lighter as she looked down at the pavement and saw their feet keeping time. Left, right, left, right, until they reached the car and made their way quietly home.

## CHAPTER THIRTY-FOUR

'And when we got back, Jake and Edie were both asleep on the sofa,' Jess said.

'So he did it,' Gemma said. 'A whole afternoon on his own with her. That's a big step.'

'Yes, and there's something else. He's moved in with his aunt and uncle down the road for a few months. He got a transfer from his supermarket to the local branch.'

'That's brilliant,' Gemma said.

'Is it?' Jess asked. 'I feel like he's waiting for me to die.'

'He's trying to be here for you, and for Edie,' Gemma said.

'Until I die?'

'Stop saying die. It's freaking me out.'

'Well, if me saying it freaks you out, I think you're in for a bit of a shock.'

Gemma laughed and threw the pillow she'd been resting on at Jess. They were side by side on Jess's bed. Jess had realised that Gemma was the only person she could joke about dying with, and she was so grateful for that. Sometimes the tension and sadness in the air was palpable, but when Gemma was around, it dissipated slightly, and Jess felt more able to breathe.

'He's coming over in a bit,' Jess said.

'Today?'

'Yes. He wants a crash course in looking after Edie.'

'I thought he'd just had that.'

Jess shrugged. 'Well, he's coming back for more.'

'I think it's great, Jess. He's fallen in love with her.'

'Who wouldn't?'

They both looked over at the travel cot beside Jess's bed, where Edie was sleeping. She'd started having her daytime naps in there, because she'd grown out of her Moses basket, but Jess liked to have her close and she was spending a lot of time in bed. Edie was on her back, her arms up beside her head as if she was doing a little, silent cheer. Jess wondered how long she would sleep like that, so open and vulnerable and trusting. Jess slept curled in a ball on her side, and she had done for as long as she remembered. She added to the list of things she would miss: seeing Edie sleeping in different positions, putting her to sleep in her first proper bed, picking her up the first time she fell out of bed in the middle of the night. She hadn't written the list down. She couldn't. But she added to it, mentally, most days.

'I was thinking we should have an adventure,' Gemma said. 'It might be the last one.'

'I hope not. But maybe. Are you up for it?'

Jess nodded. She'd hoped Gemma would think of this. She charted their friendship through the adventures they'd had, and she didn't want to think about them being over.

'What do you have in mind?' Jess asked. 'It probably can't be too far away, just in case…'

She didn't need to finish that sentence. Gemma knew she couldn't be too far from the hospital now. None of them knew how long she had, and she was getting weaker and more tired. The adventure would have to be a fairly tame affair, compared to some they'd been on in the past. Jess hoped that Gemma would be able to come up with something fitting for this final fling.

'Never you mind,' Gemma said. 'Leave it to me. I'll talk to your mum or Jake about having Edie, and I'll run it all past your oncologist. All you have to do is come along. Okay?'

Jess nodded again. Sometimes, talking was an effort. Sometimes, she needed to nap as much as Edie did.

'I'm going to leave you to have a sleep,' Gemma said.

And Jess wondered at Gemma's ability to always know what she needed. Did Gemma, perhaps, know her better than anyone else? Or was it just that Jess was always tired these days, so she was easy to read? Jess tried to focus on these questions, but the thoughts started to slip away from her, and she gave in to sleep.

When she woke again, Edie was gone. Jess stood up slowly to avoid feeling dizzy and put her dressing gown on. As she walked downstairs, she could hear voices in the kitchen.

'...any way they could have got it wrong?'

It was Jake. Jess stopped where she was, halfway down the stairs.

'I don't think so. She's really weak. You can see how much weight she's lost. And I've been with her at the appointments. They know what they're talking about, and they seem sure.'

That was Gemma.

'I'm just not ready. And I know how selfish that sounds. It's not about me, I know that. I just...'

After that, the words were muffled, and Jess imagined that Gemma was hugging Jake and he was speaking into her shoulder. Jess thought about turning around and going back to her room, but she decided that was silly. She carried on and went into the kitchen where, as she'd thought, Jake and Gemma were holding one another. It wasn't until they pulled apart that Jess saw Edie was between them, in Jake's arms. She went cold suddenly. Was this the future? Would these people she was leaving behind make up their own family? In a way, it would be wonderful. For Edie to be brought up by these two people who loved her, who Jess loved. But the stab of jealousy was overwhelming.

'Sorry to interrupt,' she said.

'Jess, we were just...' Jake trailed off.

'I know, talking about when I die. I heard.'

For a moment, nobody said anything. Jess wanted to reach forward and take Edie from Jake, but she knew she shouldn't. He was learning how to be her dad, and she knew, deep down, that she wanted to encourage that. It was just that he had all the time in the world to hold their daughter, and she did not.

'What's up, Jess?' Gemma asked.

Jess shrugged.

'Look, I can't imagine what it must be like to hear people talking about your death, but we love you. We're doing our best.'

Jess knew Gemma was right. She was always fair, always calm. But how could she explain that sometimes she was just angry with everyone for having a life ahead? How could she explain that she was jealous of the fact that Gemma and Jake might get together in the future, even if they were to say there was no chance of that happening, simply because that option was open to them? They had time, and it was the only thing she wanted. And at the same time, how could she expect them to understand how lucky they were, and how precious that time they had was? She hadn't, until hers had been cut short.

'Sorry,' she said. 'I'm just feeling a bit weird.'

'Weird how? Do we need to call someone?' Jake asked.

This is what it had come to. Her best friend and the man she'd loved, worried enough to call the hospital at the mention of her feeling 'weird'.

'No, I don't mean like that. I'm fine.'

Jake nodded and gave her a weak smile and it was only then that Jess registered that Gemma had said they loved her. Did he? Did he love her the way she loved him? It was impossible, surely. If he had any love for her left, it must by now be mixed up with pity and worry and fear. And that wasn't the same thing. She wondered, then, whether she'd had her last ever kiss. Whether that afternoon with Dan had been the end of that part of her life. A door closed. She hoped not.

There was still a little tension in the room and Jess wasn't sure how to clear it. But luckily, Gemma stepped in.

'I've made a list, of the things Jake needs to learn. First up is bath-time. Fancy a bath, Edie?' She reached forward and tickled Edie under the chin, and she laughed.

'But she always has her bath just before bed,' Jess said.

'But only because she always has, right? Just because you've always done something a certain way, that doesn't mean it's the only way to do it.'

Jess wanted to say that all the blog posts and pieces she'd read online advised bathing as part of the bedtime routine. Advised teaching your child that one thing followed another, to encourage going to sleep without getting upset. She was going to say it. But then she made herself step back. What did it matter, if they changed the routine this once? And what was the point of her sticking her oar in when they were going to have to find their way through this without her soon enough? When she was going to have to trust them and leave them to do their best for her baby.

'Fine,' she said. 'Let's do it.'

They went upstairs together and filed into the small bathroom. Jess put the lid of the toilet down and sat on it, determined not to take over. She and Gemma gave instructions and watched Jake sit Edie down on the carpet and run the bath. Gemma played with her while he put the bubble bath in and tested the temperature. And then he knelt down to take Edie's clothes off, and Jess had to bite her tongue to stop herself from telling him he was doing it wrong. There was a difference, she knew, between offering useful advice and butting in. And there was a danger in criticising. She'd been new to all this not so long ago, hadn't she, and she'd learned? Jake would get there. So although she had to hold her breath when Jake lowered Edie into the water, terrified that it would be too warm for her, she didn't say anything, and she was proud of herself for that.

Edie splashed in the water. She'd always loved bath-time, and since she'd been able to sit up, it had been so much easier. Jess looked on as Jake poured water from one of her cups to another and then on to her tummy and she giggled, lifting up her hands in her excitement and touching Jake's face. This was being a dad, wasn't it? This was bonding.

Once Edie was wrapped up in a hooded towel, Jess led them through to Edie's bedroom and showed Jake where everything was. Edie's nappies, her clothes, her hairbrush. Jess picked up her tiny hairbrush and felt something break inside her as she handed it to Jake and watched him try to brush Edie's hair as she sat on the floor, a toy car in one of her pudgy hands. Her mum had bought the hairbrush — it had come in a pack with nail clippers and a comb and she'd picked it up one day on her lunch hour, before Edie was born. Jess had held that brush and imagined not a baby but a little girl sitting on her lap, had imagined herself brushing flyaway hair and pulling it into a ponytail, or doing a plait while the little girl chattered on about the world that only existed in her imagination. Like so many things, she would have to say goodbye to that image. Or at least remove herself from it. Edie would grow to be that chatty girl, she believed, but Jess wouldn't be there to feel the weight of her three-year-old daughter on her lap.

Gemma had big plans. She was going to show Jake how to feed Edie. Show him how to peel and chop and puree apples and sweet potatoes. Jess excused herself, saying she needed to lie down. Gemma and Jake looked at her, their faces full of concern.

'Are you okay?' Jake asked.

Jess nodded, because there was nothing to say. She was tired, but she was always tired. And she could have sat through the rest of Jake's crash course in parenting, there was nothing physically preventing her, but she needed to go easy on her heart, which felt like it was cracking. It felt like she was looking into the future, like she was already gone. So Jess went back to bed and swallowed down her next dose of medication, and she picked up her book but didn't read it. Instead, she listened to the noises her friend and her ex and her daughter were making. Their laughter, their low talk. And she seethed a little. It wasn't them she was angry with. It was the cancer.

She must have fallen asleep because the next thing she knew, Jake was in the room and he was pulling the open book from her hand and watching her intently.

'Can I get you anything?' he asked.

Jess pulled the covers up, scared that too much of her thin body was showing, and thought. What did she want? She'd been eating bland food lately, because of the chemo, but her taste buds felt pretty normal today and she had no reason whatsoever to deny herself.

'Do you mind walking into town?' she asked.

Jake's brow furrowed. 'I guess not...'

'I really want a tuna and cheese melt from Dave's,' she said.

She did. As soon as she said it, her body reacted. She could almost feel herself salivating. Dave's was a sandwich shop near the school they'd both gone to, heavily frequented by Year 12 and 13 kids in their free periods. Jess and Gemma had gone there at least twice a week while they'd been doing their A Levels, and Jess had had a tuna and cheese melt every single time. And then hadn't had one at all since.

'Dave's?' Jake laughed. 'Is Dave's even still there? If it is, it's a BLT you want, surely.'

'I know what I want, thanks. And yes, I drive past sometimes and it's still there. Still full of teenagers.'

Jake went quiet and Jess wondered whether he was thinking what she was. How cruel it was that they hadn't known each other in those years. That they'd attended the same school, bought their lunch from the same sandwich shop, walked the same streets their entire lives, and never met until they were both miles away, in a different city. But then, there was nothing to say that they would have got together sooner even if they'd met earlier. Teenage years were a funny thing, and a two-year gap that felt like nothing once you were an adult seemed like something much more when you were fourteen or fifteen.

'Tuna and cheese melt it is,' Jake said, turning to go. 'Anything to drink?'

'If he still does those enormous milkshakes, can I have a chocolate one?' Jess asked.

She knew she wouldn't be able to finish it. She'd never been able to, and these days her appetite was small, but even if she just had a few mouthfuls, wasn't it worth it to be transported back to those carefree days, when she'd thought she had a life in front of her, and not just a few paltry years? Jake nodded and pulled the door closed behind him, and Jess waited for him to come back, anticipation fizzing in her tummy. Perhaps, when he returned, she would get up and they would eat at the kitchen table, like they had so many times in Manchester. Perhaps she would be able to pretend they were still a couple.

When Gemma burst through the door with Edie in her arms, it took Jess a moment to come back to the present.

'Edie just crawled!' Gemma shouted, giving the stunned Edie a high-five and dancing her around the room.

'What?'

'She totally crawled! Do it again, Edie!' Gemma set her down on the floor beside Jess's bed, and Gemma and Jess watched her as she got on to her hands and knees. She'd been doing this for a while, and then rocking forwards and backwards. Everyone had said she was getting ready to start crawling, and privately, Jess had hoped she would get to see it. As they looked on, she did her rocking and then stopped. After a few moments, she collapsed on to her tummy and started to cry. Gemma scooped her up.

'Maybe she wore herself out doing it downstairs,' she said.

'Did you film it?' Jess asked hopefully.

'No, I didn't think. I wasn't expecting it. She didn't go far, just a bit of movement forward. She'll do it again, Jess.'

She would, of course. She would crawl again and get better at it, and faster, and then she would pull herself up and start to walk, holding on to the furniture at first and then, tentatively, letting go. She would walk and she would talk and she would go to school and she would read a book and write her name and draw a picture on Mother's Day and have no one to give it to. Jess nodded, fighting tears.

'Can I hold her?'

Gemma scooped Edie up and put her on Jess's lap, and Jess pulled her close and tried to hold her against her chest, but

Edie had other ideas and she pulled away, keen to be on the move. She rolled around on the bed, grabbing her feet. Gemma looked up at Jess and they shared a sad sort of smile. Jess knew, without saying anything, that Gemma understood what she felt: that she was losing Edie, little by little. Losing her to other people and to her own independence. Perhaps that was better, in a way, than losing her all at once, when she died.

# CHAPTER THIRTY-FIVE

*Dear Edie,*

*I wanted you to know what it's like to be a daughter and a mum. We haven't had long, you and I. It's such a wonderful and fraught relationship, mothers and daughters. I wonder, sometimes, how we'd fare if I wasn't going to leave you. For the first years of my life, I idolised my mother. It was just the two of us, so I thought she was everything, because she really was. I feel like we rarely left one another's sides. She's told me, since, that we slept together in her bed until I was five, and I feel like my body remembers that. The warmth and proximity of her, her hair on my cheeks. And then when I went to school and started to make friends and meet other people's mothers, I realised that my set-up was quite unusual. That there was usually a dad at home, often a brother or a sister or two. And very slowly, I began to pull away from her. I was angry with her, for not providing me with a whole family, for trying to be enough, just on her own. We had a few turbulent years, especially when I was about fourteen. I told her I wanted to live with Dad more than once. Which was ridiculous, because he'd never shown an interest in having me to stay, let alone live with him, but must have hurt my mum nevertheless.*

*I wonder what we would argue about, Edie. I wonder what faults you would find. How would you feel about the fact that we live here, with your grandmother, rather than with your dad? How would you feel about the fact that you, like me, are an only one? I felt lonely a lot as a child, and I always swore I'd have at least three children, that I'd have a little gang who could entertain and love and help raise one another, and now here we are, and it's just you, and it always will be.*

*When I became a mother, when they placed you in my shaking arms just after I'd given birth to you, I began to look at my mother a little differently. You won't get to do that, of course. But I understood her in a way I never had before, I saw where she'd been coming from, why she'd said and done certain things. I saw, so clearly, that she hadn't always had enough money and she'd done everything in her power to hide that from me, so that I'd never have to worry. I saw that she'd had a lonely life, too, with no partner to share the burden and the joy. I saw that she'd been protective and worried, but that her refusal to let me do certain things had never once been out of malice. I was the only thing she had. And you are the only thing I have, so I know now, how it was for her. And before we get to some of those difficult years, I have to go.*

*Try not to be ashamed of your family, Edie, your particular set-up. It might be that you live with Mum but sometimes stay with your dad and that you see Gemma a lot. I don't know. I can't know exactly how it will work out. But I do know this: they'll do their best for you. They'll muddle through. Mum wasn't perfect when I was growing up, but I can't think of any examples of times she got it really wrong. She'll do as good a job as I would have done. Better, probably. All those people I've mentioned love you so much. All of them will give you the love that I would have given you. I trust that. And I'm giving you all the love I can now, while I'm still here, and just hoping that it means something.*

*Edie, you will see examples of what looks like the perfect family among your friends and classmates. You will see families who live in big houses and have fancy cars and go away on exciting holidays every summer. Families with a mum and a dad and two or three children, and maybe a dog or a cat. Don't envy these people. They will have their own things going on, I assure you. Secrets, shameful things that they hide away from the light. That perfection you think you see there, it doesn't exist. So just focus on what you have rather than what you don't, and you'll be fine.*

*I wanted you to know what it's like to be a daughter and a mum. I hope you'll get to find out.*

*With love,*

*Mum*

## CHAPTER THIRTY-SIX

Jess knew that Gemma was planning an adventure, but she didn't know what it was, or when they were going. She thought of it as their final adventure, but Gemma told her off whenever she said that. There was no denying, though, that time was short. Jess was spending a good portion of each day in bed, and she was finding it hard to manage the stairs. She was on a lot of medication. She hoped that Gemma had a clear understanding of her limitations, otherwise the adventure could turn into a disaster.

It was a Tuesday morning when Gemma appeared and said it was time. She clapped her hands, visibly excited, and Jess felt a cold stone of dread start to form in her stomach.

'We're not going too far, are we?' she asked. 'I mean, if anything happens, I don't want to be far from Edie, and Mum.'

Gemma frowned. 'Jess, trust me. I wouldn't do anything that might upset you.'

Jess considered and realised this was true. Throughout this, Gemma had been a constant, a rock. She had helped her navigate everything. The stone began to dissolve a little, and she swung round to sit on the edge of the bed. She didn't have a lot of energy, and her mum and Gemma had started to help her with getting dressed. At first, she'd been embarrassed, but that had soon passed. This body was failing her, it was running out of steam. It didn't matter what it looked like, just that it kept working for a little longer.

'What are we wearing?' Gemma asked.

'I don't know, you know what we're doing. You choose.'

Gemma pulled out a pair of jogging bottoms and a T-shirt. It was the kind of thing Jess would only have worn around the house until a few months ago, but she was pleased because she wanted to be comfortable. Gemma knew. Gemma understood. She lifted her arms and legs as required, thinking about how, at the end of her life, she was reverting to babyhood. This was how she dressed Edie, poking her limbs through little holes, manoeuvring her. And when she was dressed and she'd brushed her teeth, she made her way slowly down the stairs. The last thing she wanted was to trip and fall now and ruin this day.

Her mum was standing in the hall, holding Edie. She was obviously in on it, whatever 'it' was. She looked happy and a little nervous, and as she passed her, Jess paused and kissed Edie's forehead. She'd asked whether there was time for breakfast, but Gemma had patted her backpack and said it was all taken care of.

'Have a nice time, love,' Caroline said.

Jess felt as if she might cry and she wasn't sure why. It was something about the thought that had gone into this, the planning. And the fact that it might be her last trip out with her best friend. She thought of the teenagers they'd been, going into town on the bus and never thinking about anything more serious than which boys they liked and what they should wear. If they'd known where Jess would be these few short years later, would they have behaved differently? It was better, Jess thought, that they hadn't known. That they'd had those years of being carefree and self-centred. That's how teenagers were, after all.

Gemma opened the front door and Jess saw that there was a wheelchair outside. They must have borrowed it from the hospital or something. More planning she'd known nothing about. A few weeks ago, she probably would have railed against this, not wanting to be seen to need this help, but now, she was grateful for it. She sat down in the chair and Gemma pushed her, and her mum and Edie stood in the door and waved. It was when they got to the bus stop and Gemma put the brakes on the wheelchair that Jess knew what they were doing. They were repeating those teenage trips one last time. It was perfect. Their friendship had been built on bus trips to town, and anything else wouldn't have felt right. Jess smiled up at Gemma.

'No playlist?' she asked.

'Just you wait.'

There was a bit of a hiccup when the bus driver didn't know how to lower the ramp for disabled access, but after a couple of tries, he managed it and they were on their way. Gemma pulled *pains au chocolat* out of her bag and Jess tried to really focus on the sweetness of the chocolate and the buttery pastry.

'Thank you,' she said.

Gemma waved her words away and smiled, and Jess wondered what else was coming. And then Gemma pulled her phone out of her pocket and plugged her earphones in, putting one in her ear and handing the other one to Jess.

'Playlist?' Jess asked.

'Playlist.'

'What's the theme?'

'Just... us.'

The first song was 'Toxic' by Britney Spears, and Jess laughed as she recognised it.

'Remember?' Gemma asked.

They had loved this song. Aged about eight or nine, they had made up a dance routine to it and performed it in front of their class. Jess closed her eyes and tried to remember the moves. She thought she could probably do it now, despite not having thought about it for years and years. Memory was funny like that. It hid things away, but they were still there.

'Think of all the hours we spent practising that in front of my dad's full-length mirror,' Gemma said. 'Imagine what we could have done instead, with all that time.'

'I'm glad we did that, though,' Jess said, brushing away a tear.

Next up was 'I Kissed a Girl' by Katy Perry. This had been an obsession in their early teens. Gemma's dad had even driven them into Manchester to see Katy Perry play, and Jess had felt like she would never have a better night than that one.

Gemma pulled the earphones out. 'Sorry, we're here, but we can listen to more on the way home, and I'll send you the link to the playlist, of course.'

The bus pulled up outside the shopping centre and Gemma wheeled Jess down the ramp and along the high street. Many of the shops they'd visited as teenagers were gone now, or turned into charity shops, and Jess wasn't sure where Gemma would take her. But she decided to stop trying to guess and to just let herself be carried along by the day, by the nostalgia. So when Gemma came to a stop outside a tattoo shop, she wasn't expecting it.

'This is a stand-in for the one where we had our belly buttons pierced,' Gemma said. 'That one's gone, I'm afraid. Fancy getting something done?'

Jess laughed. They'd been fifteen, and neither one of them had asked their mum for permission, knowing that the answer would be no. Gemma had convinced Jess that they could hide it easily, and Jess remembered wanting to say that if they could hide it, was there really any point? She wasn't the type to wear tops that showed off her belly, wasn't confident enough. But as soon as Gemma had suggested it, she'd got a fizzing feeling in her tummy and she'd known she would go through with it.

'What about a tattoo?' Gemma suggested, as she pushed Jess inside.

Jess thought about it. She'd never really wanted a tattoo. Gemma had one of a mermaid on her left foot, had turned up to visit Jess at university and showed her, and Jess had felt a little wounded that she hadn't asked her to go with her. She'd asked whether it had hurt, and Gemma had shrugged, as if it wasn't her who'd had it, or she'd had it years ago. Perhaps the fact that she'd never wanted one had been tied up with the fact of being stuck with it forever. And that wasn't something she needed to worry about now.

'I don't know,' she said.

They were at the counter by then and a heavily pierced and tattooed man was looking at them expectantly.

'Sorry,' Jess said. 'I'm still thinking.'

'No hurry.'

There was a table at the front of the shop with a big folder full of designs and Gemma started flicking through it, pointing out the ones she liked. Jess tried to pay attention, tried to feel a little less detached. Of course, the fact that she didn't have a future meant that she didn't need to worry about the consequences of this, or about growing tired of the design she'd chosen, but it also meant there was very little point, didn't it?

'I love this,' Gemma said.

She was pointing to a picture of a tree in blossom. It was tiny, and Jess tried to imagine it on her wrist or shoulder.

'I don't think it's me,' she said.

Gemma closed the folder and leaned down to look Jess in the eyes, her hands on the arms of the wheelchair.

'If this was a mistake, I'm sorry,' she said. 'You don't have to have something done. I mean, obviously you don't. We can leave right now.'

'It's fine,' Jess said. 'I just don't think I want a tattoo. I never have and the fact that I don't have long left doesn't really change that. I mean, it's slightly tempting to have 'Fuck cancer' tattooed on my forehead, just to see what my oncologist says, but then what if they realise they've got it all wrong, and I have to live to eighty with it?'

Jess had been aiming for light-hearted but the mention of her living to eighty made her feel wistful, and when she looked up, Gemma's eyes were a little too bright.

'Let's go,' Gemma said. 'It was a mistake. I'm sorry.'

She flicked the brake off and moved behind Jess to push her out of the shop.

'No, wait,' Jess said. 'I could have my nose pierced. I've always wanted that.'

'Have you?'

'Yes! That's what I wanted to do when you talked me into getting my belly button pierced, but you wouldn't hear of it.'

'Harder to hide,' Gemma said, shrugging. 'Can you imagine what your mum would have said?'

'Well, we don't have to imagine. We can find out what she'd say this afternoon.'

Gemma went up to the counter. 'Can she have her nose pierced?' she asked, gesturing towards Jess.

'Sure. That's £25.'

Jess moved to get her purse from the bag on her lap, but Gemma batted her hand away. 'This is on me.'

Jess felt a bit nervous, then, and she wasn't sure why. She'd had surgery and chemo, countless blood tests. Needles were nothing to her. But she was usually in a hospital and not in a slightly grimy shop two doors down from the pound store. The man went through to a back room and Gemma followed, pushing Jess. A minute or so later, it was all over, and they were back out on the street, Jess with a small silver ring in her right nostril. It hadn't hurt, not really. And now that it was done, she felt quite excited about it. She kept reaching up to touch it, to check it was really there.

'Where next?' she asked Gemma.

Gemma smiled and pulled a packet of tobacco from her bag.

'Oh, so we're really going back in time, are we?'

'God, I wish we could.'

They'd never been proper smokers, either of them. But from the time they were fourteen until Jess's pregnancy, she'd smoked on and off. Mostly when she was drinking. She'd forgotten that these trips into town had often involved a roll-up or two. Gemma rolled two cigarettes and handed one to Jess with her eyebrows raised.

'What have I got to lose?' Jess asked, taking the lighter Gemma was holding out.

The first inhalation was like a time machine, and Jess closed her eyes and was fifteen again. She shut out the passers-by and their chatter, the sounds of cars nearby. She was with Gemma, and they were looking for something to wear to Kate's birthday, and Jess was wondering whether there was a way to find out if Dan was going without letting on that she fancied her best friend's brother. And then she exhaled, and opened her eyes, and she was still dying.

'Are you hungry?' Gemma asked.

Jess wasn't, not really, but Gemma's face was lit up with anticipation and she didn't want to ruin things.

'I could eat,' she said.

So when they'd finished their cigarettes, Gemma wheeled Jess to McDonald's, where they ate cheeseburgers and fries with vanilla milkshakes. Jess felt slightly sick halfway through and slowed down, remembering how she used to finish this meal in a couple of minutes and sometimes check the coins in her purse to see if she could afford another portion of fries.

'Not hungry?' Gemma asked.

Jess almost reached for a lie, but then she remembered that this was Gemma, and there was no need.

'Not really. I'm sorry if none of this is how you planned it.'

Gemma shook her head. 'Don't be silly. It doesn't matter. I just wanted you to have a good time, to make you laugh. We can go home at any point, just say the word.'

Jess tried to decide, objectively, whether she was having fun. It was good to be out, there was no doubt about that. She was getting so sick of her bedroom, and the whole house, and it was great to see the faces of different people and feel the air on her face. But she was tired. She was worried about falling asleep here, out in public, like an old person. She knew she couldn't stay out for much longer.

'Maybe one more stop?'

Gemma smiled. 'Perfect,' she said. 'I didn't want you to miss this next one.'

Jess didn't say anything, but she was pretty sure she knew what the final stop would be, and the closer they got, the more sure she was. They were heading for an awful 80s-themed pub which was where they'd first got served alcohol as over-confident fifteen-year-olds in heels a little too high to walk in. It had always had a reputation as a place where anyone could get served. Jess wondered whether it still did. She hadn't been inside for about four years. Once they'd turned eighteen, and could legally drink wherever they wanted to, there had been no point.

When they arrived, Jess tried to pretend she was surprised.

'The Cube, no way!'

Gemma grinned and nodded at the man standing outside with an e-cigarette who opened the door for them. It was just the same. Sticky floors, a black and white dance floor right in the middle with wobbly tables around the edge. It was empty except for a bored-looking girl behind the bar and a couple who were sitting at one of the tables, looking like they'd come into the wrong place by accident and were too embarrassed to leave.

'What can I get you?' the barmaid asked.

Gemma looked at Jess. 'What do you think? I mean, we don't have to have a proper drink, if you don't, if you can't...'

'Two vodkas and coke,' Jess said, reaching for her purse.

'Are you sure it's okay?'

'I don't know,' Jess said. 'I haven't asked recently. Not since last time I went out with you and ended up in hospital...'

At this, the barmaid raised her heavy eyebrows.

'Fuck it,' Jess said. 'Seriously, fuck it. What's the worst that could happen?'

Halfway through her drink, Jess felt like she'd had three or four. But she decided that was a good thing, because she had things to say to Gemma that it was hard to find the words for. And she thought that having lower inhibitions might help with that.

'Thank you for today,' she said.

She shouted it, over the sound of Spandau Ballet. Jess only knew the name of the band because her mum liked this song. That made her think, briefly, of all the things she didn't know.

That she'd never know, now. All the films she hadn't watched, the books she hadn't read, the songs she hadn't listened to. She'd been reading a book on and off for weeks; it was a novel about a little girl who'd gone missing and she thought it was the grandmother who'd taken her, but perhaps she'd never find out. Perhaps she'd never reach the end. And what then? If she left that book on her bedside table, unfinished, her bookmark holding her place, would that be something else for her mum to be sad about, to not know what to do with? She would put it back on the bookshelf, she decided. She would do it when she got home. Slip the bookmark out and return it to her shelf, and pretend she'd never started it.

'It's nothing,' Gemma said.

'No, it's not nothing. You know me better than anyone. And you've put a lot of thought into reminding me of some of the brilliant times we've had. It's not your fault that I'm not well enough to fully enjoy it.'

'It's just...' Gemma trailed off.

'What? You can say it, whatever it is.'

'While I've been planning this day, I haven't been missing you as much.'

Jess didn't know what she meant.

'I think about losing you all the time,' Gemma said. 'And I miss you when we're not together, even if I've seen you that day. I already feel the loss of you. And I don't want to burden you with this, because it's so much worse for you, and I just need to get over myself, but putting this adventure together was such a welcome break for my brain, because I've been thinking about when we were younger and the things we did and that's meant I haven't had to think so much about now, and the things we're facing. The things we're about to face.'

Jess took a deep breath.

'I try to think about it from everyone's perspective,' Jess

said. 'But it's hard. I try to imagine how Mum feels by putting myself in her place. I can do that so much better now I have Edie, but it's just unbearable, so I can never do it for long. And I think about how it might be for Jake, and for Edie, when she's old enough to understand what's happened. And you, of course. And then I think about people I've known but who aren't really in my life, friends from school who I hardly ever see now, friends from university. And I wonder about them, how they'll hear the news and when, and whether they'll be sad about it, and for how long. But it's pretty exhausting. My head gets in a bit of a spin with it and I have to force myself to just go back to being me. To thinking about how it is for me.'

'Yeah, that sounds pretty full on.'

Gemma laughed, and it wasn't a real laugh, but it had the potential to be.

'Do you remember that time we came in here looking for Ali Hassan, because you fancied him, and you'd heard he was coming here with his mates? And it turned out to be just him and Josh Hardman, and we spent the whole evening edging closer and closer to where they were standing in the hope that they'd come over and talk to us?'

'I remember,' Gemma said, the corners of her lips curling upwards.

'And then they finally noticed us and came over and started talking about their girlfriends, which we knew they didn't have, as if they were terrified of us? God, I haven't thought about them in years. I wonder where they are now.'

'Ali works in Costa just down the road,' Gemma said. 'Josh moved away. Uni, I think. Anyway, do you remember how that night ended? You in the corner with that dude from the college and me being sick all over Josh's shoes?'

Jess hadn't remembered that, but as soon as Gemma said it, she did. His name had been Matt, and Jess could remember the way his hands had felt on the back of her neck, the way he'd looked at her as he'd leaned in to kiss her. He'd been unshaven, and it was the first time she'd kissed someone with so much stubble. It was unusual for her to be the one who ended up with someone. Gemma killing time on her own. How had she forgotten it? And what else had she forgotten?

'Embarrassing,' Jess said. 'About the shoes, I mean.'

They both laughed, and Jess was relieved. She hoped that when Gemma looked back on this day, on the adventure she'd planned, this would be the bit she'd remember. Not Jess leaving half of her lunch or the fact that they'd had to go home early.

'Time to go,' Gemma asked.

Jess nodded, grateful that she didn't have to ask.

They didn't say much on the bus journey home. Jess was concentrating on staying awake. She couldn't wait to get back into bed, to feel her aching limbs supported and to close her eyes.

'It wasn't our best adventure,' Gemma said, a little sadly.

They were nearly back at the bus stop around the corner from Jess's house. Jess realised that Gemma hadn't bothered with the playlist on the way home.

'Maybe not,' she said. She couldn't bring herself to lie. 'But it's the one I'll remember, I think.'

## CHAPTER THIRTY-SEVEN

Jake called in, unexpectedly, the day after Jess and Gemma's adventure. Jess was lying on a sun lounger in the garden with a blanket across her knees. It had been her mum's idea. She had said that perhaps Jess would benefit from a bit of spring sunshine. Jess wasn't all that comfortable, and part of her was keen to get back upstairs to bed, but she was enjoying the feel of the cool air on her cheeks and looking at the garden, how it was coming to life.

'Hey,' Jake said, appearing on the patio, framed by the French doors.

Jess looked up and took in the sight of him. He had his hands stuffed in the back pockets of his jeans, and he was wearing a tatty black T-shirt with a couple of holes near the hem. Jess wondered whether he knew that he would always be the only man she'd ever loved. That her dying was securing that position for him, immortalising it.

'Have you come to see Edie?' she asked.

'And you,' he said.

Jess hadn't been expecting that. She'd been about to say

that Edie was inside with her mum, but then she realised that it must have been her mum who let him into the house. And he'd said he was here to see her, anyway. She couldn't help but smile at that. Jake came over. He pulled the other sun lounger a little closer to hers and sat down on the edge of it before swinging his legs on to it and adopting the same reclined position as her. Casually, as if it were nothing, he reached out a hand and took hold of Jess's. Jess felt herself catch her breath and then tried to let it out without him noticing.

'I came here to tell you something,' he said. 'Something I should have told you a long time ago.'

Jess's stomach was in knots. But she dared to hope, finally, that he was going to say the thing she'd wanted him to say for so long. Every second that passed was painful. She looked over at him and saw that he was struggling to speak. Sometimes the words wouldn't come. She knew that. But then he found them, and she let them wash over her, let them cleanse her.

'I love you, Jess. I'm sorry we spent those months apart and that I wasn't around when you had Edie. If I could go back…'

They couldn't go back, none of them could. But knowing he wanted to was enough. Jess looked at him hard. He was trying not to cry, and she hoped her eyes were making it clear that that was okay. That she didn't need him to be strong all the time.

'I just didn't know, Jess, that we'd run out of time.'

'None of us knew,' Jess said.

It was a bit dreamlike, him coming here and saying this. Jess had wanted it, and it had come to be. She wasn't sure whether she could trust it. What if Gemma had asked him to do this, to make her happy at the end of her life? She couldn't bear the thought of Gemma trying to talk him into it, telling him it wouldn't be for long and it would make Jess so happy.

'Do you mean it?' she asked.

'What? What I just said? Of course I mean it. Why would I say it, if I didn't?'

'Because I'm dying.'

He didn't say anything for a moment and when Jess screwed up her courage and looked over at him, she saw there were tears in his eyes. Her instinct was to comfort him, but she wouldn't always be able to, would she? They were all in this, the people in her life, and she couldn't make it easier for them.

'Jess, I wouldn't lie to you. Not about something as important as this. I love you. I wish I'd been a proper dad to Edie, and I wish I'd stayed with you when it mattered.'

There was so much time, Jess thought, for him to be a good dad. He'd missed out on the very start, and that was a shame, but Edie would never know if no one told her. And he had this chance, now, to change things for the better. To step up and be there. To be a parent. But she didn't say any of that because she wasn't sure she could speak it without sounding bitter. Because all the time he had, she didn't. And they both knew that.

'I wish that too,' she said.

'Can you forgive me?'

Could she? She could. What was there, in any case, to forgive? They had had that awful row, and she had told him to stay away from her, and he had. Perhaps it was she who should be asking for forgiveness. Perhaps it was she who had kept them apart.

'Yes.'

'Do you think, if none of this was happening, we could have made it work? The three of us?'

Jess closed her eyes against the pain of that question. If she hadn't had cancer, would she have got in touch with Jake? She wasn't sure. She was stubborn and she could hold a grudge. It wasn't something she was proud of, but it was part of who she was. She might well have just continued going it alone if cancer hadn't come into the picture. How cruel it was that the thing that had caused her to reach out to him was the same thing that was preventing them from having any kind of a future. How cruel it was that he loved her, and she loved him, and they couldn't be together.

'Let's pretend,' she said.

Jake looked across at her, his brow furrowed in confusion.

'Let's pretend there's no cancer. Let's see if we could make it work. Just for today.'

Jake nodded and Jess knew that he couldn't speak for tears. She got up and went inside the house, slowly. Her mum and Edie were in the living room. Edie was sitting on her playmat, knocking two wooden blocks together, and her mum was copying Edie's movements, smiling at her encouragingly.

'I need to ask you for a favour,' Jess said.

'What is it?'

'Could Jake and I look after Edie for the rest of the day?'

'I'm going out in half an hour, Gemma is coming over to look after her.'

Jess could tell by her mum's tone that she didn't approve, but she couldn't find it in her to care. She pulled her phone out of her pocket and sent Gemma a quick message to say she wasn't needed. Jess put a thank you and several kisses at the end of the message. She hoped Gemma knew how grateful she was for everything she was doing to help. The last thing she wanted was for her to feel snubbed, not needed. But on the other hand, she'd probably be glad of the free time to catch up on sleep or do something for herself. Not many women as young as Gemma were taking on childcare in addition to work when they didn't even have a baby of their own.

Jess crouched down and lifted Edie up. It was getting

harder to do. Edie was getting bigger and more mobile just as Jess was getting weaker.

'Just don't overdo it,' her mum said, watching Jess struggle with a task that had once been second nature. 'Promise me.'

'I promise. I'll get Jake to do everything.'

'I've seen the way you look at him.'

Jess was surprised. She spun around to look at her mum. 'Then you'll know that this is important,' she said.

Jess didn't feel she could relax until she heard the door shut behind her mum. She'd had a message from Gemma saying she was going to have a lazy day, and that Jess should get in touch if anything changed. Jess hadn't told her that she and Jake were looking after Edie, but she wondered whether Gemma knew, somehow. Whether she'd had a hand in this.

For the rest of the morning, Jess allowed herself to pretend that she and Jake were a normal couple, that this was their house. She fought against her tiredness and told Jake not to worry whenever he looked like he was about to say something about her going back to bed.

'Let me have this,' she said, at one point. 'I'll go to bed this afternoon, I promise.'

At ten, Jake put Edie down for her morning nap, and when he reappeared in the kitchen, Jess felt tingly with anticipation. He had told her he loved her, but he hadn't kissed her. Perhaps he hadn't meant it the way she meant it. Perhaps there was pity mixed up with that love, and no desire. She didn't look the same, after all. She was thin and bald and butchered. She wasn't the girl he'd fallen in love with. But all those thoughts disappeared when he walked into the room and kept walking until he was standing an inch away from her body. She was leaning against the kitchen worktop, and he folded her up in his arms and leaned in to kiss her.

It was like a second chance at a first kiss. Jess felt just as electric as she had the first time, just as nervous and excited and aroused. She closed her eyes and let herself fall into it, knowing this would be the kiss she would return to in her memories over her remaining weeks.

'How long does she usually sleep for?' Jake asked, his voice thick.

'At least an hour.'

'Can we go upstairs? I don't mean, I mean, it's okay if you don't want to... I just want to lie with you for a while.'

Jess laughed. It was strange to see Jake getting flustered about the suggestion of sex. When they'd been together, he'd had so few inhibitions. Jess remembered the confidence he'd had, how it had rubbed off on her a little. She took his hand and they went upstairs, to her bedroom. She lay down on the bed and he lay next to her and kissed her again. It was freeing, to just lie there and kiss the man you loved, Jess thought. It was like letting go.

Slowly, they removed their clothes. It was nothing like the frantic rushes of their early days together. Jake put his hands on her face, behind her head, on her back, and the warmth of them stilled Jess. She was trying not to think about how he would react to her scar, to her uneven breasts, to the sagging skin of her stomach. She was trying to pretend she was still the girl she'd been, before. If she kept her eyes closed, she would never have to see a flicker of disappointment or, worse, pity.

They made love lazily, as if they had all the time in the world. As if death wasn't knocking. Jess knew, somehow, that this would be the only time they would do this. The only time circumstances would allow them to be alone, together, with Edie asleep in her room. They had to make this count, because it was a last as well as a first. Jake was gentle but not so much that she felt her cancer was there with them, in the room. He said nothing about the changes to her body, and he kissed along the line of her C-section scar, and she knew she would always be grateful for that.

Afterwards, they lay side by side, the covers pulled over them. Jess wanted to say thank you, but she wasn't sure how. Wasn't sure whether it would alter something between them, cause a shift in this perfect day. So she said nothing, and they held hands, and Jess felt restored and happy and like a woman and not a patient for the first time in a long time.

She didn't remember falling asleep, but she must have done, because the next thing she knew Edie was in the room, lying between them. Instinctively, Jess put her arm around her daughter and pulled her in towards her. How many nights had they slept like this, the two of them? When Edie was teething or restless or unwell. Jess had brought her into bed with her so many times, her body aching for sleep. And Edie had kicked and rolled, moved so that her hair was tickling Jess's face, slept diagonally. Jess had lain awake, watching her, unsure how she'd get through the following day but so in love she couldn't look away. Who would hold Edie like this in the nights ahead, in all the nights to come?

For the first time, Jess wondered how long it would take Edie to know she was gone. She couldn't speak yet, of course, wouldn't be able to express her loss verbally. But she knew Jess, the sight and the smell of her. The sound of her voice. She'd known the sound of Jess's voice since before she was born. Would she miss it? And years later, when her mum or Jake or anyone played her a video clip that Jess was in, would the sound of Jess's voice strike a chord in her? There were so many things Jess didn't know and didn't know who to ask. She looked across at Jake. He'd pulled on boxer shorts and his T-shirt and he was smiling at her and Edie. He looked content. There was no way she could tell him what she was thinking.

Jake put his hand on top of Jess's, which was on Edie's shoulder, and they lay like that, the three of them connected by warmth and touch, for a few blissful minutes.

'Are we... back together?' Jake asked.

Jess nodded. 'I think so.'

She wasn't sure what difference it made, putting a label on it like that. Whatever they were to each other, they wouldn't be for long.

'Jake, I want someone to tell her that I love her, that I loved her, every single day. Can you do that? On the phone or in person or whatever. But I want her to know every day.'

'I can do that.'

'Thank you.'

It was something she'd been working up to asking her mum, but she hadn't known how her mum would respond. And anyway, Jake was the right person for the job. Because they had made her, together. Edie was part him and part her. And she felt like he understood.

## CHAPTER THIRTY-EIGHT

*Dear Edie,*

*I wanted you to know what it means to me to be back together with your dad at the end of my life. The three of us are a little unit, bound with blood, and even though it's been me and Mum raising you so far, there's something that feels so perfect about the three of us being together. If there's a lesson in this, I'm not sure what it is. Something about keeping hold of the people you love, not letting fear or jealousy or anger rip you apart. Not wasting time apart when you could be together, because you never know what's coming, or how much time you have left.*

*Truth be told, I don't know how much you'll want these letters to teach you things. Perhaps you'll just want them to be a way to get to know me a little. I can't imagine not having had a mum, and I'm sure you've felt the loss in a hundred different ways. I hope these letters can go some way towards filling that gap. Even if only for a moment. Anything I can do to close it, I will.*

*I can't help but wonder whether we'd have found our way back to each other without you, Edie. I'm not sure we would. I never stopped loving him, but we are young and not many first loves survive. But the fact of your existence, the fact of a person separate from each of us but connected to both of us, that pulled us back. That, and cancer. Now we're that tragic thing. A pair of young lovers who are about to be ripped apart by death.*

*The day after we got back together, your dad turned up at mine and mum's house. I'd wondered whether he would, whether the previous day might have been a daydream or whether it was real, but he might have gone home and reassessed, based on the awful prognosis. But he was there, on the doorstep by nine in the morning, his hair wet from the shower and a bunch of supermarket tulips in his hand. And he told me, that day, that he wasn't going anywhere. Not while I was still alive, and not afterwards. He told me that he wanted to look after you, to be a proper full-time parent, to teach you to write your name and ride your bike and to help you with your times tables. He looked like he hadn't slept much. He was slightly manic. I asked about the band, and he waved his hand, as if to say that it wasn't important.*

*You might think it was enough for me to know that there are people who want to look after you, and that they love you. That I can't know whether you'll end up with Mum or with Jake or with a combination of the two, because I won't be around to see how it all plays out. But I felt sick with worry as soon as he said the words 'full custody'. I knew that Mum wouldn't take that lying down. I knew that there would be a battle, a winner and a loser. And I wanted to make sure that the loser wasn't you. That the loser was never you. Because none of this is your fault and you shouldn't suffer from having too many people who love you, just as no one should suffer from not having enough.*

*I said that we were going to sort this out, and we went downstairs and found Mum in the kitchen, giving you your lunch. You were like a little bird, your mouth open and ready, and she was spooning something in, and you were delighted. Real food was still a novelty, and everything was exciting. I told Mum what your dad had told me, and I saw her mouth set in a line, and I knew that she was already in the midst of it all, in her mind. Arguing that she'd been there since the day you were born, making a case for Jake being young and irresponsible. I begged them, Edie, to think of you. At that point we all looked at you, and you opened and closed your mouth, wondering why there was no food in it. Wondering what had happened, with the arrival into the room of me and your dad, to knock things off kilter.*

*I made a plea. I said that you were what mattered in all of this. Not me, not my illness. Not either of them. Not Mum's mistrust or Jake's pride. Just you. I asked them to put you at the centre of everything and make this work. I told them that I wanted both of them to be a huge part of your life. I said that I was relying on them to do as I'd asked. I reminded them that I was dying. I'd tried not to play on that too much, but sometimes you have to let your awful luck work in your favour. I said that if they loved me, they would respect my wishes. They both dropped their heads, and I felt like they were beginning to understand.*

*Edie, if what I said that day hasn't worked, if you haven't lived your life being loved and looked after by Mum and your dad, if they haven't got on for the sake of you and my wishes, I am sorry. I did everything I could. I couldn't stay and referee. I couldn't stay.*

*I hope that when it was parents' evening at school, one of them went to see your teachers and the other one looked after you. I hope that he took you to swimming lessons and she took you to Brownies. I hope they made you feel that, although your set-up was different from other people's, it was a good one. I hope they made it work. I'm choosing to believe that they did.*

*There won't be many more letters now, Edie. One or two at most, I think. This one has exhausted me. The end is getting closer and I'm scared, but I'm also ready for it. I picture you reading these, and I hope they've been enough. If I'd had longer, I would have written more. I love you, now and then, as a baby, and as a young adult. I love you in a way I can't describe. I love you in every way.*

*I wanted you to know what it means to me to be back together with your dad at the end of my life. It means everything.*

*With love,*

*Mum*

## CHAPTER THIRTY-NINE

Things happened very quickly after that day, and Jess often wondered if her body understood that she'd had to hold herself together for those final, important things, and now it was giving up. Jake was around more, and there was always someone offering her something. A cuddle with Edie. A cup of tea. A piece of toast. Jess always said yes to the cuddles and, though she rarely wanted the food or drinks, she tried to say yes to those, too, when she could, because she recognised that the person offering just wanted to be able to do something for her.

One Wednesday, in the early evening, her GP came over and asked to speak to Jess alone. Jess's mum looked alarmed, but she did as she was told, shuffling out of the room and closing the door behind her.

'I've spoken to your oncologist, and she doesn't think it will be long, now, Jessica,' he said, when he was sure they were alone.

Jess looked directly into his eyes. She'd seen him with countless coughs and colds over the years. He'd done the six-week check after Edie was born. He was sad, she could see that. He looked defeated. She suspected that this wasn't part of the service. That this kind man was making this visit in his own time, after a day at the surgery dealing with chicken pox and depression and tummy bugs.

Not long now. She'd been waiting to hear these words and had expected to feel panicked by them. But actually, they came as something of a relief. She knew he was right. It was days, now, she felt. It was a matter of days. She nodded.

'I was wondering what you wanted,' the doctor said. 'I mean, whether you'd like to stay here, and have more regular visits from me and perhaps a nurse, for pain management. Or whether you'd like to go to a hospice, where you can be looked after all the time, but you won't be with your family.'

Jess had thought about this. She wanted to ask to stay at home, to spend her last few days in her childhood bed and have Edie and her mum as close by her side as possible, but she had made a decision. She didn't want them to associate that room with her dying. She didn't want them to worry and have to stay up all night and see her in pain. She wanted to free them.

'I'd like to go into a hospice,' she said.

The doctor nodded. He didn't ask if she was sure, or what her reasons were, and she was grateful for that, because she felt like she didn't have the ability to speak much more on the subject. It was a defeat of sorts, she felt. It was a giving in. But she'd always known it would come to this. At least, she'd known for long enough.

'I can talk to your mum and arrange that,' he said.

Jess nodded and hoped it would suffice as a thank you.

The doctor stood and left the room, and Jess lay there, wondering how quickly it would all happen, and what it would be like. When her grandmother, her mum's mum, had died, she had been in a hospice for her final weeks. Jess had been ten, and she remembered the smell of disinfectant and vegetables that had been cooked for too long. Whenever she'd walked down the corridor to her grandmother's room, she had found herself looking into any open doors along the way. All of them were filled with people who looked very old and very ill. But she didn't suppose they had hospices that were especially for young people. There wouldn't be much call for them.

After the doctor left, Jess drifted into a fitful sleep, and when she woke, Jake was sitting on the other side of the bed, a book in his hand. He wasn't reading, Jess noticed, he was staring into space. Perhaps he was waiting for her to wake up.

'Jake,' she said, her voice weaker than she'd expected.

He turned to face her.

'I have a job for you.'

Jess asked Jake to get her laptop from downstairs. He brought it up, frowning.

'Are you about to ask me to witness your will, or something?'

Jess laughed. 'I don't have any money. Well, hardly any, anyway. But strangely, yes, this is about that.'

Jess had made some phone calls and moved money from a couple of savings accounts and into her current account. She didn't have much, but it was all in one place and it seemed like more, as a result. She logged into her account and showed it to Jake, who whistled. It made her laugh.

'I'm going to transfer this to you,' she said. 'But I need you to promise to put it somewhere safe. I have plans for it.'

'Plans?'

'It's for Edie. I've chosen some things I want you to buy for her, for her birthdays and Christmases, from me, but I thought you wouldn't appreciate me actually buying them all now.

Plus, things change. I'm trusting you to find the equivalent if these things aren't the right things to have any more when the time comes.'

Jake was looking at her, his eyes wide. She wanted to say that she wasn't finished yet. She opened the spreadsheet she'd created, with Edie's age down the side and links to the presents she had chosen.

'I've had to guess what kind of a person she'll be,' Jess said. 'So don't buy these things if they're not right for her. I've tried not to go too far down one path or another. Nothing princessy, but nothing too tomboy-ish either. I've tried to choose games and toys that any child might like.'

Jess broke off, the poignancy of what she was saying getting to her in a way it hadn't when she had done this work. The fact that she'd tried to find presents to suit any child, and not her child in particular, was heart breaking. But the truth was that she simply didn't know who Edie was going to be. She saw flashes of possibility in her, sometimes, when she raced a car along the floor or built a tower with frowning concentration. Jess had her ideas, but she didn't know anything for certain.

'God, this is... I mean, I don't know what this is. Considerate, heart breaking, brilliant. Thanks for showing me.'

'Do you think you can do it?' Jess asked.

'Of course I will.'

Jess nodded her thanks.

'I want her to go to university, but only if it's right for her and she wants to. But don't let her not go just because she's afraid of how much it costs. Don't let that be a factor, if you possibly can. And she should go somewhere that means she has to move away. It's so much better that way. You learn so much more. How to manage a budget and how to cook and do your washing and all that stuff. If she doesn't go, kick her out anyway so she has to learn those things.'

Jess said all of this in a couple of breaths, the words tumbling out. She was scared, now, that she would run out of time to say all the things she needed to. Jake reached out a hand and put it on top of hers, and she knew it was intended to steady her. It worked.

'I promise, Jess.'

'It's going to be soon,' she said, daring herself to look straight in his eyes as she said it.

'I know,' he said.

They both began to cry, and Jake pressed his forehead against hers. Jess didn't realise how tightly she was holding his hand until she looked down and saw her tight little fist. When she pulled away, she saw that her nails had left little indentations on the back of his hand. It struck her that perhaps that's how she would have held on to him in labour, if he'd been there.

'If you're with someone else…'

'Don't do this, Jess.'

'No, I have to. It's okay. I don't expect you to never meet anyone else. You're twenty-three! I want you to be happy, I really do. I just have one thing. I want Edie to always know that I was her mum.'

Jake looked confused.

'Of course she'll always know. What do you mean?'

'I mean, if you met someone in, say, a year, when she was still little, she might think that…'

Jake put a hand on the back of Jess's head and gently tilted it upwards, so that she was looking into his eyes.

'I would never do that, Jess. No one is going to erase you. I'll show her photos and videos and talk about you. She'll know you, Jess. She will.'

'Thank you.'

Jess didn't doubt that he meant it, but she knew how things could change over time. How she would fade and get further away. How someone new that he fell in love with would become everything. But there was nothing more she could do. She'd made herself clear. She had to trust him. Him and her mum and Gemma: trust them with Edie, and with her memory.

Jake put a film on after that, on Jess's laptop. It was one of her favourites, *About Time*, and she remembered that he'd refused to watch it with her more than once when they were first together. It had been a couple of years since she'd last seen it, and she thought, then, about what moments she would revisit if she could travel in time. Would she go back to that argument with Jake, and do things differently? Would she go to the doctor much earlier, so they could catch the cancer and she might have a chance at recovery? She would do both of those things, and more. She looked up at Jake. His eyes were fixed on the screen. She wished she had the words to tell him that, if she had a life ahead of her, she'd want to spend it with him.

'I can't believe I had to get terminal cancer for you to agree to watch this with me,' she said. She was going for humour but neither of them laughed.

Jess was sleepy and knew she wouldn't be able to stay awake until the end.

'Will you stay, until I'm asleep?' she asked.

Jake leaned over and kissed the top of her head. 'Of course I will.'

Jess closed her eyes and let the familiar words bounce around in her head. She could see the images without looking at the screen. She resolved to ask Gemma to gather her favourite films and songs for her to listen to in her final days.

It would be comforting to die that way, with the sounds she'd loved playing in the background. And then suddenly, she jerked awake, sitting up and gasping for breath.

'What's happening?' Jake asked, his voice full of fear. 'Jess, are you okay?'

'I'm scared, Jake. I'm scared of dying.'

It was the first time she'd said it, but it was the truth. She'd been so busy trying to make sure everything would run smoothly without her that she'd hardly given any thought to the actual mechanics of what was going to happen to her. Would she just fall asleep, drift away, or would it be violent and painful? She had never seen anyone die, and she didn't know.

Jake was holding her very tightly. He was rocking her, slowly, back and forth. It was comforting, like being a child again. And that's how she fell asleep, in his arms, on her bed, her fear abated for now, but lurking just below the surface.

# CHAPTER FORTY

When Jess's GP confirmed that her place in the hospice was going to be available the following day, Jess knew she was going to have to say her goodbyes. She hadn't told anyone about the hospice, or her plan to be alone there. She didn't want any of them to see her die. It was bad enough that they'd seen her like this, in pain and losing weight and barely anything left of the person she'd been. She wanted to say goodbye on her terms and then go. Whatever the last few days held, she would face them on her own.

So when her mum came into the bedroom with Edie and Jess awoke from a nap, Jess decided it was time.

'I need to talk to you about something,' she said. She knew that her voice conveyed that this was something serious, something important. By then, though, everything was important. Everything was intensifying with each day that passed. There were rarely conversations about trivial things, by this point.

Caroline sat down on the edge of the bed and put Edie down between them. Jess reached to touch her daughter's face, and Edie broke into a grin and Jess saw that a new tooth had broken through. Edie's third. Already, she was losing touch with what was happening in her baby's life.

'Doctor Osborne has booked me into a hospice,' she began.

Caroline breathed in sharply, audibly. 'But you should be here! I thought you wanted to be here, at home, where we can look after you.'

'And I have been,' Jess said. 'But I don't want to die here. I don't want this house and this room to be forever associated with that. I don't want you to avoid coming in here because of the memories. I want you to be able to remember when I was seven and I had pink wallpaper and my doll's house in the corner, and when I was sixteen and covered the door and walls in pictures from magazines. I've thought about this a lot, Mum, and I want to say goodbye to you all and then go to the hospice. I don't want you to visit once I'm there.'

Caroline's face had softened while Jess had been speaking about her childhood, but it hardened again when Jess said those final words.

'But I don't want you to be on your own! I can't let you do that, Jess.'

'It's not up to you, though, and it's a decision I've thought about a lot. I want to say my goodbyes while I'm still well enough to say them.'

Caroline went quiet. She was crying but she wasn't making any sound. They both looked at Edie. Jess thought they were probably thinking the same things. How cruel it was that she would never know her mother. How sad it was that Jess was leaving her, and Edie had no idea.

'I've asked Dad to come round later,' Jess said.

She knew her mum would hate this, too. But she was putting herself first, in this.

Caroline raised her eyebrows. 'Later, when? Shall I make dinner?'

Jess wanted to hug her then and thank her for understanding. She had never sat at a table with her mum and her dad and had a meal. She hadn't expected it to happen, but once her mum suggested it, she couldn't stop thinking about it. She would get up, sit at the table for the first time in weeks. She would make an effort to eat something. And she would say goodbye to the people who'd brought her into the world. The one who'd been everything to her, and the one who'd been almost nothing. And with each goodbye, she'd be a little bit more ready to slip away.

Jess spent most of the day drifting in and out of sleep, but the dinner was arranged for seven, and at six, Gemma arrived to help her get ready.

'Can you believe the three of us have never sat at a table and eaten a meal together?' Jess asked, as she moved her legs to the side of the bed and started to get up, leaning on Gemma for support.

Gemma looked concerned.

'What?'

'I just hope you're not putting too much hope into this one evening. Your parents don't get on, you know that. That's why you've never had a meal together. I just don't want you to expect it to be perfect, tonight, and be disappointed.'

Jess thought this over. It was true that a part of her had hoped for something great to happen. It wasn't that she wanted her parents to get back together – she wasn't a child, and she wasn't going to be around to see what happened anyway, but she had entertained thoughts of them bonding over how well she'd turned out and how they felt about her. The rational part of her knew it would be nothing like that. But she didn't know how to tell Gemma that if they just took their positions and played their parts, ate their dinner without screaming at one another, that would be enough for her. That would be something her younger self would never have dreamed could happen.

'I won't be disappointed,' she said.

'What are we wearing?' Gemma asked.

Jess thought about the clothes in her wardrobe, how most of them drowned her now. She'd been living in pyjamas, changing them every day. Her mum had bought her plenty of new pairs to keep her going. Jess acknowledged this, silently. Her mum had done so many things, these past few months, to keep her going.

'Just comfy trousers, maybe a nice black top,' Jess said.

Gemma said nothing, just went over to Jess's wardrobe and found the clothes she'd asked for. All the time she was helping to get Jess dressed, she was quiet, her face lined with a frown. She reached for the wig that lived on a stand on top of Jess's chest of drawers and held it out, raising her eyebrows.

'Yes please,' Jess said.

Gemma walked over and helped put the wig on Jess's head. She was close enough that Jess could smell her floral perfume, and the mint she was sucking.

'What is it?' Jess asked.

Gemma smoothed the wig and held out a mirror for Jess to see her reflection. She looked gaunt, and pale, but it was as good as it was going to get, at this stage.

'I'm just wondering when my goodbye will be,' Gemma said. 'I mean, is this it? Tonight?'

'No,' Jess said, shaking her head to blink away her tears. 'Tomorrow. I thought you could take me to the hospice, if you don't mind.'

Gemma nodded. 'Okay,' she said, 'tomorrow.'

She helped Jess walk down the stairs and then she took

Edie, calling over her shoulder that she'd bring her back in the morning, and she was gone.

Jess's mum had laid the table with care. Three places. Throughout her childhood, Jess and her mum had sat opposite one another, talking about Jess's schoolwork and her friendships as they ate the food Caroline had cooked for them. Jess realised something she'd never noticed before – it had always been about her. She couldn't recall her mum telling any stories about her own work or life. It was like that, she guessed, being a mother. And then she had to stop herself from thinking about all the meals she wouldn't share with Edie, because there was a knock at the door and her dad was here.

Caroline had made a chicken pasta dish that had always been one of Jess's favourites, and Jess was grateful, despite having almost no appetite. She sat down in her usual spot and her dad sat next to her, her mum opposite, in the space she'd occupied for all of Jess's life. It was a little awkward, because it was so unusual, and Jess longed to fill the silences with stories and life, but she didn't really have the energy.

'This doesn't feel real,' Jess's dad said. 'That we're saying goodbye, I mean. It just feels like there must be something else they can try...'

'Tony, you haven't been to a single appointment or treatment session. It's ridiculous to come in now, at the end, and say they haven't tried hard enough.'

Jess sighed. Perhaps this had been a terrible idea. But she couldn't have gone without seeing her dad, could she? However little he'd been involved, there was no getting away from the fact that he was her father.

'Dad, it's okay. Everyone has done everything they can, and this isn't anyone's fault. It's just time. It's just luck.'

He hung his head. None of them had eaten much, but Caroline stood up and started collecting the bowls anyway.

When she was in the kitchen and they could hear her scraping the uneaten food into the bin, Jess's dad looked up at her beseechingly.

'Should I go? I mean, the two of you must have things to talk about. I feel like I shouldn't be here.'

'Give it half an hour,' Jess said. 'Mum's made a cheesecake. And we can do our talking later.'

But even as she said it, Jess felt tired at the thought of staying up much longer. When Caroline appeared with the cheesecake dish in one hand and bowls in the other, Jess smiled.

'My favourite,' she said.

Her mum had made this lemon cheesecake for Jess over and over. Every birthday, every Christmas, every minor or major celebration. Jess was determined to eat a slice. Because she knew it was the best thing she'd ever tasted. And she knew it was made with love. She caught a look that passed between her parents and wondered what it was. Reconciliation, perhaps. Not permanent, but an agreement to put their differences aside for this one evening, for the time it would take them to eat this one dessert. Jess hoped so.

'Thank you,' Jess said, taking the bowl her mum was holding out to her.

No one said anything while they ate, and Jess knew that she wasn't the only one forcing herself to eat. Her mum was broken, she knew. Making her daughter's favourite dinner for the final time had broken her. Jess wasn't sure she would ever be the same again, and she didn't know whether there was anything she could do about that. And her dad looked old and tired, and like he was so full of regret that it was starting to cause him pain. Jess had thought that they might spend this evening going over old memories, but none of their memories was shared, so it didn't work. She had a handful of memories with her dad, and a million with her mum, but none that crossed over. And she knew that if she brought anything up, it would only serve as a way for her parents to bicker over their respective roles in her life.

'Jess, I need to say something,' her dad said, as he put the spoon in his empty bowl and pushed it away from him. 'I'm sorry. I'm sorry for everything I never was to you.'

Jess felt tears spring easily to her eyes. She had waited twenty-two years for him to say something like this. Would he have ever said it, if she hadn't been dying?

'I wish I could make it up to you, but it's too late now.'

'It isn't,' Jess said. Both of her parents turned to look at her, as if they thought she might suddenly say that it had all been an elaborate joke. 'I mean, you can make it up to me by being a granddad to Edie. I always felt different and like I was missing something, and I know she will too. But I want that to be minimised as much as possible. I want her to be surrounded by love.'

Jess's dad nodded his agreement. 'Of course.'

'Don't bullshit me, Dad. If you have no intention of being in her life either, just walk away. Don't pretend you're going to do one thing and then do another after I've died.'

'I just... I'm not sure I know how,' he said. 'I've never known how to get close to people. I just feel like there's something missing in me.'

Jess ignored her mum's thinly disguised snort of amusement and kept her eyes fixed on her dad's.

'All I'm asking you to do is try,' she said. 'That's all. I'm not expecting you to suddenly be grandfather of the year. I just want her to know you, and to be able to come to you. I want her to feel safe and loved. Just be with her, that's all.'

'I can do that.'

He looked like he was going to cry, and Jess almost wished

he would. It would help her to know that she had meant something – anything at all – to this man, who was virtually a stranger.

'Okay then. Now I think I owe Mum a bit of time alone,' Jess said.

Her dad stood up to leave and Jess saw him to the door. He put on his jacket and Jess opened the door. It was dark and a little bit windy, and Jess shivered.

'I couldn't have known, when your mum told me she was having you. I couldn't have known that you'd turn into this assured, wonderful young woman.'

Jess was taken aback.

'I got it wrong, Jess. And I'm so glad Jake is getting it right. And I'm so, so sorry.'

He pulled her into a hug that took her breath away, and she was almost lifted off her feet by the force of it, and then he released her, and he was gone. She hoped he would keep his promise, and spend some time with Edie, because Edie would teach him how to love, this man who had never really known. That was the great gift that children had. Jess closed the door and leaned heavily on it, before going back to the dining room where her mum was clearing away the dishes.

'Let's leave that,' Jess said.

But even as she was saying it, she felt bad, because in the morning she was going to leave this house for good, and she wouldn't have to worry about the dishes that needed washing or loading into the dishwasher, and her mum would still be here, daughterless and yet expected to carry on.

'It's done,' Caroline said, straightening up.

'Can I make you a cup of tea? You sit down.'

Caroline left the room and Jess put the kettle on to boil. She thought about all the things her mum had done for her over the years, all the meals she'd cooked in this kitchen. The scraped knees she'd kissed, the crafts she'd helped with, the stories she'd listened to. Did it feel like it was all for nothing, in the end, if your child died? She hoped not. She thought of Edie, the things she'd done for her. The fact that she'd never regret a single second of it. The kettle had boiled without her noticing. She took a teabag from the cupboard, reached into the fridge for the milk. This was the last thing she was going to do for her mum. She tried to do it with love.

When she took the tea into the lounge, her mum was sitting on the sofa, and her eyes looked like they were focusing on something that wasn't really there. Jess wondered whether she was going over old memories, too. Perhaps she could see Jess in this room as a baby, as a toddler. Perhaps she was wishing she could go back. Not to do it differently, but just to do it again. The years ahead were bleak, but the years behind were gone.

Jess wanted to say thank you, but it didn't seem enough. This woman had raised her, and now she was leaving her with another child to raise. And she didn't know whether that was compensation or just another achingly hard job. Edie would need so much, over the years, and Caroline was getting older. She shouldn't be starting again, like this. But what was the alternative? It was too late, now, to start changing their minds.

'Do you remember when I was about seven or eight and we went to that theme park and it rained all day?' Jess asked.

Her mum smiled, and Jess knew she was remembering.

'It was so quiet and there were no queues and we went on that rollercoaster about six times in a row. That was such a good day.'

'I hated that rollercoaster.'

Jess was surprised. She tried to pull up some more images from the day. She had loved every second of it, had thought her mum did too.

'Did you really?'

'It scared the life out of me. We were supposed to take one of your friends with you that day. Lucy Brand, remember her? Anyway, she had the flu and couldn't come, and it was too late to ask anyone else. And I just knew I'd have to go on all the rides with you.'

Jess could remember the rollercoaster gliding to a stop, looking across at her mum and asking if they could stay on and go around again. Her mum saying yes. But she couldn't picture the look on her mum's face. It was like a smudge on a screen that she couldn't wipe clean.

'I thought...' Jess didn't know how to finish the sentence. She had thought her mum was having the time of her life, just because she was. Just as Edie probably thought she loved to read that book about the cat and the mouse over and over.

'It's what mums do, isn't it?'

It was, Jess saw. 'You don't have to take Edie there,' she said, attempting humour.

'I think I'll leave that to Jake. Or Gemma.'

'Do you think they'll get together?' Jess asked.

Her mum shot her a surprised look. 'Jake and Gemma? No, love, why would you think that?'

Why did she think that?

'I don't know. I just, they're together a lot at the moment and they get on well. They kissed once, you know. Before we got together.'

'Jess, those two love you. They're together because they're trying to help you. That's all.'

Jess nodded, blinking away tears.

'I'm sorry I invited Dad over,' she said.

'You don't need to be sorry. I'm sorry you don't have a better dad.'

They were silent, then. Jess was going over their arguments, the cruel things she'd said when she was a teenager, the rage she'd seen, sometimes, on her mother's face. And then the times they'd worked so well, cooking dinner side by side, shouting out answers in unison while watching quiz shows on TV, taking care of Edie.

'I need to go to bed,' she said. She wished she could make the evening last longer, but she was exhausted.

'Okay,' her mum said, getting up and preparing to help her up the stairs.

When Jess was in her pyjamas and she'd brushed her teeth, she got into bed, her body aching with tiredness. Her mum stood in the doorway.

'Thanks, Mum,' she said.

And she hoped her mum knew, that she didn't just mean for the help that evening, or since she'd got ill. She hoped her mum knew that she meant all of it. Every last thing.

# CHAPTER FORTY-ONE

When Gemma turned up in the morning, with Edie, Jess felt a primal urge to say she wasn't ready. It had seemed right, this hospice plan, these considered and planned goodbyes, but now it felt like it was happening too quickly, like she'd lost control of it. She lay down with Edie for an hour while Gemma sat downstairs with her mum, and she tried to put a fraction of the love she felt for her daughter into the way she touched her. It was impossible, she knew that. All she could hope was for someone – the people she was leaving behind – to tell Edie what she had meant to Jess. To show her photos and the letters and tell her, over and over, that she was loved.

Edie slept and though Jess ached to sleep too, she stayed awake, because this was the last time she would spend with her baby. When Edie woke, she sat up and gave Jess a sleepy grin, and Jess felt her heart twisting, felt it crack. She put her arms around Edie and kissed her on the head, and Edie put one chubby hand on Jess's throat, and it left a mark. And Jess imagined how her body would look if every touch of Edie's had left a permanent mark. Criss-crossed with fingerprints. A map of love.

'Do everything, Edie,' she whispered. 'Be everything.'

And then she had to stop, because she was crying, and her tears were falling on to Edie's hair, and Edie was beginning to struggle because Jess was holding her too tightly. Not quite one year old, and ready to break free.

She called Asha. Thanked her for being so kind.

'How are you doing?' Asha asked. 'I mean, really.'

'Most of the time I have a handle on it,' she said. 'But every now and again, it just crushes me, how unfair it all is.'

'Did I tell you that I lost my twin sister to breast cancer?' Asha asked.

Jess was stunned. 'No.'

'We'd just turned thirty. I trained to be a nurse afterwards. I wanted to help people like her. You remind me of her in some ways. She was mostly accepting, mostly calm, while the rest of us were screaming about how it wasn't fair.'

'What was her name?' Jess asked.

'Pari. It means angel. She was nothing like an angel. She was the naughty one, when we were children. Full of mischief.'

'I'm so sorry,' Jess said.

'Thank you. I just told you because I wanted you to know that the people you leave behind, they do survive it. And sometimes it shapes them in a positive way.'

'Thanks,' Jess said. 'Thank you for telling me.'

After the call, Jess called to Gemma to help her bring Edie downstairs. She looked around her bedroom while she waited for her friend to appear. It was full of memories. The air was thick with them. But she couldn't bring herself to care, too much. What was a room when you were saying your goodbyes to the people you loved? She closed the door behind her and gave Gemma the closest thing to a smile she could manage.

'Let's go,' she said.

The arrangement was this: Gemma would drive Jess and Edie to the hospice, help her settle in. And then when Jess was ready, Gemma would take Edie home. Later that day, Jake would visit for the last time. It was Jess's plan, and she was determined not to back out of it. She was saying her goodbyes one by one, she was taking back control. But it didn't make it any easier.

Downstairs, Jess's mum held her tight.

'I'm sorry,' she said.

Jess was taken aback. 'What for?'

'For the things I didn't get right. For taking Edie, for being difficult about Jake. For not giving you a reliable father.'

Jess didn't know what to say. They were standing in the kitchen, their faces too close together for people who weren't hugging. They were both crying.

'What about the things you did get right?' she said. 'What about those? Too many to count.'

And then neither of them said anything else, because they couldn't. After a loaded minute or two, Jess kissed her mother's cheek and walked away. Gemma was putting Edie's car seat into the car, and Jess got into the back seat and held Edie's hand for the twenty-minute drive to the hospice, her face wet with tears that she was sure would never stop.

Jess hadn't wanted to visit the hospice before being admitted, because she had known that she wouldn't want to go there. That she might back out of the whole thing if she saw how depressing it was there. Gemma had visited and given it the nod. When they pulled up outside, Jess wasn't disappointed or pleased. It was just a building where she was going to die. Gemma carried the car seat inside, and they were greeted by a nurse who showed Jess to her room.

She'd expected that old people smell, but the hospice

smelled of nothing. It was like a blank space. In her room, there was a single hospital bed with pale pink covers, cream-painted walls. Darker pink curtains. There were a couple of pictures on the walls, of flowers. It was nothing that Jess would have chosen, but it was nothing she could find fault with, either. Gemma helped her to get into her pyjamas and she climbed into bed. And for a while, Edie lay beside her while Gemma unpacked Jess's wash things and folded her pyjamas and underwear into the drawers.

'Will you come here, to get my stuff, afterwards?' Jess asked. It was the first time she'd thought about that, but she knew she didn't want her mum to come. It was best, she thought, if her mum never saw this place. If this was a part of Jess's life she knew nothing about.

'Of course,' Gemma said.

Edie was teething. Her cheeks were red, and she had a runny nose. She began to wriggle, and Gemma picked her up and put her down on a playmat she'd brought for the floor. Edie was crawling well by then, just starting to pull herself up to standing when there was something solid at the right height for her. She did it then, with Jess's bedside table, and Jess gave her a little round of applause.

'I thought I might see her first steps,' she said.

Gemma looked at Jess but didn't say anything. What was there to say? It didn't really matter, Jess thought. She'd been longing to see it but even if she did, she wouldn't see her run or jump or be there when she lost her first tooth or when she started her period.

'Don't let Jake forget to tell her about periods,' she said.

Gemma laughed, and Jess did too. Over the past few weeks, Jess had given Gemma countless instructions like this, and every time, Gemma assured her that she would or wouldn't do the thing that was most pressing in Jess's mind.

'I won't let him forget,' Gemma said.

They both looked at Edie. She'd fallen from standing on to her bum, and she was grinning up at them, a string of dribble hanging from her mouth. Gemma leaned down and wiped it with the bib Edie was wearing. They were still and quiet, the three of them. There wasn't much left to say, or to do.

'Do you want me to leave you two together for a bit?' Gemma asked, at last.

Jess did want that, but she knew she couldn't look after Edie on her own anymore. She needed someone else there, in case Edie fell or twisted out of her grasp. She didn't have the strength.

'It's okay,' she said. 'Could you just bring her here to me again?'

Gemma did as Jess asked and then retreated to a corner of the room. Jess knew that she was trying to make herself invisible while still being there in case Jess needed her, and she appreciated it. She couldn't have asked for a better friend. Jess was lying on her back, and she placed Edie on her tummy, sitting up.

'Baby girl,' she said. 'There's so much to say and now I can't think of any of it.'

Edie babbled. She wasn't so far away from saying 'mama'. Jess closed her eyes against the pain of that.

'I knew you, baby girl, and you knew me. You won't remember, but it's true. We were the very best of friends.'

Jess took hold of Edie's hand and pressed it to her own.

'I won't be there when you start school or fall in love or get that job or have a broken heart. I won't be there, physically. But I'll be here, in your heart...' Jess put hers and Edie's hands to Edie's chest. 'I love you, baby girl. And I'm leaving you in the safest hands I know. I need you to look after Nanna, because she's going to be really sad. And Daddy too.'

'And me,' Gemma said. She was crying, her voice shaking.

'And Gemma. They're all going to be sad, for a while. But they're going to be okay, because you're going to fix them. They all love you so much, and their love for you will get them over their sadness. And then when you're older, and you learn about losing me, you might be sad, and they'll repay the favour. It's all about the love, Edie.'

Jess pulled Edie to her chest and Edie didn't resist. Jess wondered whether a part of her knew, somehow. She was quiet, and she snuggled into Jess's shoulder and Jess held her and tried to remember the weight and warmth of her body, the particular sensation of Edie's head resting against her neck, the snuffly sound of her baby's breath. Jess closed her eyes and tried to fix this moment in her mind, so she could keep it with her in the coming days, when things got tough. She put her hands underneath Edie's T-shirt, felt her soft, soft skin. And then, at last, she held Edie a little bit away from her, so she could gaze into her eyes. Their faces were close, their eyelashes almost touching. Edie laughed, thinking it was a game of some kind.

'You are the greatest love of my life,' Jess said. And then she broke down, and when Gemma came and lifted Edie out of her arms, she didn't resist.

'Shall we go?' Gemma asked. 'Shall I take her?'

The two women were crying. Jess could hardly see.

'Yes please,' she said. 'And thank you for all of it. You'll never know, really. It's meant the world to me. To us.'

Gemma had strapped Edie into the car seat and Jess was purposely not looking at her. She wanted to keep hold of the memory she'd just made — Edie's body against hers, her eyes bright, her little laugh. Gemma leaned down and took Jess's body in her arms and Jess could feel how insubstantial she was, these days. She was almost weightless. She was almost gone. But not quite.

'I don't know what I'll do without you,' Gemma said. 'I wish I didn't have to find out.'

'I love you,' Jess said.

Gemma kissed the tips of her fingers and pressed them gently on to Jess's forehead. And then she released Jess and turned to go, and Jess closed her eyes until she heard the door close behind them.

## CHAPTER FORTY-TWO

Jake came after lunch, as planned. One of the staff had brought Jess a plate of sandwiches with a few crisps, and a yoghurt. She hadn't touched any of it. The plate was still sitting on her tray table, along with a cold mug of tea. When Jake appeared in the doorway, he looked over at it.

'Not hungry?' he asked.

'No.'

Even though she'd already said goodbye to three of the most important people in her life, Jess had no idea what to say to Jake. All those years they'd been at school together and never met, then they'd had those couple of years, lost one another, and come back together when it was almost too late. It was painful, the unfairness of it.

Jake walked slowly across the room and sat down on the edge of her bed.

'I don't want to do this,' he said.

'Goodbye?'

'Yes. I don't know whether I can.'

He looked like he'd been crying. He looked tired. Jess reached out and took his hand. It was a little cold.

'Are you sure about doing it this way? About none of us seeing you after today?'

Jess nodded her head. She didn't want to allow room for doubt. 'I can't keep saying goodbye over and over, and if I don't say goodbye each time, I'll never know. I think this is the best way.'

Jake nodded, and Jess wondered whether he agreed, or whether he just thought it was best to let her choose, at this stage.

'How's Edie?' she asked.

Jake shrugged. 'She's okay. She's the only one who is. She's lucky not to understand.'

'Well, she might not feel that way when she's older and she does understand. She might feel angry that she missed out on the chance to say goodbye properly and didn't get to have me around. You'll need to help her through that.'

'I know.'

He looked a little overwhelmed, then, and Jess worried that she'd gone too far.

'All of you, I mean, not just you. You all need to help her through that. Look, I know this is a lot. You weren't a dad until recently and now… this. It's ridiculous. Unfathomable. But it's happening anyway. Don't feel like you have to do everything and get it all right. It's hard, all this parenting stuff. It's so hard. Just do your best for her. That will be plenty.'

Jake looked at Jess, hard, and she wondered which would be the first of them to cry. Which would be the first to say goodbye, how he would leave, and when.

'I want so much to get it right,' he said. 'She needs me.'

Jake was making small circles on her thumb with his hand.

He leaned in, then, and kissed her, and she gestured for him to get up next to her on the bed, and he did. They'd slept together in a single bed in her student room in halls and she had loved it, their bodies pressed close like that. But he moved a lot in his sleep, and she knew he'd found it difficult. Now, he lay alongside her for the final time, put his hand on the small of her back. They were facing one another, breathing slowly.

'I would have spent my life with you,' he said. 'More kids, marriage, all of that.'

'Do you believe we get another chance?' she asked, in a whisper.

'What do you mean? Reincarnation?'

Jess wasn't sure what she meant. She was just hoping this wasn't the end of everything. 'Reincarnation, ghosts, heaven. Just... something.'

'I don't know, Jess. I hope so.'

'I'm scared,' she said.

'Me too.'

She felt her eyes getting heavy, and she must have drifted off to sleep, because the next thing she knew, Jake was sitting in the armchair in the corner of the room.

'What time is it?' she asked, and then she wasn't sure why it mattered.

Jake looked at his watch, his eyes glassy. 'It's a little after four.'

It won't be today, Jess thought. But it might be tomorrow. She had so little energy, so little drive. It was getting harder to speak. Harder to stay awake. She was glad she'd had this day, and that they wouldn't have to see her deteriorate further. She hoped, once Jake had gone, that it would be quick. Tomorrow would be fine. The day after. She didn't want it to drag out.

'I think it's time,' she said.

Jake raised his eyebrows at her, surprised.

'Not for me to go,' she said. 'For you to go.'

'I don't want to go,' he said, getting up and coming back over to the bed.

'I don't want you to go either,' she said. 'But I'm so tired. And I don't want you to remember me like this.'

'Do you know how I'll remember you?' he asked. He pulled his phone out of his pocket and started scrolling through his photos. Jess wondered what he was going to show her. 'Like this.'

He passed his phone to her and she looked at the girl on the screen. Her, undoubtedly her. Healthy, vibrant, young. Laughing. Her eyes dancing. She remembered the party where it had been taken, how they'd arrived, holding hands, and she had drunk a bottle of wine and danced, her head thrown back. But that was later, the dancing. She had been beautiful, Jess realised. Why had she never known?

Jess passed the phone back to Jake, trying to smile.

'I'll always see you like that, but with Edie superimposed into the picture, because it just seems like she's always been with you, now.'

Jess smiled properly at that. 'It does, doesn't it? Imagine if I hadn't had her.'

Jess didn't say what she was thinking, which was that if she hadn't had Edie, she wouldn't be leaving anything behind. No legacy. Despite the pain of leaving Edie, there was some reassurance there, that a part of her was living on. That Edie would grow up and do all the things she hadn't managed to do.

'I can't,' Jake said. 'And I've only known her such a little while.'

'She gets under your skin,' Jess said. 'Latched on to my

heart the second I saw her. It was like a thunderbolt, like something you see in films. Love isn't a big enough word.'

'What is?' Jake asked. 'We should come up with one.'

'One what?' Jess was confused.

'A big enough word, for how we feel about Edie.'

'I'm not sure we could.'

Again, Jess became aware of herself drifting off to sleep. She didn't want to, because she wanted to get this done, to say goodbye to Jake and see him leave and know that she was finished. She was planning to write a final letter to Edie, and then she would let herself relax. She would have finished with her body, then. But there was no stopping this sleep, which came over her like a wave. When she woke, the room was empty, and she felt a little cold.

She began to cry and pressed the button for a nurse. Within a few seconds, one appeared. He was young and he looked tired, and Jess wondered how long he'd been on shift.

'Did my boyfriend leave?' Jess asked.

She was cross with herself as soon as she said it. This man was here to take care of people who were dying. He had better things to do.

'I think so,' he said. He came into the room and picked something up from the chest of drawers. 'Looks like he left something,' he said.

It was a piece of paper, torn from the notepad she used for her letters to Edie. In big capital letters, he'd written:

I WATCHED YOU SLEEP, AND THE BEST I COULD
COME UP WITH WAS FLOOGLE.
I FLOOGLE YOU, JESSICA. AND I'LL FLOOGLE OUR
GIRL AS LONG AS I LIVE.
SEE, WE DIDN'T HAVE TO SAY
GOODBYE, AFTER ALL.

'Are you okay, Jess?'

Jess hadn't realised the nurse was still standing there, in the doorway of her room. She looked across at him. She didn't know how to answer.

'Do you want me to call him? See if he can come back?'

'No,' Jess said. 'No, thank you.'

## CHAPTER FORTY-THREE

*Dear Edie,*

*I wanted you to know so many things. I wanted to tell you them in person, as you grew. But it wasn't to be. I'm writing this final letter from my hospice bed. I'm not scared. I know about pain, and when it gets too much, it will just end. That doesn't worry me. It's just you I worry about. I relied on my mum so much when I was growing up. I still do. And you'll never have that. I would do anything for you to have that.*

*Summer is coming. The sun is getting stronger, and I love to feel it on my face, on my arms. I'm so grateful I got to see the blossom and the daffodils one last time. I'm grateful I got to show them to you, your arms around my neck, your cheek touching mine. God, I love you. More each day, each minute. Occasionally, I see you as an older child, or even a young woman. And I weep each night at the reality that I will never see those things come to pass.*

*Sometimes, I'm relieved that this is happening when you are too young to understand it. That you won't have to grieve, or worry about me, or even really know you've lost me. And yet it's the other side of that that causes me so much pain; that the photos people will show you of me will mean nothing to you. That I'll be a stranger to you. And that's why I wanted to write all of this down, really. And why I've been honest about it all, keeping nothing from you. I wanted you to know me, at least a little bit. I wanted you to have a mum, if only on paper.*

*I've thought for a long time about telling you the whole truth in these letters. I know some of it must be hard to read. But I wanted you to know the entire story, to really understand the people in your life and how they acted when things got as bad as things get. I've asked Gemma to give these letters to you when she thinks you're old enough to read them. I imagine you, fifteen or eighteen or twenty, and I wonder whether they're all still in your life. I know that Mum and Jake will be, providing nothing's happened to them. I'm sure Gemma will be. I hope that Dad is. That he's woken up to how wonderful you are. Edie, I'm sorry. I'm sorry that I couldn't stay. I would do anything at all, to stay.*

*I've been seeing a lot of my oncologist. Dr Singh. She's probably ten or so years older than me. I know she's very sorry that this is happening. I know she wishes she could do more. But the treatment options have been exhausted, and they haven't worked, and I understand. It's not her fault, but the way she looks at me sometimes, I feel like she's offering to take the blame. She has said that she's used to patients getting angry with her, or just crying through every appointment. She tells me I'm very calm. I don't know, perhaps I'm unusual. But I've accepted what's happening. The only sticking point is you.*

*I asked her why she chose this job, and she had her answer ready. She must be asked a lot. She said that she sees the very best of humanity; how much people love one another, what they'll do to survive. I liked that. I was glad I'd asked her.*

*This morning, before I came here, I lay with you in my bed beside me. I was tired and so were you. It was time for your morning nap. You fidgeted before going to sleep. I offered you another story, but you shook your head. You were too sleepy. I watched you close your eyes and I put my hand gently on your back, felt your warmth. All the times I'd wished you would go to sleep; I wanted to take them back. I wanted you to stay awake. I wanted to play with you, one last time. I had to settle for feeling your warm breath on my cheek. I lay awake, aching. And you, you slept on, peaceful. I envied you that.*

*I hope that you can be strong, and brave. I hope that you can live a wonderful, long life, unhindered by my absence. And I know that's unrealistic, but it doesn't stop me hoping. You will have your heart broken. You will break someone else's heart. You will tell lies, and break the rules, and do the wrong thing. You will also do something wonderful. Perhaps many wonderful things. You will do things every day that would have made me proud. You will be luminous, and perfect, and do things I can't even imagine.*

*Here's my advice to you, for what it's worth. Don't give your heart too easily, but don't be too scared to give it at all. Don't feel you have to marry the first person you love. Do take good care choosing your friends, and be loyal to them, and work at those relationships too. No one ever tells you about the work a friendship takes. If you are able to, and you want to, have children. You have been my greatest joy, and I want you to know that kind of happiness and pride.*

*Choose your career carefully; I hope you'll do it for a long time. Think about what you're good at, and what you love doing, and forge a path that incorporates both of those things. Stick with anything you enjoy and are good at, whether it's a sport or a musical instrument or a hobby or a school subject. I thought only school subjects were important, but I was wrong. It's good to have a wide range of skills, to be great at all kinds of things. You never know where one of those things might take you.*

*Take your health seriously; understand your own importance. Check your breasts, go for your smear tests, get things you're not sure about checked out. Don't sit out in the sun all day long, even if you rarely burn. When you are young, it doesn't seem like anything will catch you out. But I'm the proof that things can. Your body is worth looking after. I won't tell you not to drink or smoke or take drugs; I know it's unrealistic to expect you to be sensible enough to avoid those things. And perhaps you shouldn't. Perhaps you have to push things to the edge to understand where the edges are and come back from them. Take care of your mind, too. You've got a lot to deal with as a child, having lost your mother. Take time to grieve and talk to someone if you feel lost.*

*It's nearly time; I can feel it. I don't have long left. There are so many things I want you to know, but they've slipped away. And who am I to tell you how to live your life? I only made it to twenty-two. And the only thing I got right was you. Do it your own way. Don't make yourself less than you are. Make yourself more.*

*Edie, I'm reconciled to losing the rest of my twenties, my thirties, my forties and so on. I just can't bear losing your first birthday, missing the rest of your teeth coming through, and the first time you hop, and opening Christmas presents. Those, and so many things. Tell me about them, even though I won't be here. Tell me.*

*I wanted you to know so many things. I wanted to tell you them, one by one, as you grew. And I can't. Know this: I won't be here, but this love I have for you will survive me. I believe that.*

*I floogle you, baby girl. Ask your dad about that.*

*With love,*

*Mum*

# ACKNOWLEDGEMENTS

I don't think I'll ever write another novel quite like this one. When I wrote the first draft in a month, breast cancer was still breathing down my neck. I'd just finished chemo and had multiple operations ahead of me (still one to go). My editor, Kate Evans, saw something in that raw draft and I'm so grateful for that. And I'm grateful that she kept turning down my rewrites (although I didn't feel it at the time!) until I got it right. Huge thanks go to Sam Brace and Peyton Stableford at Agora Books, too, for everything they've done for it. A novel is such a team effort, despite there being only one name on the cover.

Thank you so much to the authors who've read and been kind about *Missing Pieces* and *Nobody's Wife*. I hope some of you enjoy this one, too. And of course, to the bloggers and the readers — I know how many books there are to choose from, and I'm honoured when someone chooses one of mine. Special thanks to readers in The Motherload Book Club, who are so endlessly supportive. Huge thanks to Alison McGarragh-Murphy, Kate Dyson, Hannah England, Sarah Buckenham, Gabrielle Clapp, and Clara Wilcox for helping with the book club in various ways that are sometimes invisible but never unnoticed.

Many thanks to some very special women who answered questions about having secondary breast cancer for me: Julie Wolfarth, Carolyn Gammon, Jenny Rhodes, Jackie Davies, Pauline Burt, and Jo Taylor. I think of you often and wish you the very best. And enormous thanks to Danni Hunt, one of my chemo nurses, who read this book to check I had my medical stuff straight. Any mistakes are my own.

Thanks to writing friends old and new. I mostly interact with these people online and some of them I've never met in person, but they are vital. Gillian McAllister, Rachael Smart, Rebecca Williams, Lia Louis, Steph Chapman, Nikki Smith, Lauren North, Zoe Lea, Clare Empson, Francesca Jakobi, Louise Mangos, Hannah Persaud, Nicola Crosskey, Louise Beech, Susie Lynes: thank you.

Thank you to the friends who helped pull me through my cancer experience. There are too many to name, but please know that every small kindness made me stronger. Thanks to Pete Wallroth at Mummy's Star for coming to visit and sharing his own story, and to Victoria Yates at Younger Breast Cancer Network for starting the group that I relied on so heavily.

Thank you to my parents and my in-laws for propping up our family at that time, and always. I'll never forget it. Thank you to my sister Rachel for too many things to name. Thank you to my husband, Paul, who makes everything possible, and my children, Joseph and Elodie, for giving me the very best of reasons to get better.

During the final checks and edits of this book, my wonderful friend, Deb Chambers, died, leaving behind two young daughters. Deb died suddenly, and not of cancer, but still the parallels with this novel were startling. I'm still adjusting to her loss, and I don't really have the words, but I wanted to say something here to her girls:

Your mummy was loved and loving, and I believe that, just like in this book, you two are the key to fixing the broken hearts around you. You will show your dad and your grand-parents and your mummy's friends how to laugh and live again, just by being you. When you are old enough, I will tell you stories of our friendship, and you can add them to what you know and remember of her. For now, I just send my love.

# missing pieces

LAURA PEARSON

# 1

## 5TH AUGUST 1985

### 21 DAYS AFTER

The coffin was too small. Too small to contain what it did, which was not only Phoebe's body, but a large part of Linda, too.

At the funeral parlour, a man touched Linda's arm and asked, gently, whether she wanted to see Phoebe, and even as she was nodding her head, she knew that it was a mistake.

'Are you sure?' Tom asked.

Linda knew that this was a decision she couldn't unmake. Knew, instinctively, that she was wrong. She would wish, later, that she hadn't seen their daughter like that, because no matter how peaceful she looked, she was still gone. Knew that the memory of her lying there, surrounded by silk and dressed too immaculately, would interfere with the memories she held of Phoebe laughing and running. Alive. And still, she nodded her head and followed the man down the corridor towards a lifetime of regret.

Linda looked back, once, at Tom and Esme. They were standing hand in hand, quite still, dark heads bowed. Esme's fringe needed cutting, and it was covering her eyebrows and, when she looked down at the thick carpet, her eyes too. This is my family, Linda thought. This is what's left of my family. And then she looked down at her swollen belly, touched it as her baby flipped over like a fish, felt nothing.

When they reached the room, the man told her to take as long as she needed. He opened the door for her and then disappeared down the corridor like a ghost. And Linda approached the coffin slowly, looked in at the girl who couldn't possibly be Phoebe. Who was too small, and still, and quiet, to be Phoebe.

And Linda felt like getting inside it, curling up with her daughter and going to sleep.

But the coffin was too small.

## 2

## 13TH AUGUST 1985

## 29 DAYS AFTER

Linda set her hands on her rounded stomach, interlaced her fingers. Tom was beside her in the sparse, white waiting room, and neither of them reached for a magazine, and neither of them spoke. The receptionist was eating her lunch, and the smell of her egg sandwiches made Linda feel sick. She unlaced her fingers and gripped the sides of her chair, willing the waves of nausea to pass. She'd given birth to both of her daughters in this hospital, had sat in this room waiting for numerous scans, and she'd always found it cold. That day, though, it seemed stuffy. She thought about standing and opening a window. She lifted her thick hair from the back of her neck, rooted in her bag for a band to tie it up.

When her name was called, Linda stood. Tom held out a hand for her to take, but she didn't reach for it, and he let it drop, followed her down the corridor. When they opened the door, the doctor stood and offered them a kind smile.

'I'm Dr Thomas,' he said.

'You were here when Phoebe was born,' Linda said. 'I remember.'

He smiled again, but didn't confirm or deny it. He saw hundreds of babies being delivered, Linda told herself. He wouldn't remember hers. She sat down on an uncomfortable blue plastic chair and crossed her legs. She couldn't look at Dr Thomas, and she couldn't look at Tom, and so she set her eyes on the abstract painting that hung on the wall to the left of Dr Thomas's head. Every time she blinked, she kept her eyes closed for a fraction too long, trying to ignore the strong smell of ammonia that hung in the air.

'I heard about your daughter. I'm so sorry.'

Linda wanted to ask why he didn't say Phoebe's name.

'Thank you,' Tom said. 'It's been very hard.'

Since Phoebe's death, almost everything anyone said seemed ridiculous to Linda. She wanted to shake Tom, to punish him somehow for reducing their pain like that.

'Of course,' Dr Thomas said. 'That's why we wanted you to come in today and have another scan. The stress of something like this can be very tough on a baby. We just wanted to have a look and check that everything's all right. Try not to worry, though, I'm sure it will be. Now, Linda, would you like to get up on the bed?'

Linda did as she was told. As she pulled her legs up, the paper that was covering the bed tore a little, and it sounded loud in the quietness of the room. Six weeks ago, they'd come here for her twenty-week scan. Esme and Phoebe were being looked after by Maud, their next-door neighbour. Tom had closed his travel bookshop and they'd driven to the hospital, and Linda had felt a clutch of excitement in her throat, like she had on the day they'd run away from their families, when Esme was growing inside her. On the way to the appointment, Tom had turned the radio up loud and they'd sung along, the car windows open and the breeze whipping Linda's dark hair against her face.

It was hard to reconcile that memory with the question that wouldn't go away. The question that had come to Linda, formed and ready to be spoken, a few nights before. That was rising up in her throat, like bile.

'Dr Thomas?'

He turned to her, and she met his eyes for the first time.

'Yes, Linda?'

'Is it too late to have an abortion?'

Linda heard Tom's intake of breath and saw the flash of shock that Dr Thomas tried to hide. She wouldn't back down, or retract the words. How could she? How could she be expected to have this new child, and love it, when her love for Phoebe had brought her to this? When she could barely take care of her remaining daughter, barely look Esme in the eye?

Dr Thomas cleared his throat and the sound brought Linda back into that room, and she glanced at Tom. He was looking at her like he didn't quite recognise her. Squinting slightly, as though trying to work out whether he'd seen her somewhere before.

'It is too late,' Dr Thomas said. 'But if you don't think you can care for this baby, there are options we can discuss.'

'Adoption?' Linda asked.

She considered this, briefly. Going through the labour, feeling the baby emerge from her like a miracle, and then handing it over. Would she hold it first? Would she be told the sex, be given a chance to think about a name? No, she decided. That option wasn't for her. But before she could speak, Tom spoke for both of them.

'No,' he said, his voice soft but firm. 'We're having this baby, and we're keeping it.'

'Let's get this done,' Dr Thomas said. 'And then we can talk some more.'

He smeared the cold jelly on Linda's stomach and she

almost laughed at the tickling shock of it. She waited to be told what she knew, that the baby was fine. She was aware that Tom was worried that her grief, her refusal to eat properly, and her inability to sleep, had caused the baby harm. But she could feel it moving, turning and probing. And more than that, this baby was a part of her, and she felt sure that she would know instantly if there were anything wrong. Just as she had known, that night, that something had happened to Phoebe.

And so, when the image appeared on the screen and Dr Thomas said the heartbeat was strong, Linda wasn't surprised. But she saw Tom, saw his hand fly to his mouth in pure relief, saw the love in his eyes that was ready and waiting. It was simpler, somehow, for him.

Despite what Dr Thomas said about it being too late, she knew there were ways to rid yourself of a baby. Ways that women had relied on for centuries. Painful and dangerous ways, but possible. But she wouldn't do it, because of Tom. She closed her eyes briefly, tried to imagine herself as the mother of a newborn again. Tried to imagine them being a family of four again. But it didn't feel right, when Phoebe wasn't one of them.

'Well,' said Dr Thomas, 'everything looks fine here. Come and take a seat at my desk again, when you're ready.'

He wiped the fluid from Linda's belly and she pulled her clothes back into position, pushed herself up and off the bed. Tom waited until she was ready. When she stood, he placed a hand on the small of her back and guided her the few steps back to the waiting chair. Linda anticipated a lecture, a talking to about how she would get through this. How other women had. You don't know, she wanted to scream. She wanted to open the door and let her voice bounce and echo along the empty white corridor. None of you knows.

'I'd like you both to think about having some counselling,' Dr Thomas said.

'It won't change anything,' Linda said.

'Not the situation, no. But I really think it might help you to come to terms with things. To accept what's happened, and start to move on. I'm not asking you to make a decision today. Just think about it.'

Linda took the leaflets he was holding out to her, and stood, ready to leave. When she was at the door, she felt Tom's breath on her neck, and she was sorry, for a moment, that they were leaving together. That they would have to suffer the car journey home, and then the evening, and the days and weeks to come in that too-empty house, with the words she'd spoken hanging there in the air, like a threat.

Tom didn't speak until he was behind the wheel with his seatbelt on. He reversed neatly out of the parking space, and Linda watched him, waiting for the accusations and the blame. He was handsome, this man she'd chosen. His profile was strong. They were both still young, him thirty and her twenty-eight, and yet small flecks of grey were starting to show in Tom's neat, dark hair. Once, he'd mentioned colouring it, and she said that she liked it as it was, and Esme commented that he looked like he'd been caught in a tiny snowstorm, and he left it. Tom must have felt her eyes on him then, and he glanced at her. It was his eyes that she'd noticed first. Green in some lights, grey in others. Kind, open. There was kindness in them still, she saw, even though she expected to be met with disgust.

When Tom did speak, it wasn't what she expected at all.

'I do understand,' he said, his voice calm. 'I lost her too. Just—'

His voice cracked, and Linda watched his face, saw the tears welling.

'—Just try not to shut me out.'

'I'll try,' Linda said, because she wanted to offer him something other than hurt.

THAT NIGHT, AFTER TOM FELL ASLEEP, LINDA LAY AWAKE BESIDE him, listening to the occasional sounds of people and cars on the street outside. Sometimes, even before Phoebe's death, Linda woke up wondering how she'd ended up here, in an unassuming semi on a residential road in Southampton, so far from home. The night before she'd left Bolton with Tom, they had sat in his car with a map of England spread out on their laps. Linda's eyes were drawn to the edges, to the places beside the sea, and she'd pointed at Southampton, smiling. She had known almost nothing about the place. Her grandparents had holidayed there once. It was where the *Titanic* had sailed from. Linda had pictured a crumbling sort of house by the sea. Fish and chips, walking along the beach, her hair salty, being lulled to sleep by lapping waves. And when they had arrived, and it was nothing like she imagined, she hadn't cared much, because it was still a fresh start, a new life. But almost a decade had passed, now, and that freshness had long since faded.

Linda was aware of the sound of her breathing. She watched the clock crawl through half an hour, and when it got to one o'clock, she sat up carefully, trying not to wake Tom. She took her white cotton dressing gown from the hook behind the door and left the room, looking back once to check that he hadn't been disturbed. He was lying on his side, his breathing deep and slow, his mouth open.

She didn't turn the light on in the kitchen. After almost eight years in this house and two babies, she knew her way around in darkness. The kitchen had always been her favourite room. When they had come to look at the house, weary with unsuccessful viewings and the knowledge that they couldn't afford the kind of place she would choose, Linda had gone to the kitchen first. She'd looked around, at the drawings on the fridge that were held in place by colourful magnets, at the old pine table in the corner still messy with breakfast crumbs. The walls were painted a bright yellow and the cabinets were a pale wood, chipped and marked in places. It was the kind of room where a family gathers at the beginning and end of each day. And she'd known, then, that it didn't matter that the bathroom was small and the garden was a bit wild. This was the house where she would have her family.

For a while, Linda stood at the window, watching the stillness of the dark garden. It was mid-August, late summer, and although she was hot with the weight of her pregnancy, she wasn't ready for the season to change. Because when that summer had begun, she'd still had Phoebe. And it still seemed impossible that she was gone for good.

Linda opened the narrow cupboard in the corner of the room, stared at its contents. And then she took out the bottle of vodka and unscrewed the cap. She did it quickly, as though afraid of being caught. The bottle was three-quarters full, and she calculated that it had probably been there since the previous Christmas, when they'd had a party for some friends and neighbours. That night, she'd taken the drinks Tom had handed her, and she remembered feeling light-headed, feeling that the room was spinning slowly, as girls in bright dresses darted in and out of the small groups that had formed. She remembered catching sight of Phoebe, and dropping to her knees, catching her youngest daughter's wrists and kissing her forehead. Phoebe had wriggled from her grip, dashed off after her sister and the other older girls, and Linda had poured herself another drink.

Now, alone in the dark while Esme and Tom slept upstairs,

Linda longed for the edges to blur a little, to take a break from the heaviness of her thoughts, and alcohol was the only way she knew. She lifted the bottle to her lips, tipped it, gulped. The baby inside her kicked, a quiet protest. And Linda tipped the bottle again, swallowed, and put it back in the cupboard. She sat down at the kitchen table, waiting for something to change, for some of the darkness to lift.

# WANT TO HEAR MORE FROM LAURA PEARSON?

Sign up to Laura Pearson's Book Club to get:

1. An exclusive author Q&A with Laura and topics for your book group;
2. Details of Laura's publications as well as a sneak peak at her next book, and;
3. The opportunity to receive advance reader copies and win prizes

Interested? It takes less than a minute to join. You can get your Q&A and first newsletter by signing up here: www.laurapearsonauthor.com